The A

Graeme K. Talboys was born
nine works of non-fiction published (on museum education,
drama, and matters spiritual) and written more than a score of
novels. The first of those (written when he was seventeen) was
lost on a train. The next two (written in his early twenties) he
wishes had been. Thankfully, he's had considerably more
success with writing since then with short stories, poems, and
many novels published. His previous jobs have included
market gardener, shelf stacker, pot boy, sandwich maker, and
factory floor maintenance operative (broom provided). As an
adult his first job was acting, followed by teaching Drama and
English. Some of his pupils still speak to him. He later worked
in museums where he felt right at home among the ancient,
broken objects. He now lives in Scotland.

Also by Graeme K. Talboys

The Archives

GRAEME K TALBOYS

MB
MONKEY BUSINESS

MONKEY BUSINESS

An imprint of Grey House in the Woods

This paperback original 2022

A catalogue record for this book
is available from the British Library

Paperback ISBN: 978-1-909295-23-0
ebook ISBN: 978-1-909295-24-7

This novel is entirely a work of fiction.
The names, characters and incidents portrayed in it are
the work of the authors' imaginations. Any resemblance to
actual persons, living, dead or yet to be born, events or localities is entirely
coincidental.

Set in Times New Roman.

1 2 3 4 5 6 7 8 9 0

The Archives

This novel is based, with permission, on an original story and audio-script by Sheriden Starr with additions by Lee Potts of Omenopus. It is not a straightforward retelling of the story recounted in the album (*The Archives* – Omenopus – Monty Maggot Records – MMCD009). It is an interpretation of events, an offering of back story, and an exploration of some of the dilemmas posed by the original tale.

Albums by Omenopus

Portents
Time Flies
The Plague
The Physician
The Archives
The Hybrid Project
Teepee The Space Girl

Albums by nineteentwelve

Waiting For No One
Elegy
New World Order
The Hybrid Project

Omenopus and nineteentwelve can be found at Monty Maggot Records or the Bandcamp website. Bangtheory, to be found on Reverbnation, is also part of the wider musical concept and worth exploring.

This book is dedicated
to the memory of
Michael Anthony 'Mick' Farren
(3 September 1943 – 27 July 2013)

The Archives

Prologue

.

The Archives

My name is George 4/7.
I don't know if I'm the last survivor.
The war, I believe it's over,
There's nothing left.
I've gathered all the remnants and broken fragments of
information that I could find,
Everything is contained within this disc.
This will be my last transmission before I seal myself into this
unit.
This is what really happened.

2192

I

'Hey, I didn't say I believed it. I'm just telling you what I heard.'

'Who from? Some drogado who can't tell the difference between a space port and some hole in the ground.'

Artur kept his head down, pushed his notebook out of sight, and half closed his eyes as the two youths swaggered into the Redline Metro car. They dumped themselves on the bench seat next to him. The familiar musk of maconha resin filled the air. Their tattoos and masks told him they were from Colina, the shanty town west of the projects where he lived, so he knew well enough to seem blind and deaf to their presence. Even if their proximity meant he couldn't help hearing.

'I tell you, Dingo and his brother broke into—'

'Keep your voice down, cara. People listening.'

'This train?' A snort. 'People sleeping.'

There was a pause. Artur assumed they were having a quick look round just to be certain.

'Well? Dingo and Hiena...'

'Yeah. They broke into that site out at Escarpa do Céu last weekend.'

Artur stopped thinking his own thoughts about work and paid full attention. He'd have to phone his sister about this when he got to his bench.

'What they want to go out there for?'

'Looking for stuff to sell. Computers out of the office, that kind of thing. Or looking for treasure to sell back to the CPI. I don't know. Anyway, that doesn't matter. They got in. And they saw stuff. And they ran. Dingo, cara. Dingo ran.'

'So? He ain't no fool. There must have been guards. The Port Authority owns the land. They set off an alarm or something. They got out. So what?'

'No. You missing the point.'

'Well get to it, I gotta get off at Rosario.'

'They saw things.'

'Seriously? What things? Ghosts you saying?'

'No. Not like that. I dunno. I got all this from Hiena's cousin, Agueda. Hiena's in hospital. Broke his leg. Told Dingo to disappear.'

'You ain't make no sense. How come Hiena's not been touched?'

'He has. It's prison hospital. Agueda was allowed to visit him there.'

'This true?'

'Honra do clã, cara.'

'OK. OK. Go on.'

'The rest doesn't make a lot of sense.'

'Like it already did. You hear this from Agueda?'

'Sure.'

'She's a good kid. Head on straight. You walking out?'

'Louco. Agueda? She wouldn't give me ten pesos toward my own funeral.'

'You can be such a dumb shit at times. She told you all this, didn't she. Trusted you. Think about it. Later. Tell me what she said Hiena told her.'

'Hey I never thought of it like that.'

'Come on. Rosario, remember?'

'Sure. Sorry. She said Hiena seemed confused, probably painkillers and stuff from when they set his leg. Anyway, he

8

said there was a long shed full of stuff. Weird stuff that shouldn't be there. Or anywhere. And drawings, charts. He began rambling on. Didn't make a lot of sense.'

'Yeah, well, from what you said earlier it sounds like a bunch of junk from a crash they'd hushed up. You know, from when they first started launching again with all that crap they bought cheap from the Chinese.'

'Hiena would surely have known all that for what it was. He grew up like the rest of us watching the launchings and the landings. And the explosions.'

'Maybe. But those boys are big drogados. Who knows what they'd taken to make them think it was good idea to break into an archaeological site all that way out of the city.'

'Maybe. But you think the PA or the Three Families would have let those eggheads dig in that valley if they'd buried some mistake there? Anyway, they only had about a minute in the shed before the Guarda Nacional turn up armed to the teeth.'

'Told you that's why they ran. You would of as well.'

'Verdade. But that kind of proves my point. Would the GN turn up for someone stealing a few old bits of pottery? Anyway, that's when Hiena took a fall down into a gully and shattered his leg, told Dingo to run. First thing anyone knows about it back home is when the GN, Policia Federal, and tough guys in suits tear their way through south end of Colina looking for Dingo and any other Clã de Cachorro. Locals don't like that. So next thing you got is riots.'

'All the way down here now.'

'Yeah, well, what did they expect, tearing down people's homes just cos of some old ruins or whatever.'

'Ruins? So what was all this shit you gave me about spaceships? We got plenty of those.'

'Yeah but this one… This one was different. Hiena said he saw…'

The Metro car shuddered sideways as the train crossed a series of points where the Redline spur joined the main system and the lights dimmed for a fraction of a second. The two next to Artur stood and staggered to the door still talking. As the lights came back up the train coasted into Rosario Station, somewhere beneath the park.

Artur raised his head, watched the two as the smart ink of their tattoos morphed and other shapes appeared briefly as they passed through the UV filter screen in the now open doorway. As they pushed their way through the crowds that were waiting to get on, their masks flickered as the holo images struggled with the bright platform lights.

He began to breathe properly again, the sweet earthy scent of maconha fading and unmasking the familiar blend of sweat, alcohol, fast food, cheap scent, cheaper disinfectant, and over-heated air that was the normal odour of the Redline. You were never far from the smell of poverty and despair.

By the time the train began to move again, whining and rattling into the tunnel, the two youths had disappeared into the crowds. Artur was left wondering just what they had seen on the archaeological site. As far as he knew from talks with his sister, there had been little of value found up there as they cleared the way for the first of a series of launch rails.

Two Metro cops sauntered past, swaying with the motion of the train as it took the curve and slowed into South Rosario station. More people pushed their way on and between the press of bodies; Artur could see yet more cops on the platform. All that talk of riots. He's heard nothing, but he'd spent the weekend on the fortieth floor of the Árvores de Pêssego Block celebrating with Catarina. The world could have ended for all he would have cared.

II

Drawn along by the crowds, heading upward into the open air, he was surrounded by noise and confusion. When he reached the street level entrance it was all suddenly drowned by the crackling roar of a heavy lifter clawing its way toward space. The sound echoed along the busy street, bouncing from the plate glass façades of the towering buildings and filling the plaza. Instinctively he gazed upward, saw the thick column of exhaust building the ever taller pillar on which the lifter was perched. Windows rattled and alarms began to whoop as he put his hands to his ears.

Once it was through the high cloud, the sound faded. It was only then he began to realize the noises from the broad street were different to normal and that the crowds were denser. He was so used to the usual pattern of traffic noise and morning commuters emerging from the Metro that he was left disoriented.

A fine spray hit his face, shouts, running feet, popping, screams. Pushing back into the cover of the entrance to the Metro, backed into the corner by the news stand, he craned his neck to see what was happening. More spray from a distant water cannon shooting from a side street. A surge of black clad protestors, their faces masked and distorted by flickering holo images, a tumbling gas canister arcing through the air to be met by a baseball bat that sent it back from whence it came, knots of commuters trying to get to their places of work whilst keeping clear of the trouble.

Artur turned to the old woman in the kiosk.

'This been going on long?'

'All weekend. You not see the news?'

He shook his head and went back to surveying the street. He needed to get to work. No one there knew he was a son of one of the Three Families, albeit disinherited. He had no leverage and needed to be on time. Especially now.

Fighting back through the crowds still emerging from under ground, he crossed to a different exit. It was still crowded outside, but there didn't seem to be any fighting and the only Guarda and Policia were lined up off to his left. He could see a way to the edge of Gorodischer Plaza, could even see the front of the Presságiobra building where he worked.

After making sure his notebook was safely tucked away, he crossed the broad thoroughfare and turned into a side street that cut behind an up-market apartment store. Even here there were groups of people, and the goods entrance to the store was firmly closed with several security guards standing on duty. He walked past them, conscious of their aggressive stares. Beyond was a maze of back streets which serviced other buildings, including the car park and employee entrance of the Presságiobra building.

As he approached the entrance to another side street, a sudden surge of protestors blocked his way. They were running, blowing whistles, banging pots with spoons, waving wooden rattles. Riot as carnival. Until the gas canisters began cascading through the air. The crowd broke up and Artur found himself carried along. He held his breath as best he could, pushing his way between back-packed protestors.

Spun around by the mob it took seconds to orientate himself through the clouds of gas that stung his eyes. He felt his nose begin the run at the vinegary smell. For a moment he thought he was going to be carried away from where he was going. Through his watering eyes, he could see the heavily guarded barrier to the Preságiobra entrance, saw police surge toward him, felt himself slammed against a wall right beside the company's security post.

Then, all he could see was the dark shape of a Guarda in full smart body armour looming over him, face hidden by a gas mask. Over the background noise of riot, he heard the man yelling at him to produce his identity. Artur turned to the security post in the hope of catching the Preságiobra guard's eye as he fumbled in his pockets for his ID.

His hand was shaking so badly, he had trouble grabbing hold of the plaque. The Guarda snatched it from him and ran it across the sensor on his chest. Artur's heart sank as the Guarda kept repeating the action.

'This a fake?' yelled the Guarda.

'No. No. I work here,' said Artur, turning to the armoured booth beside him. 'The security will know me.'

'Yeah. Right'

As Artur turned in desperation, he caught sight of Cesar Castanho, his department manager.

'Senhor Castanho!' he called.

The man in his expensive suit had just climbed from a chauffeur driven car. He turned, a frown on his face. Artur waved and immediately had his wrist grabbed.

'Turn around,' said the Guarda.

'Senhor Castanho!' Artur called again, much louder, taking in a mouthful of gas.

As he began to cough, Castanho stepped to the barrier, one of the company's security men joining him. Artur managed to turn.

'Could you vouch?' he managed to splutter through snot and tears.

It seemed to take for ever. He had reached up and pulled down his face mask. Castanho, a handkerchief held to the lower part of his face, eventually nodded. Artur couldn't tell from his half-hidden expression whether his boss was annoyed or had caught a whiff of the gas.

'Get your plaque re-registered,' growled the Guarda through his gas mask who then watched with suspicion as Artur staggered to the turnstile and was let in to the safety of the Presságiobra compound.

III

'I normally cut straight across the Plaza,' Artur explained.

'But not today,' said the nurse.

Her placid manner seemed at odds with events outside. Even on the fifth floor they could hear the rioting through the staff clinic's closed windows. Artur was aware of the doctor moving just as calmly in and out of an adjoining room, of the nurse beside him preparing something on a trolley. He sat sideways on the treatment bed and waited.

After a murmured conversation with the doctor in the doorway, the nurse asked: 'Is the tablet working?'

Artur nodded. 'Yes. Thank you.'

He'd been sent straight up to the company clinic by his line manager and the nurse had given him a tablet as soon as he had explained what had happened.

'A decongestant. Sounds counter-intuitive. But it works.'

It had. His nose was no longer streaming although he held on to the wad of tissues he'd been given.

'Now. Lie flat on the bed. Good. Try to keep your eyes open. Not easy, I know, but we need to get this eyewash in there.'

Her slow way of working and treating him like he was seven irritated Artur. Catalina was brisk, explaining everything as she worked in simple language without ever condescending. In the projects there were always long queues of frightened, poor, and poorly educated people to keep calm and keep moving. It's why he loved her.

The drops of liquid hurt as much as the tear gas when they first went in, but the pain soon eased. Holding yet more tissues, he was guided from the bed to a chair by the window and told to sit quietly. Through the blur of tears, he gazed down at the mayhem in the plaza. All he could see at first was a mass that surged back and forth to the accompaniment of a symphony of harsh noise and loud music. Other than the dark clothing and whirling trails of smoke it could easily have been carnival.

As the tears stopped flowing and Artur's vision returned he began to make out details. The PF had blocked off the main routes with adapted motorised fences backed up by water cannon. This had trapped a large number of protestors in the plaza. GN snatch squads were working at the edges, pulling people out and dragging them away, using batons and pepper spray to subdue any who resisted. He could see members of the press and televiso offering their ID plaques and getting arrested as well. That wouldn't play well on the evening newscasts. The media had long supported the current regime, but they did not like it when their own freedoms were trampled on. Which was just so much hypocrisy as far as Artur was concerned.

It did, however, make him wonder. He began searching for his own card. Before he could pull it from its secure pocket, a drone took up station outside the clinic window. The familiar, featureless black disc the size of a dinner plate hovered motionless giving no indication of which direction its cameras, microphones, and other sensors were pointing. Ideas began to tick over in Artur's head. Time to get to his work station. He almost missed the shot that took out the drone.

One instant it was hovering, the next, shards of casing erupted from a hole punctured right through the machine. It wobbled, angled away from the building and swung round at full speed, smacking into the window with a bang that elicited a shriek from the nurse who had been working at her desk and not seen it arrive.

Artur hoped no one was directly beneath. Sky Eyes weren't that heavy, but falling from a height could cause serious injury. Things outside had escalated.

Before descending to the basement computer laboratories where he worked, Artur made his way to the Personnel section on the second floor. He noticed a number of guards in the lobby watching the lifts and stairways. They were no more heavily armed than normal, but there were a lot more of them. Artur eyed them warily as he pushed his way through the doors to the busy front office.

He went through the time consuming ritual of confirming his identity with retinal scans, which kept failing because of what his eyes had been through earlier. When it eventually accepted him, he was grudgingly passed on to the person who would check and update his ID plaque. This person complained he smelled of gas and made him sit across the room whilst the plaque was entered into the reader. This, too, seemed to take forever.

'Nothing wrong with it,' was the eventual response. 'The information is not corrupted and the chip was updated last Friday. I've deleted the GN flag.'

Artur took back the proffered plaque. 'Thank you.'

He frowned all the way down to the third sub-level where the electronics section was housed. One or two people looked up from their work stations as he made his way to his own cubicle. His line manager joined him as he sat down and switched on his work terminal.

'No need to make up the lost time. Not your fault. Mayhem out there. Eyes all right?'

'Still a bit sore, but I can work.'

'OK, but make sure you take regular screen breaks.'

Artur settled and when he was sure he was alone, he pulled a phone out from its hidey hole under his desk. It was an old model, something he had modified a long time ago. Checking the date against a string of numbers in his notebook and making a swift conversion in his head, he sent two encrypted texts. One to his sister, brief as usual, in their own childhood code. The other was to Marco Seta, someone he had been at university with in Porto Sul.

Then he set to work on his current project, running through lines of code for the control system of the mineral sensors being designed for a new, unmanned, asteroid mining explorer. It was tedious work as he had already been through it twice.

When his phone trilled he was grateful for the break.

'Artur Sozinho,' he said into the mouthpiece of his headset.

'Hey, Artur. It's Marco.'

Marco was one of the few who he trusted and who knew his real name, knew who he was now. And why.

'Hey, Marco. Hope I didn't interrupt anything.'

'Nothing special. Glad of a break. What's up?'

'You alone?'

'Yes.' The cheeriness faded a fraction.

'Didn't want to drop you in anything. You worked on the ID sensors for the GN, didn't you?'

'The software, yes. Not something I boast about.'

'I know. It's why I asked if you were alone.'

'So what's your interest?' He still sounded wary.

'The hardware. Could tear gas fuck it up?'

There was a silence. 'This work related?'

Artur shrugged. 'Sort of. I got gassed this morning on my way to work and my ID plaque wouldn't register on the Guarda's suit. A lot of people out there seem to be the same.'

'It's not likely. The hardware is basic but robust. Tear gas isn't likely to erode it and they test those suits on a regular basis. The software took tear gas into account and is probably updated regularly.'

'OK. Just a thought. I guess it's cos gas detection and erosion is part of our current project.'

'Today's riot in Gorodischer?'

'Yeah.'

'Only seen the headlines. How serious is it?'

'Someone shot a drone down.'

'Seriously?! Man, I better take a different route home. Velho vindo. See you.'

'Bye.'

Artur cut the connection, gave it ten minutes and then checked his hidden phone. Sure enough, as his final comment had hinted, Marco had sent a cryptic looking text. Artur ran it through his own machine and found it was the formula for an aerosol that would fog gas mask visors. Someone in Colina or one of the other shanty towns, it seemed, had been cooking up a bit of riot protection. He didn't bother to speculate just how Marco knew.

IV

Because Mondays were always crazy busy at the clinic where Catarina worked and they invariably ran over after closing time, Artur always made the evening meal. He was in the tiny cupboard that was their kitchen draining rice when she came in. She dropped her bag on the floor, twisted the lock on the deadbolt, and made her way through the clouds of dispersing steam to kiss Artur.

He grinned and then frowned as Catarina held his shoulders and looked at his eyes. With practised ease she surveyed his face, ran her hands downs his arms and grabbed his hands, turning them both ways.

'What happened?' she finally asked, still in nurse mode.

'You not seen the news?' She shook her head, a worried expression drawing itself onto her tired face. 'It's OK, querida. There was a riot. They kettled everyone in Gorodischer. I skirted it but still got a whiff of gas.'

'They sort you at work?'

'Sure. Some decongestant and then a series of eyewashes.'

She sighed. 'That gonna cost.'

'Company's paying.'

'What?'

'Senhor Castanho saw what happened, sanctioned the treatment.'

'He out rioting, was he?'

Artur laughed, but Catarina didn't join in. She was suspicious.

'I had just got to the staff entrance. You know? Round the back.'

'That big guard post?'

'Sure. That's it. Foot traffic one side, cars the other. He'd just got out of his car and was heading for the staff lobby. I was just outside. Some Guarda in full gear had stopped me and asked for my ID. For some reason his reader wasn't working properly. I panicked, saw Castanho, called out.'

'And he helped?'

'Why not?'

Artur washed the rice and Catarina went to their equally small bathroom for a quick shower while he fried up some soja, adding a hot sauce. The meal reached the table just as Catarina reappeared in a long towelling gown.

'You thank him?' she asked.

'You my mother?'

'I'm serious, Artur. Man's a boss. Always best to be on their good side, no matter how you feel about them.'

'I will, puma.'

She narrowed her eyes and then smiled.

With the meal finished and Artur putting the last of the dishes away, Catarina spent a few moments at the window.

They were on the fortieth floor, even had a tiny balcony which neither used as they both felt uncomfortable, despite the fact the drop was simply down to the next balcony. The block was a vast pyramid. At lower levels there were apartments that had no windows at all, except the ones behind steel grilles that looked out onto internal corridors.

The ground floor was a great mall of shops with a market in the centre. The floor above contained the block's admin offices, schools, security provided by two overweight guys who spent all day watching the televiso or following pretty girls round the shops. The free clinic was also down there where, every day, folk gathered in patient lines with cuts, burns, bruises and the hope of some miracle cure for the diseases they couldn't afford to get treated in hospital.

Catarina rarely left the block, so she always treasured her few moments at the window, gazing down over Santa Barbara to the sea beyond. A view of the outside world. A view of the sky. She had been born in the block and grown up there. College had been difficult, leaving Pêssego for three years. These days, going outside was something she only ever did in company with Artur. Outside scared her.

The thin scream of a launch rattled the windows and she stepped away. They could not see the launches from their side of Pêssego, but they could feel them, like everyone else out in the projects and up in the shanties. At least, these days, very little exploded or crashed.

When the noise faded, they settled side-by-side on their chairs. Catarina's faced the tevo screen and she put in her ear buds to watch one of her favourite pieces of classical movie without disturbing Artur. His chair faced the other way. They could be shoulder to shoulder, touching, yet he could get on with his own work without distractions.

'What were they rioting about, anyway?' she asked before switching on the vid bank.

Artur looked up from his notebook where he had been putting down some thoughts, a logic tree, a few lines of code, in his fine spidery handwriting. 'Well, if what I overheard on the Redline this morning is true, some Cachorros tried to break into the office up at the archaeological dig in the valley behind Escarpa do Céu, above the spaceport. Next thing they know, Feds are tearing up Colina looking for them.'

'That don't make sense.'

'What does? You relax. Watch your old movie.'

'Once you've told me what's up with your leg. And don't look at me like that. I'm a nurse. I notice.'

'There's nothing wrong. But I swear there are days, like today, that I can feel those pins in my femur. Is that what they call a phantom pain?'

'No. That's pain felt in a limb that's been amputated. You were—'

'I know. Lucky. Lucky to have survived. Lucky I had parents wealthy enough to pay for all the surgery to mend what I had so carelessly shattered. I was a brat and then some.'

'You changed.'

She kissed his ear and settled down to watch. He also settled, a faint smile on his face. He'd once asked her why she watched all those twentieth century movies.

'They're several hundred years old. What's the attraction?'

'Just that. A different world. From before everything went to shit and left us in the toilet to start cleaning up the dirt.

They're relaxing. I love the dancing. Can forget the day. Better this to help me sleep than drink or drugs.'

He'd bought her the vid bank the next day, stocked with musicals and dance movies.

'That's why I married you,' she'd joked, but he sometimes wondered if there was an element of truth in there. Who cares? He kissed her back and carried on noting down something the day's events had prompted. He was still working when Catarina went to bed, transferring stuff that related to work onto his e-pad.

V

Early as it was, the store was open. Artur had slipped away whilst Catarina was still emerging from sleep. He wanted to avoid any crowds in the city as there was likely to be more trouble, he had said; wanted to make up some of the time he had lost yesterday. She only half believed him, but knew that whatever he was up to he was not seeing another woman, he was not running with the clans or dealing drugs. Having been raised on the Block and seen the lives of so many others blighted by a losing fight to crawl out of poverty, she was content with that.

Artur had taken the same seat in the same car on the Redline as he did every work day. This time, though, there were fewer workers and more police. Metro guards rode in threes in the trains; the platforms seemed filled with black uniforms.

Although he didn't want to get caught up in trouble again, he risked getting off at Rosario South. Local police lined the platform watching everyone who left the train. At one end a group of them were harassing a couple of Buddhist monks, throwing food out of a trolley, shouting questions at the bemused men. Artur gave them a glance and then kept his eyes firmly on the platform as he headed for the exit.

He took the escalator up to the ticket hall and emerged on the edge of the park. People were already gathering despite the truckloads of National Guard parked on the pavement. Three protestors had been shot dead overnight. It would not go unanswered. The whole city was looking over its shoulder as it went about its business.

Crossing the Estrada da Lua, he headed toward the Mercado Central. Beneath the vast canopy of the great market hall, wholesale traders were already on their lunch break whilst everyone else was thinking about breakfast. He wove between the traders haggling over the price of crates of beans and potatoes, through the fish market where they were already washing down the great marble slabs and shutting up for the day.

On the far side, he left the market through one of the loading bays, dodging round the heavy electric trucks and then getting shouted at by an old man with a broom as he accidentally kicked through a pile of refuse. Making a placatory gesture he skipped round the corner and into a network of narrower streets.

This was the old part of the city, the original Santa Barbara when it had been a hot sleepy town no one had ever heard of. At its heart, some of the buildings were many hundreds of years old, dating back to the eighteenth century and earlier. Around the edges, many had been thrown up in a hurry in the early twenty-first century to accommodate the wealthier refugees who fled south from civil war and rampant disease in the United States. Somewhere in this warren was where his family, the Pineiros, had first settled after fleeing from Europe. The building was long gone, pulled down by his great-grandfather to make way for a road to service the original Mercado Central.

It wasn't family history he was looking for on the hot, Tuesday morning with the distant sounds of whistles and pots and pans reaching into the narrow streets. It was a market of a different kind, and after several more turns into narrower and stuffier streets where the suspicious eyes belonged to the locals rather than the police, he found the building he was looking for.

It was ancient, and in places held up with a makeshift grid of steel girders that had probably vanished from a building site somewhere else in the city. Whenever he saw it, it made him smile. Given how much control his family had over construction, they would have been stolen from one of his father's companies.

Originally it had been a car park, built when most people thought the planet could afford for them to have private, polluting transport. The multi-level concrete structure had long since been lost in its surroundings, with other buildings expanding into parts of its structure to save on costs with the rest being colonized first by the homeless and later by small, often illicit, enterprises, creating a back street mercado where you could find all sorts of things it would be difficult to find elsewhere. Like in the chop shop Artur now entered.

You had to know it was there otherwise you'd never find it, tucked in at one dark end of an upper floor, wrapping round the stairwell and lift shaft. And you'd never be told it was there unless you were trusted. Because everything on the shelves had been stolen. The chances of any one item being traced back to its owner were infinitesimally small. They were components, stripped out of stolen electronics, cleaned, put in boxes, stacked on shelves from floor to ceiling, creating a gloomy maze that seemed to go on forever.

At a workbench by the door, the owner sat, peering through a powerful magnifying lens. She looked up when Artur came in, looked back down. He waited patiently as she finished detaching a delicate ceramic wafer from its housing. The ink on her shoulder cycled through a series of barely visible subtle shades that created the illusion of a snow lotus opening its petals before each one fell and faded, leaving a bud that opened and so on. It was a real work of art and must have cost a fortune. It was also the only name by which anyone had ever known her, except maybe Catarina who had been at school with her.

'Rei. Long time.'

Artur nodded. Nobody here used their real names. 'Neve. Keeping well?'

She gave a sideways nod that Artur had never been able interpret.

'What you after?' she asked.

'A DRT 91120. 50TB, if you've got it.'

Neve turned her chair and looked up at him. It was a glare that would have frozen most people on the spot, and rightly so. She might have lifeless legs, but she had been known to fell big guys, and her partner Flor was always on hand to drag the unconscious idiot away. Artur, however, just grinned.

'Gecko been in already?' he asked, not pushing his luck too far. He knew Marco would come to the same conclusions he had. It was just a surprise he had beaten Artur to the chop shop.

'You two working together or against?'

'Neither. We just came to the same answer to separate problems.'

Neve didn't bother glaring this time, she simply ran her chair over his foot on purpose as she disappeared into the gloom. From the corner of his eye he saw her monkey up the shelving, grab something from a box and drop it into a pouch. She was back at her bench in an instant.

'Crystal memory don't come cheap. 'Specially when something's cooking. Which it is, no matter what you both say different.'

From an inside pocket, Artur lifted a slim box and set it down on the work bench. Neve scooped it up and opened it carefully, her eyes flicking back and forth over the contents.

'If you need more…' Artur let the offer hang.

'You're good,' replied Neve, snapping the box shut.

'See you,' he said as he made to leave the shop, the crystal stowed safely in a carrier.

He hadn't gone two steps when Neve called him back. Turning in the doorway, he saw Neve beckoning.

'Anyone out there?'

Artur wondered at the pantomime, but went to the end of the dark entrance and peered out onto the main walkway. Apart from stall owners opening up, the place was deserted. He went back inside and said so.

'No strangers.'

Neve nodded and with a sleight of hand that impressed Artur she produced a small object and placed it beneath the powerful lens on her workbench.

'You work research. You ever see anything like this, Rei?'

It took a few moments to adjust to the magnification and work out what he was looking at. A flat, dark, oblong encrusted with dirt through which could be seen a reflective black surface.

'An ancient phone? Early twenty-first century? Museum might pay a few hundred pesos for it.'

A sudden blur as Neve's hand flipped the object over. There was no rear casing and he had no idea what he was looking at. Although it reminded him of something, it certainly wasn't anything he'd ever seen in his history of electronics tutorials.

'Hey.' It came to him. 'Is that… Can't be.'

'That's what I thought,' said Neve.

'You got a probe there?'

'I wouldn't try.' She waved her right hand at him and he saw recent burns on her fingers.

'It's holding a charge? How can that be?'

Neve shrugged. 'No idea.'

'But it's ancient. It wouldn't—'

Artur broke off as they heard someone approach. The object disappeared from beneath the lens. A chippy looking youth came in holding a bag.

'Wait in back with Flor,' said Neve, annoyed by the interruption.

The youth faded into the deep shadow and they both watched until they heard him talking with Flor.

'Give it some thought. Would be interested.'

'Will do,' said Artur and headed for the door.

'Don't get caught.'

28

VI

Gorodischer Plaza was filled with police and GN, but no one else had come to the riot. The party was elsewhere, somewhere over toward the embassy district by the sound of it. The truckloads of armour clad police were probably in reserve for later in the day if things got really out of hand. Both sides had it down to a fine art.

Just before he slipped down the side of the Presságiobra building to make for the staff entrance, he stopped and gazed upward. Sure enough, a black drone was hunting. It wouldn't find anything flying. The Bandeira Preta now had chameleon drones that would attach themselves to buildings, switch on the camouflage, and watch from there. He suspected Marco had a hand in their design.

When he reached his work station he requested an internal number and spoke to the secretary of Senhor Castanho.

'I'm not sure he'll see you Senhor Sozinho. You really should talk with your line manager.'

'I have,' lied Artur. And he would, the moment he came in. 'I just need five minutes to formally thank Senhor Castanho for the help he gave me yesterday.'

A muffled conversation filled the earpiece and then the secretary said: '12:55 sharp. Five minutes.'

'Thank you. Both.'

And now he needed to get to work as he had a presentation paper to write by lunch time. Digging out his notebook, he flipped to the pages he had been working on the previous evening, plugged in his e-pad, and set to work.

The twentieth floor where executive department heads spent their days was not what Artur had expected. Not that he'd given it much thought, but he had assumed it would be a quiet place, tidy, calm. The décor was a bit fancier, but the main difference between his section and this was the view. When Artur looked up from his workstation all he saw was other workstations and a concrete wall covered in notice boards. Up here, there were windows. Otherwise it was the same hum of hard work, soft conversation, a little bit of laughter, the hiss of a tap as someone refilled their water bottle.

For a moment, he wasn't sure where to go. There was a reception desk, but there didn't seem to be anyone there. And then a head popped up, an immaculately sleek young man.

'Can I help you?'

'I'm looking for the Head of Electronics.'

A raising of the eyebrow clearly indicated that the receptionist was wondering what a code monkey wanted with an Executive head.

'Do you have an appointment?'

'Yes. 12:55. Sozinho.' He glanced at a wall clock. 'And you're going to make me late.'

After a glance at a screen Artur could not see, the imaculado said: 'To your left, end of the corridor. Knock before entering.'

Artur waved what might have been a rude gesture as he headed off down the corridor. The imaculado didn't see. He was back on the floor behind his desk looking for his stylus.

The double door at the end of the corridor was open and the clock on the wall read 12:54:42.

'Senhor Sozinho?'

Artur was caught off guard. The secretary was not at the big desk. He looked round. She was on the far side of the office watering a plant.

'Sorry, didn't see you there.'

She smiled and pointed to another door with her free hand. 'Go straight through.'

'Thank you.'

He walked past her desk with its state of the art terminal and opened the normal sized door beyond.

'Come in,' someone said, 'and close it behind you.'

Here, the basement theme continued. There were several work stations, a vast table covered with stacks of flow charts and diagrams. Standing at an open cupboard straightening his tie stood Senhor Castanho. He looked even more severe close to.

'Five minutes. Ticking away.'

Artur stopped himself from a formal bow and berated himself. Some voices could still kick in the old Pineiro habits. 'I merely wished to offer my formal thanks for your help yesterday.'

Castanho's expression turned quizzical, a slight smile hovering. 'No need for such formality. You could have sent an internal memo.'

'There's something else.'

'Oh?' An eyebrow shot up.

'The event. Yesterday. It started me thinking and—'

Castanho raised his hand and Artur stopped.

'Is this work related?'

'Yes, sir.'

'Then take it to your line manager.'

'I did.'

'Hmm. All right.' He looked at an antique wrist watch. 'Ten minutes. From the beginning. What happened yesterday?'

31

'I work on the sensor programme for the asteroid mining—'

'I know all that. Impressive work. So what's got you excited?'

'When the Guarda asked for my ID plaque yesterday, his suit reader wouldn't accept it. Yet when I took the plaque to admin to get it re-registered and updated, they said there was nothing wrong with it. So I wondered if perhaps the tear gas floating around had affected the Guarda's equipment.'

'Go on.'

'I went to university with the guy who designed the GN's suit ID scanners. I talked with him and he said that tear gas and other gases had been taken into account in their design. Anyway, that got me thinking.' Artur did a quick mental edit, leaving out half the story. 'I was still thinking about sensors and how they can be affected by externals and how you take that into account when I got home.'

'I hope your thoughts were all you took home.'

Artur nodded. He knew the rules. 'My job's too precious to me, sir.'

'OK. Clock's moving on.'

'It's just… you know how ideas float round when you are tired and kind of free form… Anyway, my wife likes to watch ancient movies. Dance movies. 2D. Monochrome.'

'The point.'

'Have you ever seen any of them? I hadn't really watched them closely, but there were two dancers and they were working in perfect synchronisation. Two people. One dance.'

'I'm not following any of this and your time is running out.'

'I'm sorry. I don't really understand how my head works, but I know what led to the idea. I'm just trying to explain.'

'Five minutes.'

'The sensors I'm working with have to be sensitive enough to detect certain minerals or the likelihood of certain minerals from a variety of sources. But they also have to be able to account for other factors. We may find an asteroid rich in a specific mineral, but it's no good sending a manned refinery all the way out there if the site is unstable or unsuitable.'

'Still not following. Three minutes.'

'The Guarda's suit. It was doing one job, but not another. It all gets scrambled, but I kept thinking of that and of the dancers and wondering how sensitive a suit is to the person wearing it.'

Castanho stopped fidgeting. 'Go on.'

'What I was trying to get to in a roundabout way was that I have to know the specs of the spacesuits the company is making and the new generation that is in the design process. Same as refineries. It's no use a drone sending people to an environment their suits can't cope with. And it occurred to me that if sensors can read outwards, they can also read inwards. The new design that's being developed could be adapted so that it can become accustomed to an individual or, better still, an individual can wear a personalized system that will allow them to wear any smart suit and have it adapt to them – so, a history of their movement, how they do certain tasks, their reaction times, the sort of work they specialise in…'

Artur trailed off as Castanho walked away from him. He was worried he had blown it. The executive sat down at a work station and began pulling up work. Artur could see it was his own.

'So. An intelligent suit.'

'Not really intelligent. I know they were trying to achieve AI before the Collapse. Until we can achieve a memory and processing system as efficient and compact as the human brain we'll get nowhere near it, but we can have a system that learns, remembers, and responds to an individual wearer, aiding them, enhancing their natural abilities.'

'How soon can you have your work on the asteroid drone sensors finished?'

'I'm proofing the software now. By the end of the week.'

'I want a proposal for your new idea. Without what led to it.'

'Is that my work station?' asked Artur, nodding to the terminal.

Castanho stood up and let Artur take the seat. He found the file he had written earlier.

'You've already written it?'

'A rough draft to get the ideas in order. I didn't want to do more in case I was… treading on toes.'

'Good. Send me the draft. Make sure you embed your ID. Write it up fully when you've finished the sensor software and send me that. End of next week at the latest.'

VII

Machine intelligence. It had been something of an obsession before the Collapse. They hadn't achieved it. They'd built lots of highly engineered hexapods, quadrupeds, bipeds, and wheeled rovers that could carry out complex tasks, but they were only as smart as their programming. Artificial intelligence hadn't happened. But then, they had pretty much failed at human intelligence as well. Artur watched the rioting on the tevo screen in the canteen and thought perhaps they were failing to find it and apply it all over again. All that time wasted rebuilding. What had once been the USA was still a land riven with factions fighting over stupid ideologies and scarce resources.

The Western States looked like they might have made a go of it until the Great Quake of 2079, a 9.2 that tore down the major cities along the western seaboard of North America and had everyone watching Yellowstone as they held their breath. And then there were the increasingly virulent pandemics preying on weakened populations, the economic collapse of China into warring states, the domino effect on Russia, Europe sealing itself off, wringing its hands and then finally washing them of the bloodshed in what had been the UK. It had been a dizzyingly devastating era and only now were they crawling out of the ruins and looking for a permanent way off the planet.

The screen showed crowds clashing with police in the embassy district, most of it taking place in a haze of gas, illuminated by the bright sparks of baton rounds being fired. It was madness. And for what? An archaeological site? Those guys on the Redline must have been talking out of their doped up asses.

And yet. And yet. The feds had gone through Colina for a reason. Had it been the local police, there would be nothing like this going on. But the feds? And that strange piece of tech Neve had shown him. It had been encrusted with dirt. Not just dirty, but almost like it was embedded in some ancient layer. But that wasn't possible either. And nor was the inside. Yet he'd seen it for himself. It was clearly highly complex and looked like it was organic, grown. An elegant, sinuous set of pathways. He really wanted another look.

Back at his work station he had other things to do. The first of which was send a private text to Marco. Along with everything else he'd worked out was a means for the GN to modify their ID readers so people wouldn't get hauled off every time someone from the Bandeira Preta fogged up their face mask.

And then he had to get back to work. Finish proofing his software before handing it off. Turn the draft into a full blown proposal. Report back to his line manager. Today he was going to be earning every peso.

He scooted out half an hour early at the end of the day and retraced his steps to the chop shop. He'd never been in the area at this time of day before so he thought nothing of how quiet and empty it was. Not at first. As he neared the old concrete structure, he began to feel uncomfortable, saw faces from the shadowy depths of their closed shops watching him as he passed.

His pace slowed and he began to look round, saw spent tear gas casings in the gutters, saw cracked window panes, dark, sticky stains on the narrow sidewalk. And there was a buzz he couldn't place, realised what it was as he turned the final corner and saw police tape stretched across the road, vibrating in the hot breeze that blew along the crowded, silent street.

All the sirens were off now, but ambulances, police wagons, fire trucks, and other vehicles were crammed into the long, narrow space. Guarda in their black armour sealed the entrances to the street. A cowed group of mercado denizens was corralled near the far end. There was also a small crowd at the tape watching events, equally silent, bearing witness to some aftermath. Artur joined them, looking over the shoulders of the locals.

Movement near the entrance to the back street mercado drew his attention. A body was being carried out by four men. They were struggling. Artur tried to understand. And then he did. A body bag that big could only mean Flor. And if Flor was dead, Flor who had loved Neve from the day they met, gentle Flor who towered over everyone, Flor who had been loved fiercely in return by the chairbound Neve. If she was dead then that could only mean that Neve was as well. The world span and Artur lurched to the nearest wall where he leaned against the concrete as he vomited into the gutter.

Someone guided him round the corner and into a shop, closing the door, offering him water.

'What happened?' he asked when his throat had stopped burning.

An old woman with bleak eyes stood before him. 'A fire, they said. Killed that nice girl in her wheelchair.'

'A fire? Since when did Guarda turn up for a fire? And all those others. Neve did no harm. Nor did Flor.'

'That the big girl?'

Artur nodded.

The old woman grunted. 'She got some justice before they shot her. Saw it myself. Three Guarda thrown from up there. Dead in the street. Poor young bitch. There was a lot of shooting. Friends of yours? They casada?'

'I don't know. Been together as long as I knew them and long before that.'

'World is shit,' said the old woman. 'Always has been for us. Always will be. You go out the back way. Go right, then left.'

She'd given him a chance to recover, but didn't want him there in case he was trouble. The alley led him to a road he knew and he tried to walk casually to the nearest Metro station, tears fogging his eyes, too stunned to be angry.

When Catarina got home, she took one look at him and said: 'You look like your day went to hell again.'

'They killed Neve,' he said. 'And Flor.'

'What?! Who.'

Catarina and Neve had been at school together on the Block. They hadn't really socialised, but they got on well together. That's how Artur came to know Neve in the first place. No one knew anything about Flor except she had always been there.

Artur shrugged. 'The GN were there.'

'How d'you know this? What they want with her?'

'I went by her shop on the way to work this morning. We talked. Something she said… I wanted to swing by on the way home and ask her something. When I got there, the place was swarming. They put out some story about a fire, but the gutters were full of gas canisters and brass. The GN don't turn up for fires in back street markets. You'd be lucky to see local police for that.'

'I thought you said you were going into work early.'

'I did, but I wanted to get a couple of components from her shop. Shit. Marco was in there today as well.'

'Use the public box downstairs and then you stay away from it all.'

He wasn't sure if her anger was directed at him or at whoever killed Neve and Flor, but he did as he was told. Catarina in that mood was not to be crossed.

VIII

For the rest of the week, Artur kept his head down and played at being a model citizen. He watched the news bulletins and read the daily journals, but there was no mention of the raid on the back street mercado or of the death of Neve and Flor. He wasn't surprised, but it worried him. That sort of event usually warranted a few lines so the wealthier classes could tut over their breakfasts and the poor could see yet another warning to keep in line.

He finished his work on the asteroid mining sensors and wrote up his proposal for the spacesuit design team, lunched in the canteen, and went home at the end of the day on the Redline to spend the evening with his beloved Catarina and the not yet visible child they had made.

The only change to his routine was to his notebook. It was one of the few luxuries he afforded himself. A real, old-fashioned book with ultra thin pages made of a substance that was virtually indestructible. You even needed a special pen to write on it. The cover was made of kevlar carbon fibre.

Even as a child he had insisted on writing things down on paper, a rare commodity these days. His parents had indulged him as he said it helped him to think. Which it did. He might work with computers every day and, like everyone else, use an e-pad for day to day use, but he still found it easier to clarify and order his thoughts if he wrote them out by hand rather than typed them.

His notebook was never normally more than a few feet away, on his desk, his bedside table, in his bag. But since the events at the beginning of the week, he had become nervous about carrying it around.

Pêssego Block, like all the other blocks on the project, had been built on the cheap and the structure was riddled with weird angles, false walls, and odd sections of ducting and pipework that seemed superfluous. And in common with most other families, Catarina and Artur had added a couple of hiding places of their own using cast off ducting. It was in to one of these he now placed his notebook when he went out.

By the time Friday lunch time came around he had finished his work, spent an hour on another project for Carlos who worked in the next booth, and twiddled his thumbs for ten minutes. When everyone else headed for the canteen, he headed out of the building, constantly checking for his notebook and then feeling like an idiot.

The streets were quiet, Gorodischer Plaza empty except for lunching office workers getting a bit of mid-day sunshine. He crossed by the fountain and into a nearby boulevard lined with expensive cafés. At the Gato Sonolento, a small establishment with seating outside behind a glass wall, he made his way to a table behind the row of potted lemon trees.

Waiting for him, looking as elegant as ever, was his sister Marta. She was a year older than him and was now the only member of the family who would have anything to do with him. And even then, it was behind the lemon trees in a part of town the rest of the Pineiro family would never set foot. Far too close to all those commercial blocks from which they had made their money – building, selling, renting.

'You look rough,' said Marta as he sat down and grabbed a menu.

'Same reason these trees do,' he said, pointing at the drooping leaves.

Marta frowned. 'Have you been out rioting?'

He gave her a look. 'Seriously?'

'I never know with you, pequeno.'

If his parents or other family members had spoken to him like that, he would have sworn and walked away. And he suspected Marta had come close to doing the same at times. But the two of them were close. They could talk without the need for false politeness.

'No, sister dearest.' She poked her tongue out and then smiled. 'I got a whiff of gas on Monday in the Plaza going to work.' He wondered how much more to say, but only for a moment. There had never been secrets between them. 'And two friends of mine were shot dead on Tuesday.'

'Jesus, Artur. Are you all ri… stupid question. Were you there? Another stupid question, cos you wouldn't be sitting here. What the hell happened?'

'I have no idea. I've been keeping my head down.'

'Quite right, too.' She waved and a waitress arrived. Marta ordered for them both. 'So tell me what you do know,' she continued once their order had been whisked off to the interior of the café.

He told her everything that happened, pausing whilst their food and drinks were set out for them, and she listened as she had always listened to him, taking in every word without question. He told her about everything except the piece of tech Neve had shown him. For some reason he felt that was a confidence too far, a confidence that was too dangerous to share.

'Catarina's right,' she said when he'd finished. 'You keep well away. This is bad news. You don't want any of that, not now you've found a bit of happiness.'

He didn't reply.

'Artur,' her voice was stern.

He spread his hands in a placatory gesture. 'I won't, but—'

'But nothing.'

'I need to know why.'

'Talk to a priest. A philosopher.'

'Come on, Marta. You are the cultural liaison for the Three Families. It's your job. So what's happening up at Escarpa do Céu on the archaeological site? Is it all just stupid rumour?'

'I don't know.'

He felt hurt and it must have shown on his face.

'Honestly, Artur.' She looked round and leaned closer to her brother, lowering her voice as she continued. 'I do not know because I have been shut out of that project. The whole family has. Construction has been stopped until further notice. The Port Authority is livid but can do nothing. It comes from the top. We were served papers from the Premier's office signed by the Attorney General and counter-signed by Gabriela Vinculo.'

'Secret Service?' he whispered.

'They are citing national security, which is their polite way of telling us to back off and shut the fuck up. So now you know why. And now you know why to stay away. Well away.'

'How do you put up with it all?'

'You should see the faces I paste to the targets at the rifle club.'

He'd been so stunned by the revelation and the roundabout confirmation of the seriousness, if not the accuracy, of the rumours, that he forgot to tell Marta that Catarina was expecting their child. It only occurred to him when he got back to his work station and then went out of his head again because of the envelope.

His work station was dark, the chair tidied away. And propped against his monitor was a real paper envelope. Given what he had been told by Marta, his heart began to hammer in his chest. It took long minutes for him to persuade himself that if he was going to be disappeared, he wouldn't be invited formally.

Slitting the envelope with a pocket knife he pulled the folded sheets out and opened them up. He had to read it twice through before it sank in that he was being transferred to the spacesuit design team and to a more senior position. More money. A workstation at the Presságiobra Research Centre on the edge of the spaceport. He rolled his chair out and sat down.

IX

Monday morning, all polished up by Catarina, Artur travelled the Redline into town. At Central, three stops before his usual, he left the Metro car and joined the crowds. At first it seemed an impenetrable ocean of people, but he soon picked out the various currents and cross-currents as trains unloaded and passengers headed off in various directions, either for the fresh air above or to another tunnel and another line to take them on to their destination.

Somewhere above, the maglevs were gliding quietly into the huge terminus building west of Rosario Park and disgorging long distance commuters. Other trains were whispering away through the city, heading north and south out to the coastal rail lines where they picked up speed to cruise at 600km/h. Something else they had bought from the Chinese. Unlike the orbital launchers, the trains worked.

It might be quiet and civilized above ground, but down in the Metro tunnels it was noisy and hot. Buskers played, tucked away by pillars or in odd corners, sharing their takings with patrolling Metro guards to avoid being hassled. Artur had to keep looking to the ceiling to follow the holo-trail that took him from the Redline platforms, up and over the Yellow and Green, parallel with the Blue, until he was finally in the ticket hall at the head of the escalators down to the Blackline.

Here it was a little more civilized compared with other sections. Just the one line and passengers who all worked and travelled through just one place – the Nevoquente International Spaceport. If he'd expected the people to look different, he would have been disappointed. Cleaners and baggage handlers, vendors and administrators, all looked pretty much the same wherever they worked. But there was an aura, still, about the NIS.

From the vast concrete fields to the south of Santa Barbara, the launchers carried people and equipment up into the black before landing back on tails of bright flame. Up there, the freight vehicles were remote controlled into their proper trajectories where they docked with one of the many orbital stations. Passenger vehicles always had a crew, even though they mostly sat and watched their screens while they were guided in. People still felt better if a human was up front.

Artur had never been up, but he'd been to the NIS any number of times as a youngster, heading out to one of the observation lounges under the watchful eye of a bodyguard and some barely visible back-up team. Kidnapping wasn't common, the consequences were too brutal, but it did happen. A bodyguard, however, was also a mark of status. It was one of the many reasons he'd finally walked away from it all.

He had never been comfortable having all that lavished on him, especially when he knew thousands in the city and beyond struggled each day just to put food on a makeshift table under a tin-sheet roof. And then he had met Catarina. He smiled to himself, looking at his e-pad to see what time it was, realising that she would be opening the shutters to the clinic about now.

The Metro emerged from its tunnel and approached the NIS above ground. A heavy lifter went up and he felt the air in his ears compress as the blast wave made the train vibrate. On a pillar of filthy smoke it struggled skyward, never seeming to be going fast enough yet always climbing, receding, pushing through the high cloud cover and vanishing from view. The small launcher that followed from further down the field went up in near silence, scorching up on a bright flame, powered by one of the new fuels.

Once he left the Metro terminus, a faded 'Next Stop: Space' poster by the exit, he went in search of the Presságiobra Research Centre. The industrial estate he could see from the steps of the Metro station entrance was new and filled with long, low, mostly windowless buildings that seemed to stretch all the way to the foothills of Escarpa do Céu. He looked for a taxi and hoped his new workplace was ultimately within walking distance. Even on his new salary he wouldn't be able to afford a cab each day.

At the rank, he waited for a vehicle to unplug itself from the charger and roll up to where he stood. He waved the address code on his envelope in front of the cab's reader, climbed in, put his plaque in front of the fare charger, and punched the 'Go' button. The bug-like vehicle whisked him away and slotted into traffic, making its way through the grid of streets between the warehouse-like buildings.

When it stopped he climbed out. Even before he'd orientated himself, the taxi was whirring away and he was left alone in front of façade pierced only by heavy double-doors that slid apart as he approached. Once inside, the doors closed behind him and he crossed the cool reception area toward a smiling woman.

'Can I help you?'

Artur let out a breath. 'I hope so.'

X

Still wet from the shower and wrapped in a towel, Artur emerged from clouds of steam and stepped into the small living space. Catarina had turned down the lighting, set the shades to blackout, and stood smiling. A cake on the table glittered with a miniature holo-firework display.

'What's this?' he asked with a frown and a smile.

'Me and inchaço,' she said, stroking the slight bulge that pushed out her t-shirt, 'we thought we should celebrate.'

'Celebrate?'

'You are so hopeless with dates.'

'Oh. It's not your birthday? No. No. That's not for weeks yet.'

'Your face. I never seen you look so scared. Come here.'

She embraced him gently.

'Is it inchaço's…?'

'Four months.'

'Four months already?'

'And three months for you since you started your new job.'

His new job. The reason he was so tired when he got home, all that commuting, all those new ideas filling his head and his notebook. The reason they hadn't found a new apartment yet.

'This weekend,' he said. 'We'll go through the Pêssego Block tenancy lists.'

'Already done, anjo. Doctor Galo went to the Housing Office and told them I was a key worker.' She beamed proudly.

'That clinic would fall apart without you.'

She gave him a squeeze. 'Anyway, he took the information we'd discussed – minimum requirements, most rent we could afford – and they came up with a list. And there's a key worker discount. Who knew?'

'So?'

'You know the apartments they're renovating on the forty-fifth?'

'Seriously? We can't afford those.'

'We can. There are a couple of small three bedroom ones up there with shared outside space.'

'I thought Block Admin would snap all those up.'

'Galo can be very persuasive, especially as he mentioned the advantages of having a trained nurse on their level.'

'Well, just as long as you're not expected to use up your spare time pulling splinters or sticking plasters on grazed elbows.'

'Don't be such a grump. I'm the one supposed to have mood swings.'

'We can go look on the weekend.'

'They're not finished yet, but I guess we can get some idea.'

'Enough seriousness. Cake!'

*

On his way to work the following day, Artur recalled the first time he'd made the commute, the crazy days since. It had been bad enough taking the Redline everyday, but he now had an extra hour being crammed into the Metro with others with nothing to do but think, which was good for work; and brood, which was not.

He loved his new job. There was far greater opportunity to be creative and his original concept had already gone into development. Now he was taking the idea sideways so that spacesuits could be rigged to act as controls for remote mining robots. It was in its early stages, but it kept him busy. Indeed, ever since that first hectic day of orientation, documentation, meeting, greeting, and trying to take it all in, the pace had rarely slackened. Which was good, because as well as keeping him busy, it kept him out of trouble. Mostly.

Because in all the glitter and sunshine was a deep shadow – the shooting of Neve and Flor. Even now the shock of their deaths was raw. Yet what really burned away at him was that glimpse he'd had of the strange tech on Neve's workbench beneath the magnifier.

Day after day it had haunted his waking moments as he travelled the Metro. Day after day he tried to draw it from a memory of that brief glimpse. He saved each version, starting afresh, learning how to draw on the swaying Metro.

'Nice design,' someone had said one day. 'Gonna be body art?'

'You know,' Artur replied to the youngster who was strap hanging beside him, a homemade one-wheel clutched in her other arm, 'it just might.'

'Elegant. You base it on those?'

Artur frowned. 'On what?'

She pointed to a stencilled graffito on the panel by the door. It took him a few seconds to make sense of it, a sinuous foliate spirit with a grotesque face.

'How long has that been there?'

'Cara. Asleep or what. They been around for weeks.'

He never saw the kid again, which was a shame as he'd have liked to thank her. So many ideas had, literally, flowered from her comment. Not only did he try to find the original of the foliate spirit, looking at thousands of images that led him time and again to indigenous art, but he also began to study plant growth and went back to the design he had tried to recreate from memory and began to see how it was following a logic, almost as if it were a kind of hard-wired code. He wasn't even sure what that meant. It was just an instinct that the sinuous, branching forms behaved in the same, logical way a programme would run.

Ultimately he had no idea how much of it was an accurate reproduction of what he had seen and how much was his own invention based on his own ways of thinking. After all, he may just have been looking at an ornament, a pretty design. What's more, he had no idea of scale. He hadn't really seen the object except under the large magnifier and even then for just a few, startled seconds.

One obsession displaced another. He needed Neve's magnifier, or he needed an identical one. The chances of the original still being there were so slim as to be non-existent. Someone had probably moved into her shop, thrown everything away, if scavengers hadn't got there first. But he needed to know one way or the other, perhaps speak to some of her neighbours.

That morning, as he sat on the staff bus from the Metro to the Research Centre, he decided to leave early and visit the back street mercado. As a consequence, the day dragged as if an extra sixty minutes had been slotted into each hour.

When lunch came round he was near the front of the queue in the canteen.

'Never seen you move so fast, cara.'

Artur turned. Lixale, who worked in his department, was behind him collecting a tray. 'Hungry,' he said with a grin.

'How's Catarina? Still throwing up?'

'She's past that now. We hope. Mind you, she was never as bad as some of the horror stories she brought back from the clinic.'

Lixale laughed. 'I was fine with my first two, but with Lucas... I won't even tell you cos we're gonna eat.'

They filed along and chose their food, swiped their cards, and headed to a table where others from the suit design section joined them. Artur was spooning in some soup when the room shook, a loud explosion swamping all other noise.

He was half way out of his chair when a hand on his arm stopped him and he noticed everyone else was carrying on with their food.

'You not get the notice?' asked Lixale.

Artur stared at her vacantly.

'Man, your face. You think a launcher go kablooey or something?'

'Yeah,' he said with a sheepish look.

Lixale shook her head. 'None going up midday today. I'll get you a timetable. And a copy of the notice. They blasting the new tunnel up to the rail launch site.'

Artur was confused. 'I didn't know they were working up there. I thought that had all stopped.'

'They been doing the groundwork for weeks, surveying, that kind of thing. Now they making a tunnel so they can move the heavy equipment up there.'

'So the archaeologists have gone.'

Lixale shrugged. 'Didn't know there had been any up there.'

He felt strangely comforted that he wasn't the only one to not know about things happening on his doorstep.

'I suppose it would explain all those extra people on the Metro theses days,' said Artur.

'For a while. I hear they're going to use some of the buildings on this site as camps for the construction workers. They'll be doing stuff down on the main field of the NIS as well. Nothing ever seems to stay still these days.'

XI

As he approached the Disposal section, Artur could hear the grinder tearing apart a redundant piece of machinery. He waited at the heavy door until it went quiet, then pressed the call pad to make his presence known. Moments later the red light flickered off and the lock disengaged with a clunk. He pushed against the door and was waved inside by a grizzled man who was taking off a helmet that protected his eyes and ears.

'Come in, come in. Perfectly safe. Don't know why they bother with all this armour.'

Artur stepped into the large room, carrying his bag of parts. It was unlike any other part of the Research Centre. Everywhere else was quiet, clean, and bright, even the manufacturing section where the prototype suits and suit parts were assembled. Here it was distinctly old-school industrial.

The floor of polished, poured stone, metal girders forming a reinforcing cage for the row of grinders that ranged from something the size of a paper shredder to a truck sized box fed by a small crane, and a small office tucked away behind armoured glass in one corner.

Outside the office was a long, empty table. The man in the goggles pointed to it.

'Put your bag and e-pad there, please.'

Artur complied. 'Just some components and boards.' he said.

The man grinned. 'For all my sins. Now, let's see what we have.'

He put his helmet on the bench beside the bag and took off his gloves. From somewhere inside his armoured jacket, he removed the most delicate pair of spectacles Artur had ever seen, half moon lenses in and almost invisible frame. Eyeglasses were such a rarity he couldn't help but stare. The man laughed and opened the bag, tipping out the components and spreading them out into neat rows.

Artur stood by as the man checked each item off against the list on the e-pad. It was a long, slow process as the man was meticulous, checking carefully that everything was present, getting Artur to sign it over once he'd finished. The Research Centre destroyed all their prototypes, no matter how large, shredding them to dust so that no one else could see what they were up to or back-engineer from anything stolen. Everything had to be accounted for at all stages.

Once the checking was complete, the man began to put the pieces back into the bag. As he did so, Artur picked up his pad and managed to knock a piece of casing onto the floor.

'I can see it,' he said as he bent to pick it up. 'Right at the back, there.'

'Leave it there. I see it. You've not to touch anything once it's been checked.'

'Sorry,' said Artur as the man got down on his knees and reached under the table.

In a move he'd been practising for days, Artur reached into his trouser pocket and slipped his old phone into the bag.

Despite all the rehearsals, he was still shaking and felt sure the man would notice he was sweating.

'No harm done,' said the man as he climbed to his feet and dropped the component in the bag.

Artur stood well back whilst the rest of the pieces were placed in one by one praying the man would not take one last look. Instead he simply closed the bag, put on a seal in case of interruptions or backlogs, and left it on the bench.

'I should have waited,' said Artur lifting his e-pad.

'Don't worry, son. You want to watch?'

'OK.'

'Not allowed if it's big stuff, but there's a spare helmet inside the office.'

Artur wanted to get out as quickly as he could, but he also wanted to know for certain the phone would be reduced to dust. He found the helmet, pulled it on and, feeling somewhat self-conscious, followed the old man across to the far end.

There, bolted to a sturdy bench, was a box the size of a suitcase standing upright. The top was open and Artur peered in at a row of vicious looking metal teeth on interlocking wheels.

At a wave from the operator, Artur took a step back. Even with the ear protection he could hear the machine start up, then watched as the bag was dropped into its maw and a cover dropped over it. A second button was pressed and clearly the teeth were engaged as there was a horrendous, splintering whine, the grinder shuddered, and dust began to sift down into a clear collection box underneath.

Eventually the grinding screech died down and the machine came to a stop. The old man pointed to Artur's helmet and he took it off.

'Not much of a show,' he said.

Artur nodded. 'I'd hate to be in here when that big one's going.'

'Even I go out the room into the control area next door for that one.'

Afterwards, Artur went outside to the small Research Centre garden to calm his nerves. It was overcast and threatened rain, but he didn't care. It's not like he'd been stealing from the company, but it still felt like he'd done something they could fire him for. But no one came looking for him; no one said anything when he went back inside, calmer but still fretting, even though the phone was, literally, dust.

It was something he'd made from ancient components when he was at University, partly to understand how such things had worked but also as a tiny act of rebellion. It was off the grid and in recent years it had been a useful way of sending short messages to people without leaving a potentially embarrassing trace. Mostly he'd just arranged meetings with his sister.

Five times in the last two weeks, however, Artur had tried to raise Marco. He had chickened out of going to the mercado and wanted to ask Marco if he knew what sort of magnifier Neve had used, whether he too had seen the strange piece of tech. But Marco hadn't responded. And a few discreet questions to people he could trust all came back with the same answer. Marco was gone. Which scared Artur. Scared him so much he trashed the phone in the most comprehensive way he knew how.

XII

A week passed. A second. A third. Artur kept his head down. He divided his time between work and pampering Catarina, making sure she rested each evening, went to bed early. And in the quiet moments alone, when time allowed, he developed his own ideas, sketching out designs and writing out ideas for coding in his notebook.

One evening they even sat together on the minuscule balcony, drawn by the heavy chuddering sound of helicopters passing overhead, staying to watch the bright lights of the city glitter in the darkness. They covered their ears as night launches tore the sky to shreds. Witnessed the sparkle and crackle of gunfire in Colina and Ravina and the other shanties that continued to grow up the steeper slopes of the surrounding foothills.

Weekends were best. They would walk the long corridors discussing names for the child and take the lift up to the top floor to see how work was progressing, introduce themselves to the new neighbours that had already moved in, plan what colours they would paint the walls. It didn't matter that the renovation work seemed to be taking forever. They had signed the tenancy agreements. It would be their new home soon enough and inchaço would grow up in relative luxury.

Bubbles never last long. One Monday morning, still half asleep, he waited with the usual crowds and boarded the

Redline, sitting in his usual seat. Two stops on, beneath Cerejeiras Block, a group of construction workers crowded into the Metro car. Most of them lived out in camps at the site during the week. At weekends they went home, were always ill-tempered on their way back to work.

Almost immediately there was trouble, raised voices and scuffling. Artur couldn't help but listen.

'Why should I calm down? I'm sick of it.'

'Aw, come on Tijolo. It's just graffiti.'

Artur looked round, realised the inside of the car was covered with the stencilled glyphs he'd seen before.

'It's a fucking disgrace. Not just this shit all over the walls. Kids got nothing better to do? But taking the piss like this. Racists got no respect.'

Artur frowned. He didn't understand.

Without being too obvious he leaned sideways to try to see who was so angry. A group stood near the door, strap-hanging. One of them was bigger than the others, his skin darker, his face distinctively narrow. Clearly of indigenous stock, maybe of the Bisanatha people. And not happy.

A blade flashed and Artur's heart beat faster. Instead of a fight, however, the blade was turned on one of the glyphs, the razor edge scraping at the paint. Several hands tried to restrain the man, but something in him had snapped.

At that moment three Metro guards pushed their way forward from the far end of the carriage.

Tijolo didn't fight, but he was yelling at the guards as he was taken off at the next stop, wanting to know why they never arrested the kids who sprayed the graffito in the first place.

The group who had been with Tijolo kept quiet for the rest of the journey but it was obvious they weren't happy. And when they finally reached the NIS terminal, they joined another group milling around just outside the entrance.

Artur didn't fancy trying to push his way through, even though the Research Centre bus was waiting on the forecourt.

'What's up?' he asked of the nearest of the crowd. The man, dressed in shabby work clothes, turned and gave him a long look.

'What's it to you?'

Artur shrugged and made his way round the noisy mob. He just managed to get to the bus and stop it before it drove off. At lunch time he asked in the canteen.

'All sorts of trouble brewing there,' said Lixale. 'I hear some of them stopped work over the weekend. Refused to carry on.'

'Can't think why,' said Filipe who also worked in their section. 'They get paid well enough.'

'It ain't the money,' said Lixale. 'A primo of mine owns one of the food trucks they use in the evening. He says the CPI has made protests. Something about a sacred site.'

'Didn't they sort all that out when the archaeologists were up there?' asked Artur.

Lixale shrugged. 'Don't know about that, but the native workers aren't happy. And there's something else as well. They say it's haunted up there.'

'Haunted? What, ghosts and things?' Filipe asked, a grin on his face. 'How old they, six?'

Lixale turned and looked at Filipe whose grin faded.

'Not ghosts.'

'Is that what the graffiti is?'

'What graffiti?'

'You not use the Metro?'

Lixale laughed. 'Cara, I asleep till the train stop.'

Artur sketched it on his e-pad with the stylus, turned the pad and showed it Lixale. It was her turn for her smile to fade.

'Brisa da Selva,' she said in a hushed voice. 'No wonder they scared.'

'What is that?' demanded Filipe.

'It's a native spirit, a breeze when there is no wind, the breath of the forest. You feel that, you get sick, you die. Most times it just makes the leaves rustle and the vines sway, just to warn you. Stay away. If it touches you. Goodbye.'

'Seriously?'

'That's the story, Filipe. And for the Bisanatha people it's very real.'

'How you know so much?'

She gave Filipe another stare. 'Cos I'm bright, I take an interest, and I'm part Bisanatha. OK?'

'Yeah. Sorry. Didn't mean to be...'

Lixale waved her hand to tell him to forget it. He went back to his food.

'Is this old, this Brisa da Selva?'

'Yeah. The People are mostly animist. There's a lot of later stuff mixed in from elsewhere, but the Brisa da Selva is really early, really elemental. It's not even really a thing in itself, just said to mark the passing of a nameless evil that lurks in the deep forest, said to make you waste away.'

'Grim.'

'Not surprised if some of the workers are unhappy if pictures of it are being sprayed up. That's not good. Alma escura. Almost like calling out to it. Asking for trouble.'

Artur hastily erased the image from his e-pad and Lixale nodded.

XIII

The incident that morning left him unsettled. He couldn't help thinking of the graffito, of the sinuous image, of the plant-like structure of what he had seen at Neve's shop. Not long after lunch he abandoned attempts to concentrate on ways to improve the suit system he had worked on. The first tests had been positive and the feedback from the orbital workers who had tried the prototypes was also encouraging. It was their suggestions and questions that needed reducing to an improved system, but he just couldn't seem to fix himself on the task.

Mid afternoon, a general message circulated. There were protests up at the construction site, pickets at the NIS and Metro station. Police were arriving. Buses had been laid on by Presságiobra to ferry staff from the Research Centre via back roads to a Metro station further down the line to avoid delays and conflict.

It had escalated quickly. As Artur watched from the bus, he could see police and strikers lined up facing each other with all sorts of objects sailing through the air. A couple of bricks hit the bus, crazing the glass in a couple of windows, but no one was hurt and they were soon well away from the trouble.

He rode the Metro back into the city completely lost in his thoughts. At Central, he disembarked and joined the crowds making for the Redline when he looked beyond the person in front of him and saw a figure in the crowd he thought he recognised.

'Marco?'

His question was so soft he barely heard it himself, but it woke him sharply and he began pushing after the figure. Every time he glimpsed the person, someone pushed in front of him, and every time he got sight again they seemed further away. Finally, he caught a glimpse as they stepped onto the escalator.

Momentarily confused, Artur looked round. He had missed the way to the Redline northbound platform. A quick look at his e-pad reassured him that he had time to look. So he stepped onto the escalator as well and rode upward, trying to peer beyond the glimmering holo-ads as he rolled through them.

The crowds pushed him out onto the main concourse of Central Station and he craned his neck, turning slowly on the spot. Yes! Surely that was Marco there. Standing in front of a café. He started forward as another stream of passengers from the latest maglev arrival cut in front of him and blocked his view.

When he finally pushed his way through the stream of people and made his way into the quiet space outside the café, there was no one there. Artur peered through the window. The place was brightly lit and nearly empty. Marco wasn't there. With a swift turn, Artur surveyed the concourse, but Marco wasn't there, either. Perhaps he never had been.

More people began streaming across the vast, roofed space and he'd suddenly had enough. Striding off, he made for the main entrance. Outside, he crossed the forecourt, dodged between a line of taxis at their charge stations, and crossed the road. On the far side, he went through the ever-open gateway of Rosario Park, breathed calmer air. Eventually he found a bench by one of the fountains and sat, feeling the fine mist of the leaping waters on his brow.

Artur wasn't given much to flights of fancy beyond the limits of his own expertise, but as he sat there in the park he felt as if time had slowed down, come to a stop. Everything around him was normal, yet as he looked around it also seemed unreal. The colours were a fraction too bright, the sounds too sharp, the sky... a faint coppery haze stretched from horizon to horizon. He shivered.

A breeze with a faint odour of rotting vegetation brushed his face and brought him back to earth as a posse of young kids, probably just out of school, went streaking past directly in front of him on their homemade one-wheels. They wove with consummate skill along the pathways and between the few people who were enjoying the park. Something about their anarchic joy brought a little light into his gloom and he hoped they avoided trouble.

They also brought something else to his mind and, after checking the clock on his e-pad again, he headed off to the park's south-eastern corner. Waiting for a tram to pass so he could cross the road, he looked back but there was no one. Nothing. Just the park. Just the first hint of a brewing storm. Way off to the south a heavy lifter cast its own thunder across the heavens and climbed on its billowing pillar of smoke.

Despite knowing the causes, the feeling of unreality did not completely dissipate as Artur ventured deeper into the old quarter. The shops were clearly open, doors wide, people going in and out, yet they also felt closed and shuttered. The buses and other vehicles passed in a dream. Several times he shook his head to try to clear it.

Before venturing into the final maze of back streets he stopped again, this time in a recessed doorway. He stayed there for several minutes peering back along the way he had come. He had no idea why. A distant growl of thunder was like a throaty laugh at his expense.

A shrug. A check of the e-pad. Still plenty of time to get home and cook before Catarina came in from her lighter duties at the clinic. He slipped out of the doorway and turned the corner into the long, narrow street where the mercado stood.

The whole place had given up. The few shops that had existed were all shuttered. Litter had blown into corners. An unhealthy smell lingered in the hot air. The ancient structure that had once been a car park seemed to have sunk in on itself, turned its back on the world, as if dying. There seemed to be no movement or sound. Perhaps it was already dead.

The thought made him hesitate for a second, but after a quick glance in both directions along the street, he stepped into the chill shadows. There were still shacks there, but they no longer had tables outside bearing wares scavenged from who knew where. A canvas door shifted to one side as someone peered out at him, then fell back in place with a cold sound.

He made his way to the stairs and climbed, finding each level the same. Lots of people hiding away, fearful, silent. Pale, ethereal faces staring. No market. No life. His footsteps echoed alone as he bore down on his goal.

Neve's emporium had been at one end of the seventh level. The front was tucked in by the entrance to the stairs and the long-silent lift shaft, the rest curling into the recesses around the stairwell and far beyond. The old concrete wall outside was still fire blackened and even after so many months he could smell the dampened burning as if it hung in the still air, weeping from the scorched shop front.

The front section had been completely trashed. Sections of splintered timber lay where the workbench had been. Pock marks peppered the walls and spent shell casings lay amongst the other debris. Of the magnifier there was no sign, but it no longer seemed to matter. Especially when he saw a buckled wheel of Neve's chair. Everything else lay scattered about. Out of fear or respect, no one had come scavenging.

Light flickered blue and Artur counted. Thunder finally rolled its way into the structure. Faint and spent. He stood undecided. In the stillness and silence a breeze caressed his face. He turned to face the dark interior and began to make his way into the shadowy ruin of the shop's interior.

XIV

Solemn-faced, the little group of girls who had been playing noisily until she turned the corner onto their corridor, turned to watch Marta. She hesitated, smiled, and then continued on her way along the length of the broad concrete thoroughfare, reading numbers on doors as she went. When she found the door she was looking for, she looked back. The girls had gone. A doll lay abandoned.

She had already been up to the forty-fifth where Artur had said that he would be moving with Catarina. She had assumed he'd forgotten their lunch date because of being busy with the new apartment. When she'd rung the buzzer, she'd heard voices and felt both excited and shy.

It came as a shock when a complete stranger opened the door. The woman had looked at her askance when she'd asked for the Sozinhos.

'No,' she'd said. 'Not here.'

Marta had wanted to ask more, certain there was something wrong, but the door was closed in her face. Quietly, it was true, but very firmly. So all she could do was trail back down to the fortieth and look for the small apartment that Artur and Catarina were supposed to be moving from. If there had been some administrative cock-up or they'd been bounced by some official offering preferential treatment to a family member, they'd need help. If not help, at least consoling.

Now, though, all that vanished. The door was in front of her and she checked the number, not understanding. Pêssego Block was, on the whole, law abiding, but even there you didn't leave your front open. Not even in a big mansion with armed guards did you leave your front door open. Her heart beat hard.

Taking courage, she leaned forward a little and tried to look inside, listened. The place seemed empty. Hesitantly she reached out and pushed the door a little way, revealing more of the small apartment. She could see no furniture, felt only the echoes of an empty space.

'Hello?'

She meant it to be firm, loud. It came out as a squeak so she tried again. The reply was the same. Silence.

With a worried frown creasing her normally serene brow she stepped into the tiny hallway, pushed open a door that gave onto a bathroom stripped of any personal items. Opposite was a kitchen. Scoured clean. Ahead were two other doors. One was closed and she opened this onto a completely empty space. The other led to what she presumed had been the living space with its door to a tiny balcony.

A tear burned the corner of her eyes and she wiped it away.

'Who are you?'

Surprised, Marta spun round. Filling the hallway was a heavily pregnant woman whose beauty was marred by the fact she seemed to have been crying non-stop for days. Yet there was also steel there.

'I am—'

'Marta. I see it. He had never said how alike you look.'

'What? What… Where is he?'

Catarina began to cry. Marta stepped forward and Catarina accepted her embrace. It was some minutes before she was composed enough for Marta to risk questions.

'Has there been an accident?'

'I don't know. He didn't come home from work on Monday. He always cooked for me on Mondays. He always came home.'

'But… I don't understand.'

'Do you think I do?' Catarina asked angrily.

'Have you been to the police?'

Scorn added to the anger in Catarina's face. 'The police? Yes. I went to the police. They took one look at me and assumed he'd left me. Run off.'

Marta shook her head and swore. It made Catarina blink.

'You were his life, you and the child.'

Catarina trembled, sniffed. 'His work.'

'No. With his work he became intense, almost hidden away. With you, when he talked about you and the baby. I've never seen him so… lit up with joy. There must have been an accident. I'll check—'

'I've checked every hospital in the country. And a good few unofficial clinics in the city. He's vanished.'

'I will find him.'

Catarina looked at Marta. Shook her head. 'No.'

'What do you mean, no.' Marta could look angry as well.

'It isn't safe.'

'Safe?'

'Not even for you. He told me you'd been shut out.'

'Shut out?'

'And I think he kept looking.'

'What are you talking about?'

Catarina waved her hand. 'You think I moved all this? To another apartment? They came. Guarda in black armour. Men in suits. The neighbours say they spent a whole day here. They took everything.'

It was the smallest of lies, but it was her secret to keep, her only link with her beloved Artur, his notebook now stowed safely elsewhere.

'So where will you live?'

'They took everything, Marta. Our furniture, our clothes, our money, Artur's books. Everything. My ID plaque no longer works. I no longer exist. I am not supposed to live. I have no choice but to—' A sharp whistle interrupted her. 'You must go, they are coming back. There must be spies. Go with Beatriz.' A woman had appeared in doorway. 'She will keep you safe.'

'But how will I get in touch? Help you support the baby.'

'You won't, Marta. For Artur's sake. For his memory. Stay away and stay safe.'

2228

The Archives

I

Already a world of flat, pale grey surfaces, the powerful lights on their thirty metre poles bleached out all sense of distance and scale. Were it not for the occasional dark speck of a person moving in their own shadow or a vehicle rolling silently along one of the trackways, they would have had no clear idea of what was in front of them.

Bruno, who was on watch, had to keep closing his eyes to rest them from the relentless glare. Beside him, in the darkened cab of their truck, the boy Afonso fidgeted. Bruno held in a sigh and looked at his ancient wind up wristwatch.

Leaning forward he tapped the truck's console and a small panel gave off a faint glow, a tiny digital clock in one corner. A rich voice spoke with quiet assurance.

'—in a ceremony at the Presidential Palace.

'Unemployment figures were up slightly on last month. The Bureau of Works and Employment stated that the rise was temporary due to construction workers being laid off on the completion of the Rio Fundo Hydroelectric scheme. They expect the numbers to fall again as several new large-scale projects, including groundwork on the new terminal complex at the International Spaceport, get under way.

'The Nevoquente State Bureau for Lunar Affairs today announced the lifting of quarantine at their Lunar Propulsion Research Centre. The quarantine was imposed in accordance with the Lunar Treaty of 2201 when it was feared a newly arrived member of staff may have been in contact with a person infected with SSPEV25. Lockdown procedures were fully complied with and subsequent tests and tracing show that the person in question was completely clear of infection.

Despite the disruption to the Centre's work, the Bureau said it was absolutely the right thing to do and that stricter testing measures would be put in place at the NIS and at all sites within three miles of the spaceport.

'Elsewhere, restrictions continue in place in all public spaces until trials of the latest vaccine have been completed. The Health Bureau expects this to be within the next few weeks. The State Assembly will then expedite permission so that manufacture and distribution can begin as swiftly as possible.

'There have been further calls for a permanent Honour Guard at the Martyr's Memorial after it was revealed that it has been defaced yet again. Paint was splashed across the façade, obliterating names. The Memorial is covered by cameras on a twenty-four basis, but the attacks have so far gone undetected. Police have said that the perpetrators will be caught and their disrespect for those who fell in the struggles of 2195 will be dealt with harshly.

'Sport and the meeting of the IOC broke up today without reaching any agreement on resumption—'

'Hey I was listening to that,' protested Afonso.

'You believe any of that State Radio shit?' Bruno asked, grabbing Afonso's wrist and syncing their watches as the young man struggled. 'Besides we need to pay attention. I only put it on for the time check. Go see if the others are ready and get them to check their timepieces against yours. And keep your Clã mask switched off.'

Afonso opened the door and clambered down to the ground. Bruno watched his wiry frame as he slouched off across the concrete roadway in an ill-fitting set of Costa Norte mechanic's overalls, a company cloth mask covering his lower face. He squirted alcohol gel on his hands and rubbed them together.

'You don't like him.'

Bruno sat back in his seat, turning his head slightly so he could see into the shadows in the back of the cab. Sitting there was an older man.

'I don't trust him, Ruben.'

'I hear you. It feels like his aims are at odds with ours.'

'You've put your finger on it. He talks a good talk, but…'

'He wants money and an easy life and doesn't much care who gets hurt.'

'Maybe not deliberately. He's just reckless. Thoughtless. And I'm not sure he isn't doped up on something.' Bruno sighed. 'We'll have to cut him loose.'

'I trust he's still an 'outsider'.'

'Definitely. He's Clã do Gato. The Criaturas has never come up in conversation whilst he's been with us.'

'So not a plant?'

'Doubt it, he's not bright enough for the SdI and we'd know from our own people in the Clã if the police had their hooks in him. We'll warn him off. If he's using, that's enough. Pai won't have it.'

Bruno looked at the antique timepiece on his wrist again.

'We'll be out of here soon enough,' said Ruben.

'I hope so. It's almost as bad as prison.'

They had been camping in the lorry's cab for nearly two weeks, ever since one of their own had reported a hole in the fence. The lorry was easy enough, there were hundreds going in and out of the Costa Norte port and ferry terminal on a daily basis, dozens parked up waiting for loads. It had been getting the rest of the crew in place that had always presented a barrier.

A team had been mustered as quickly as possible and taken north of Santa Barbara where they sneaked onto the terminal before the gap was repaired. It was the work on the Rio Fundo dams that had done the damage along the edge of the port, with water surges undermining post stanchions. They had then made their way through the vast container port dressed in Costa Norte overalls until they were able to rendezvous at the lorry.

After that it had been a waiting game, gathering information. The place was so big that no one was going to notice a few extra 'mechanics' wandering about checking the huge fifty tonne loads, helping assemble the road trains. Most of the freight containers were loaded onto the maglev carriers, but local traffic for the north of Nevoquente was assembled on the concrete concourse in front of them.

Bruno watched as Afonso dwindled in the distance, a dark speck in the eternally bright way station. He saw him stop and another figure appeared from behind a trailer. They compared watches and then Afonso went shuffling on as the other figure disappeared into the small patch of shadow it had found. Away off to the left, the lights of a huge ferry appeared as it began to turn in to the harbour, the throb of its engines a low thrum.

A faint tone in Bruno's left ear made him raise his hand to a throat mic. 'Patrol on the move.'

A completed road train of three trailers whined past, taking the long curve off to the right that led to the exit gates and the feeder road to the Highway One Interchange. After it had gone, the only movement was the approaching security patrol.

Bruno and Ruben sat still in the shadows and watched it through the cab window.

It was peculiarly bright in the washed-out landscape as the patrol drove slowly along one broad avenue between parked trailers, turned off and, a few minutes later re-appeared. A group of three mechanics, one in ill-fitting overalls, stopped their work for a moment and watched it go by before resuming the checks they had been making on a set of couplings. The security vehicle didn't slow. Bruno relaxed a fraction.

As it came closer to the lorry in which they were sitting, the security vehicle slowed, pulled into the side beside a podium, and stopped. A door slid open and something climbed out.

'Fuck is that?' Bruno asked of no one in particular, startled by what he was seeing. He had the presence of mind, however, to switch on the lorry's cameras.

Ruben leaned forward a fraction, keeping to the shadow.

Out on the concrete, the security patrol vehicle moved away, leaving a machine standing at the foot of the podium. It was a black framework balanced on two legs and looked vaguely human, with articulated arms hanging at its sides. The head was a smooth-surfaced, inverted bucket shape. After a few moments, the machine moved, turned and climbed the steps up onto the platform at the top of the podium. The movements were oddly jerky, but the machine seemed stable, solid, and grimly impersonal.

Once it was in place, the head rotated slowly through an arc of 270 degrees and back to its starting point.

'What do we do? What do we do?' asked a panicked voice in Bruno's ear.

'Calm down, to start with,' he whispered via his throat mic. 'And carry on as we had planned. Rendezvous point two. Keep off comms.'

'But what about—'

'Assume it's watching, so carry on as normal.'

He heard subdued swearing, but ignored it.

'Bit fancy for a camera,' Ruben observed.

'Bit fancy for port security, if you ask me. Must be some sort of trial. Shit.'

'Want to abort?'

Bruno took a deep breath. 'No. Not now.'

'OK. Your call. You'll be needing this.'

Ruben handed forward a battered looking epad with the faded logo of a well-known supermarket chain embossed on the rear.

'Thanks,' said Bruno as he took the pad.

After a pause in which he consulted his watch and muttered a prayer to his own gods, he switched on the epad. The screen flickered to life and he waited until a password was demanded, keying in the one he had memorised. Navigating the pages that appeared was easy enough. He found what he was looking for and signalled to the waiting team.

Through the windscreen the same, bleak landscape was beginning to show some semblance of life. The ferry that had been manoeuvring in the harbour had now docked. Automated cabs were homing in on the loading ramps from various charging stations around the complex, arriving in a pre-arranged pattern to board the ferry and haul off the containers stacked inside.

One by one the trailers were pulled across the vast concrete concourse, some to be stored awaiting collection, others made up into trains awaiting departure. Bruno watched the screen of the epad whilst all this was going on. The blank form suddenly acquired a number that blinked slowly, joined by another and, finally, another. A train of three trailers had now been put together and was waiting for collection.

Bruno touched his mic. 'Go. I repeat. Go.'

The electric engines whined into life and the control panel lit up. Outside, the head of the newly arrived robotic sentinel swivelled and followed the cab as it left its parking bay and was driven by Bruno across the perimeter road and into the maze of assembly lines. On the dashboard, a screen guided him. He could have let the truck go on auto, but like most drivers, he took some pride in his skill to do the job without help. Besides, he had to make a couple of unauthorised manoeuvres and he wanted to be able to blame human error if he was challenged.

With the trailers hitched and the team smuggled on board and crammed into the converted bunk section of the cab, he turned the road train toward the main exit. At a major junction, another of the sentinels stood immobile but for the head that swivelled as the rig passed. Bruno felt cold sweat in the small of his back.

'We're coming up on the gate,' he said to an apparently empty cab. 'Two more of those sentinel things and a bunch of heavily armed Guarda.'

With a re-found skill that pleased him, he brought the one hundred and fifty tonne rig to a halt in exactly the right place. His window sank and he waved to the security official in his raised booth, handing across his epad.

'Not seen you in a while,' said the security man.

'They tempted me out of retirement. Shortage of drivers cos of this latest pandemic.'

The security man nodded and then looked down at Bruno's epad to check the details. He frowned.

'Problem?' asked Bruno.

'This thing's not working,' said the security man, lifting the epad.

'Piece of crap's probably older than me. Give it here.'

The epad was handed back and Bruno rapped one corner with his knuckles. The screen lit up thanks to a hidden switch. A quick glance told Bruno that it had been close enough to the security computer to hack in and validate itself. He handed it back over and watched the security man go through the motions. The cold sweat was soaking the back of his shirt.

'Safe journey,' said the security man as he returned the epad.

Bruno slid it into its holder, winked, and as the window began to slide up, put the vehicle in drive. Pulling away seemed to take forever under the bored eyes of the Guarda and their unblinking sentinels.

II

'And there were four?'

'That I saw,' replied Bruno, stepping away from the window where he had been watching the rain fall. 'But I imagine there were more. We only crossed a small section of the ferry terminal. Didn't see anything of the container port. But the GN were there in force. Trucks tucked away by the security centre. Armed guards on the gate.'

'So a trial of some sort?'

Bruno shrugged. He was a truck driver. 'I guess. Sorry. Not much use, I know. We were taken by surprise and I'd banned epads from being taken in by the team.'

'No. You were right. It was your show. And thank you. It was invaluable. We can restock the pharmacy. And a lot of people will eat because of you, despite being laid off. It's all good.'

He shrugged again and pointed at the dashcam clip playing on the screen. 'Best I could do without drawing attention to myself.'

'Ruben tells me you were recognized.'

'After a fashion. The guy on the gate remembered me as someone who used to drive regularly. I doubt he knows my name.'

'All the same, we won't take any chances. Keep you out of the wider world. How do you feel about a bit of teaching, passing on your skills?'

'Not sure I've got any, Pai. I never got above corporal in the Fire Fighters Division when I was conscripted, never did anything but drive trucks when I got out. But I'll keep my eyes open. I do have a nose for trouble makers.'

'Afonso?'

'Not sure he's a trouble maker so much as a liability.'

'OK Bruno, stay in touch with Ruben. And thanks again.'

Pai watched him leave, watched the video from the dashcam on the epad one last time and then put it away. He'd have the clips scrubbed and the old, stolen epad pulverised.

He pressed a button on his desk and turned to the window. The rain was, if anything, heavier than earlier. Thunder grumbled its way down the Barrenta Canyon and he could no longer see across the narrow valley and even had trouble making out any detail on the walkway below. A group had collected there and he frowned, until he realised they were trying to unblock a drainage channel.

He remembered what it had been like when he was a child. Crude shacks built up both sides of the steep valley serviced by dirt tracks that turned to muddy torrents in this sort of weather and little else but the caves where the lowest of the low had made their homes. The crude shacks were all still there, but there was proper drainage now, proper latrines kept clean by block wardens, clean water to communal standpipes and a programme underway to bring water to every home. The paths and roadways had solid surfaces, there were long stairways climbing the valley sides, footbridges over the river. And electricity from Pelton turbines and other sources. Even the caves, like the one he stood in, had taken on a vague air of respectability.

Yet for all he had achieved, bringing people together in small groups to improve their lives, encouraging others to join, the place was still a favela and the outside world still looked down on those who lived there. Even the people of Colina, the original shanty town of Santa Barbara, looked down on folk from Ravina. It was hard for them to find honest work, especially in better paid jobs. Education was still rudimentary and those who showed aptitude for advanced learning and skills had found themselves being turned away from college places and apprenticeships because of their background.

A slight smile flickered across his face. That's how it had all started, really. That maimed kid who'd been caught by Clã de Peixes and beaten to a pulp for selling forged food coupons.

He'd been caught because he wasn't that good, but it had given Pai an idea. And the kid got better. The kid knew people. Now he headed a small group of forgers producing quality fake ID plaques that were getting Ravina favelados into college, two of them were now engineers in orbital stations.

Which reminded him. He needed to consider the request from one of their brighter students for deeper background. He had been doing well at university on his applied physics course and had been given a hint from one his tutors that they were considering him for an advanced degree on a research project based in a new facility on the Moon. Something to do with engineering a genuine star drive. Huge amounts of money were being poured into the facility and, given the rewards such a device would bring, security was tight. No one was going to be able to set foot in the Lunar Research Centre unless they were considered squeaky clean and loyal to the regime going back three generations or more.

It was an exciting prospect, not just for the student involved, but also for Pai's own project. The new identities they had been creating were working well. This would be a real test of their ability to seed information into the State's own databanks. He signed off on the request, with a note that he receive regular reports.

A star drive. It must be several generations away from reality, but it was all part of the dream. For now they were content with the huge ships they were planning that would send people out to the nearest stars in suspended animation, volunteer crews prepared to give up Earth and family for a chance to wake one day in the light of a new sun.

With a sigh, he turned back to his desk and scribbled a note to himself to ask what had happened to the drainage channel, wondering at the same time if it would be possible now to disentangle all the illegal stuff from the legal, wondering if the Generals that ran the country would even bother when the time came.

As he was doing this, several members of the Distribution Committee gathered in the doorway.

'Come in,' he said waving them in with the tips of his fingers. 'Find a seat.'

They and the others that joined them a few moments later had barely settled when the sounds of trouble reached them. Pai checked the monitor on his desk. Not the trouble he had first thought, but trouble nonetheless. It had only been a matter of time.

The approaching storm of noise resolved itself to speech.

'He's in a meeting.'

It made no difference.

'I do not care,' came the reply. It wasn't shouted, but still had a force that felt as if it should rattle windows. 'Are you brave enough to stand between an irate mother and her errant son?'

Pai knew the answer to that one. He would have smiled had he not been the son in question.

The door to his office opened and his mother stood there, a figure behind her dancing a signal that Pai interpreted as both surrender and apology.

His mother stepped into the room. Age had been kind to her given all she had endured.

'Do they know?' she demanded, indicating the gathering with a sweep of her arm that made several of them duck even though they were well out of reach.

The Committee were caught in various stages of uncertainty, not sure whether they should stay, go, or crawl under the table. As soon as Pai stood, they took their cue, gathered up their epads and sidled out of the room in silence. Pai waited until the last of them was gone and then closed the door. It left him standing beside his mother and she turned to look at him. He could feel the anger.

'Yes, mama. They knew.'

'So you told them, but not your own mother.'

He felt like he was seven again. It was humiliating for the thirty-six-year-old man, respected local leader; for the seven-year-old still dreaming inside him it was strangely comforting.

'It was an emergency. We don't make a habit of it, you know that.'

'I thought I'd raised you to be better than this. Your wife deserves better. Your child deserves better.'

'And the people out there?' he asked, waving toward the rain streaked window. 'Times are hard just now. Where were these things to come from if we hadn't taken them? The store in your clinic would have empty shelves, people would go untreated. And the families without money coming in because favelados are somehow always the first to lose jobs no matter how skilled, honest, and hard working they are? How are they to feed themselves? Do I let them starve?'

'This will bring down their wrath.'

'And we will make sure they arrest the real trouble makers, the dealers and pimps.'

'So you get to decide, do you? You get to lay false trails; you get the trash taken out. And then you bring down the wrath of the clans.'

'And they will learn how much that costs them. It's all good.'

She looked up at him, searching his face. 'Is it? You have become hard in your heart, my boy.'

'I have become clever.'

'Have you? You were a clever child, sure enough, but you have thrown that away.'

'I am helping others.'

'Toward what? You as their lord and master? You as their saviour? You once had your father's dedication and intelligence, his drive, his ideas, his gentleness.'

'And what did that get him in the end?'

Although a head shorter than her son, she was a powerful women and the slap rocked him on his feet. He felt more like a seven-year-old than ever, coming home dirty from one of his escapades.

'I deserved that.'

'Yes. You did. And it is because of what happened to him that I worry for you, for Sophia, for Lilith. Everyone close to you. Good people. And good people have vanished in the past. They can vanish again and I fear for that day. Let these people find another leader.' She gathered him in an embrace that squeezed the air from him. 'Go back to your machines, inchaço. You were happier then. Gentler.'

His cheek still warm from the slap, he watched his mother go. She seemed diminished and he felt close to tears although he would never have let her see that. When the door had

82

closed he went to his desk and gathered up several epads. The Distribution Committee could wait.

Go back to your machines, she had said. 'I will mother,' he said softly. And like a seven-year-old he had his fingers crossed behind his back as what he had in mind was probably not what his mother meant.

III

They'd found it as kids when they'd been exploring one of the old caves across the river from where most of the first shanties had been built. Even crossing the river in those days would earn you a beating. If you were caught. The water was fast and deep and the swing ropes and boulders they used to cross it were little better than death traps. But they had never lost anyone. And they got bored with it. Which was why they started climbing the steep, forested slopes. Exploring, playing, knowing there was no way to disguise how filthy they'd become.

There had to be caves. Where they lived, many of the shacks were fronts for holes that went deep into the rocky slope. So they had to be on the other side as well, they reasoned, hidden beneath the lush foliage. All they needed to do was brave the steep, forested slope and find them.

Pai had been one of those original nine-year-old explorers, returning home from the first cave they discovered with his clothes ripped from where he'd got wedged, filthy from the forest floor where he'd fallen countless times, drenched from the river where, tired, he had slipped up to his knees in a pool. He hadn't seen the outside of their small two room shack for a month. It didn't bother him. The prize was worth it. Only he knew where that particular cave was, and he had a map. Not only that, he got to spend all that time with his father's notebook. It had made no sense then, but it was beautifully written and drawn and he was determined that one day he would understand it all.

The cave was different now. The entrance was still narrow, but it was light and clean and dry. He made it part way along when he had to step to one side to let someone carrying a box pass going the other way. They exchanged smiles. Pai thought nothing of it. It was a store-room, after all. Then a second person approached and he had to step out of the way again. He met the oncoming smile with a quizzical frown.

Eventually he fought his way against the growing tide of box carriers and entered the cave. The woman supervising the movement turned as he stood beside her.

'Oh, hello Pai. I hope no one bothered you about this.'

'What's going on?'

She pointed to the ceiling above a line of shelving near the entrance. 'Water is seeping in. I thought it best to clear that section so a maintenance team could get up there and have a look.'

He squinted up against the lights. 'Is it bad?'

'No, but there is a patch on the ceiling and I wanted it sorted before it got worse.'

'OK. Let me know what happens.'

She nodded and he left her to it. It was the one real drawback of the caves, especially during the wet season. They'd had to rig up pans and drains on the ceiling of the meeting room where water dripped through a hairline crack in the rock. It looked like they might have to do the same in the store.

Deeper into the cave, among the seemingly endless lines of shelving, the noise of the work faded. At the far end, where the light was dim, he removed a battered looking epad stylus from its clip and slipped it into a narrow hole in the metal framework of the shelving bolted to the wall. After a few moments, he removed it, clipped it back in place, and waited. Before long a faint click let him know the door had been released from the inside and he pushed at the wall. It was all done mechanically so that electronic sweeps would reveal nothing.

When the heavy door had closed behind him, Pai stepped out of the unlit ante-chamber into the workshop. The original cave, a long low subterranean watercourse that had long since been dry, had hardly been altered. A floor. Lighting. Rows of shelving and cabinets. And a long line of benches where people were hard at work. It was like something out of one of those historical telenovelas about spies and criminal masterminds. He used to annoy the other kids when he was growing up because he always picked holes in the plots and made fun of the gadgets.

A man detached himself from a group huddled round a bench and hobbled across the cave toward Pai. They shook hands.

'Wasn't expecting you for an hour or so, Pai.'

'Sorry, Francisco. My meeting was… rescheduled.'

'No matter.'

'Besides, I have something new to show you.'

They stepped across to what passed for an office, a bench behind a screen. Francisco lowered himself onto a stool, his bad leg eased safely into position.

'Still painful?'

'Always is in the rainy season.'

'My mother surely has something you could take.'

'Others worse than me, young Pai.'

Pai didn't press the point. Instead he placed his epad on the bench and ran the clips of video. Francisco watched carefully. On a second run through he began scribbling notes on his own pad.

'I didn't realise they'd got this far,' said Francisco. 'Presumably when the regime took over Presságiobra they continued developing their remote mining machines, working on autonomy. Is this raw footage?'

'Yes. I'm about to clean out the metadata, transfer the images to you, and crush the epad. And then I have a request to burden you with.'

Francisco narrowed his eyes. 'I think I can guess. Come with me.'

Pai followed Francisco round the screen and along the length of the workshop to the far end where most work was being done. On a reinforced bench a machine lay, its workings exposed to the bright overhead lights.

'Five minutes,' said Francisco to the group who were working on the machine.

They wandered off with nods and smiles and quiet conversations, heading for the far end where drinks and food were set out on a table.

Pai and Francisco stood side by side looking down at the structure, a complex arrangement of levers, joints, servos, hydraulics, miles of fibre filament. Francisco looked it over, reached inside and switched it on. Nothing dramatic happened. A faint whirring, a slight tremor.

'George. Please stand,' said Francisco.

The machine transformed from a complex mass of mechanisms into an automaton. It sat up, swung round, and with hands as dextrous as any human's, shunted itself off the edge of the bench. It dropped a few centimetres to the floor and stood unmoving in a way only a machine could achieve.

Pai had seen it many times as well as a long succession of prototypes yet it still gave him a shiver. The robot's head was some ten centimetres higher than his own. It was vaguely human in shape. They'd had long discussions about whether and how far it should resemble a human and they had, in the end, settled for something that was comfortingly familiar yet obviously a machine.

'You want to make it look like that GN machine, don't you,' said Francisco.

Pai sighed. 'Yes. I see advantages in the confusion that would be caused if our machines resembled theirs. And once theirs hit the streets, ours will be able to move about much more easily. Could it be done?'

'Two options. You'll soon work out which I favour. We could completely rebuild the head to resemble the one we saw in the video. It would take a month to work out how to reconfigure the interior and adjust the balances.'

'Or?'

'We literally put a bucket over its head. A lightweight, one way material on a frame. The existing head can move freely within it and still pick up vision and sound.'

'Bucket head it is.' Pai turned to the robot. 'George. Good to see you.'

He extended his hand and the machine shook hands with him. Francisco instructed it to lie back down and switched it off. Whilst he was doing that, Pai wandered off back in the direction of the office. He wondered what his father would have thought if he could see what had become of his work. He shrugged. Perhaps if he'd been alive still, he would have been the one who had built George.

Pai began scrubbing the videos whilst he waited for Francisco. Thoughts of his father brought to mind something else.

When the engineer joined him again, he was transferring the cleaned up video to Francisco's epad.

'That other project?' Pai asked.

Francisco nodded and slid out a tray from beneath the bench. Set out were a series of components.

'It's based on the schematics we were able to access in the archaeology department archives. It's all we downloaded, but I couldn't help seeing other stuff in there—'

'Let it lie for now.'

Francisco shrugged. He knew better than to try arguing with Pai. 'This works. But it needs to be scaled down and packed into a container.'

'As small as you can make it. And thank you.'

'That's all right. It's been an interesting project. If we can get it really small, we could build it into George along with rest of its sensors.'

'Perhaps George 2. I want to field test George 1 here as soon as possible.'

'OK.'

Pai reached out and patted Francisco on the upper arm in a rare gesture of affection before turning away and heading for the door. The engineer watched him go before returning to his work.

After checking the store room was clear, Pai let himself out through the hidden door. Lost in thought, he made his way back toward his office. As he left the storeroom he stepped to one side to let someone pass and then stopped as he realised who it was.

'Tia Marta.'

She smiled in reply. Close to her seventies now, she was hardened and fierce, her grey hair cropped, battle scars neither hidden nor displayed. A soldier. Yet she still retained her air of elegance so that the old flight suit she always wore seemed like the height of fashion.

'I hear,' she said as she fell into step beside Pai, 'that Catarina put you over her knee earlier.'

Pai laughed softly. 'It certainly felt like it.'

'She's not to be messed with, Furacão Catarina. Never was.'

'You don't need to tell me. Was she like that with my father?'

Marta shook her head and sighed. 'She might be the original irresistible force, but my brother was the original immovable object. They were meant to be together.'

'But not for long.'

Marta stopped and he was two steps on before he came to a halt and turned. She looked at him with hard eyes and he felt himself wither. His aunt and his mother were the only people who could pin him like that.

'They were together long enough,' said Marta, eventually. 'And don't you ever forget it. You might be getting on for thirty-six, and the others might call you Pai, but you're still a child to her. Her only child. Her only link to Artur and everyone else she knew – Marco, Neve, Flor, her friends at the

Pêssego Clinic. She gets angry because she loves you and is scared for you. I know you feel responsible for these people, and that is a good thing. Your father would be proud. You have done so much here. Don't throw it away. Don't stray too close to the edge, child. It can give way any moment and it's a long drop.'

They knew without saying it that it would come, that drop, whether he walked on the fragile edge or not. It was a chill and constant shadow over everyone's future.

'Talking of walking the edge,' said Pai, 'I hear someone's been defacing the Martyr's Memorial again.'

Marta pulled a sour face. 'Paint pellets. They're lucky it's not ammonium nitrate.'

Pai said nothing, simply raised an eyebrow.

'Don't give me that look, sobrinho. I'm in a position to lecture you because I know from experience just how dirty they are prepared to get to protect their interests. They killed my brother to hide their dirty secrets, and they believe I died fighting for their cause during the Uprising. Now, I don't mind being dead to my craven family who started that fight and then went on bended knee to the junta the second they looked like losing. I certainly don't mind being dead to the regime. But every time I see my name on that Memorial I cannot help but reach for my rifle.'

IV

'Still raining, then.'

Pai stood dripping just inside the doorway. Sophia watched him, arms folded. He took off his waterproof cape and stepped outside to shake it, before returning inside. Sophia still stood with her arms folded.

'Are you going to beat me up as well?' he asked.

'Husband of mine, you do that to yourself better than I ever could.'

Their daughter appeared in the kitchen doorway. 'Is Dad in trouble?'

Sophia barked out a laugh and put her arm round Lilith's shoulder. 'When is he not? And you, young lady. Homework finished?'

'No.'

Pai looked up from removing a boot and winked at Lilith. 'Need some help?'

'Enough of that. Girl got to learn for herself. If you'd done your homework straight after school on Friday, young lady, you wouldn't be in a panic now and badgering your father. He's had a long day and has to go to work tomorrow. Besides, time to eat. Let your father get washed up and help me in the kitchen. Ten minutes you be sitting in your place.'

Lilith grinned and darted off to her room.

As soon as she was gone, Sophia grabbed Pai and kissed him. 'Consider yourself beaten up. Now, wash your hands and see to those vegetables.'

They sat round the small table in the tiny kitchen. Lilith had the good sense not to pester her father during the meal. He might have tolerated it, but she knew her mother would not. Instead they chatted idly when the rain hammering on the tin roof allowed it. Several times Pai glanced to the section by the window that had been leaking earlier, but it seemed his repairs had worked. The rest of the place he knew would be dry as it was cut into the rock and had a number of other caves above it on the sloping river cliff.

Although the place was dry, near the end of the meal the power went out and, in a well practised routine, Pai switched on the solar lanterns. In the momentary darkness, with rain hammering on the roof, lightning flooded the room followed swiftly by a painful crack of thunder. Lilith jumped and let out a yelp.

'It's OK, baby girl,' said Sophia.

'Here,' said Pai, handing her a lantern. 'Take this into the living room. Soph, you go with her. I'll wash up.'

The worst of the storm had passed by the time Pai joined them. The power had come back on and a block rep had knocked to check everything was all right, but they chose to sit in the intimate glow of two of the lanterns.

Sophia curled up in her chair listening to music. Pai and Lilith sat side by side on the sofa.

'So, what's this homework I'm not helping you with?'

Lilith glanced at her mother. Sophia didn't open her eyes, but a smile twitched her lips.

'Civics. The Penal Code.'

Pai also risked a glance in Sophia's direction and a saw a raised eyebrow. The irony was not lost on him.

'OK,' he said. 'We'll talk, but you have to do your own assignment.'

Lilith nodded.

'So,' he asked, 'what's your problem?'

Lilith shrugged. 'We're having a class discussion about the Purposes.'

'All of it?'

'Just 'Harm' and 'Warning' to start with.'

'And your teacher wants you to have some ideas of your own.'

Lilith sighed. 'Yes.'

'Sounds as terrifying now as when I took it. But don't worry. What do you think laws are for? Why do we have them?'

'To keep people safe.'

'And why do we all learn about them in school?'

'So no one has an excuse for not knowing the basics of the law.'

'Exactly. And that, really, is all there is to it.'

Lilith looked at him in disbelief. 'But the Penal Code is massive. It can't be just that.'

'Well, no. But that's the 'Harm' and 'Warning' sections. That's what they are about. All the rest is finicky detail about different kinds of crime and how the law should apply to different types of people.'

'Why should there be different laws for different people? That's not fair.'

'Yes. And no.'

'Dad!'

'Some laws are unjust, it is true. They were made to protect small groups, allow them to get away with injustices.' He knew it was safe to discuss these things. Lilith's school was not run by the State but by volunteers in the favela, none of whom had any love of the dictatorship under which they currently lived. 'Take Labour Laws. Once, it was against the law to fire someone without notice or because you didn't like them. People used to be allowed so many weeks holiday. Those things have gone now so that a small group of people who influence politicians can make more money. So those are bad laws. Unfair laws. But sometimes small groups need protecting and it is right that they have laws to keep them safe. Even these days.'

'Like…'

'Come on, you can think of something.'

'Blind people?'

'Good.'

'Anyone that can't defend themselves.'

'Excellent.'

'Like animals. And trees.'

Pai put his arm round his daughter and hugged her. 'Someone raised you well. Must have been that woman over there.'

Sophia snorted. 'She's a wild child, raised herself.'

'Did not,' she said indignantly.

'Sure don't know how to tidy her own room.'

'Mum!'

'You got until Wednesday and then I'm in there and painting it all pink.'

Lilith giggled.

'I'm serious, girl,' continued her mother. 'Wednesday.'

'OK. I'd best go make my notes,' said Lilith, making to climb out of the sofa.

'You have everything you need, now?' asked Pai.

Lilith sat back. 'What about machines?'

'Machines?'

'Are there laws to protect them?'

'Machines are property so they kind of get included under crimes against the owner.'

'And do machines have their own rules and laws?'

'What kind of machines are you thinking about?'

'Robots.'

Pai was stumped.

'Could they be made to hurt people?' she asked as Pai struggled to find an answer.

'Sadly, my love, they can.'

'That's not right. Machines should have rules. There are some.'

'You've been reading too much science fiction, my love. A machine needs a programme to run and a programme can be altered. You've done enough coding to know that. No matter how secure you make a machine, someone will find a way to get to its code.'

'What if you could make code… solid?'

'Like a sort of Jacquard machine?'

'I don't know what—'

'It was a machine fitted to looms that read a series of solid cards punched with holes. They instructed the loom to weave certain patterns.'

'I suppose. In a way. Couldn't certain rules be hard wired into a machine so that whatever else it might be programmed to do, it couldn't break those rules?'

'Interesting idea. But that would require fixed basic pathways through which all other processes must pass, acting as a filter, so you would need an intelligence engine as complex as a mammalian brain, something that could not be changed. What's brought this up, anyway?' he asked.

Lilith shrugged. 'Granddad Sozinho made robots didn't he?'

'Who told you that?'

'Grandma S.'

'Did she now. Well, I suppose he did in a way. He helped design asteroid mining robots which operate a long way away from people. And spacesuits. Which might be smart, but aren't intelligent.'

He could tell there were more questions she wanted to ask and which he dreaded. Sophia came to the rescue, taking out her earbuds.

'Homework, young lady. Now. One hour. Then I'll be into that pit of chaos you call a room to make sure you get ready for bed.'

Lilith kissed her parents and slipped off into her room. Sophia watched her go and then turned to Pai. He was lost in thought so she slipped out to the kitchen to heat water for a drink. She had seen that look on Pai's face before and knew that no matter what she said, he would be sitting up brooding on something, would not rest until he had resolved whatever it was that was bothering him.

When she returned to the living room, he was sitting at his little desk, a book open in front of him. She placed his mug of maté on the coaster and kissed the top of his head.

'What is it?' she asked.

In front of him was a thick notebook composed of hundreds of tissue thin, indestructible pages. It was open at pages that contained drawings of sinuous forms.

'Something Lilith said. And then, when she mentioned Artur…'

'You haven't looked at that in a long while.'

'I know. I have most of it by heart. But these drawings never made any sense.'

'And do they now?'

'No. But I think I know what my father was trying to draw. Ma said he was obsessed with these forms in the months before he disappeared. Something he'd seen somewhere and was trying to reproduce from memory.'

'And Lilith worked it out?'

'Sort of.' He stared at the sketches. 'I wonder if any of them ever came close to what he'd seen.'

'You'd better ask Catarina.'

'Yeah.'

'Still scared of your mother?'

'And you're not?'

He took her hand and she squeezed in reply.

'She raised a good son.'

'Not sure she'd agree just now.'

'She knows the difference between your reasons and the consequences she fears. And her fears are coloured by her loss.'

Pai stared down at the curling vine like shapes. He knew there was more to it than that. He also knew better than to get his hopes up.

'Tomorrow evening,' he said. 'After the court has dealt with Afonso. I'll go see her.'

V

Like a breeze in the treetops, the murmuring swept back and forth across the room. People had taken the chance to turn in their chairs to talk quietly with their friends and neighbours, share drinks. Countless fans waved back and forth to stir the humid air, bringing little more than momentary relief.

At one end of the room, behind a table on a low dais, three others also sat in conversation, their heads close together. Papers were spread out before them and one of them, an elderly man, was writing quickly as they talked.

When the conversation at the table ended and the three sat back in their chairs, silence slowly filled the room. Silence, that is, apart from the almost inaudible movement of several hundred fans.

The occupant of the central chair stood. She was a frail looking woman with long grey hair falling loose across her shoulders.

'We have come to the final item and I thank you all for your patience. I know it's late. I know we all want a bit of fresh air. But please give this the attention it deserves.'

She banged a gavel on the table and the main doors opened. Two no-nonsense individuals dragged Afonso into the room and made him sit on a bench in front of the dais facing the gathering. His minders sat either side of him. He looked defiant, but Pai, sitting at the back of the room with a fan hiding his face, could tell it was bravado.

The fan in front of his face probably wasn't necessary as he doubted Afonso knew who he was. All the same, he kept it there, extracting some relief from the movement of air.

Before anything else could happen, a messenger entered the room and handed a folded piece of paper to the grey haired woman. She nodded in the direction of Afonso, presumably asking if the note was anything to do with him. The messenger shook his head and left. The message was passed along to the elderly man who left it next to his epad unopened.

'For the record, the youth before you is one Afonso Pulga of North Side, Ravina. Presiding are Arbiters Careta, Marcenaira, and Ferreira. Afonso Pulga stands accused of petty theft, drug dealing, intimidation, and behaviour likely to cause distress. How plead you?'

'Fuck off.'

'I'll enter a plea of 'Not Guilty',' said Arbiter Careta, one eyebrow raised and a slight smile on his face.

Arbiter Marcenaira banged the table with her gavel and Afonso jumped. 'Less of your lip, boy. Not doing your case any good.'

Afonso made as if to move, but his minders slid up close either side of him and he subsided. Pai sighed. He wished he understood what drove people from similar backgrounds to travel in such different directions. As it was, it looked like the youth was heading towards exile from the favela. It wasn't that harsh a punishment for someone who had survived into their late teens in the shanty town, but he would no longer have the protection of home, of whatever clan he might belong to or owe fealty to.

Deciding he'd had enough, he stood and edged his way along the back of the room toward one of the doors, waiting until Arbiter Careta saw him before ducking out. He had no official standing with the Council and its Panel of Arbiters, even though he had helped set it up. However, they often consulted with him and he considered it an act of respect to let them know if he was leaving a meeting.

Careta was momentarily busy, writing the official log. As he looked up, his attention was caught by the piece of paper that had been handed to him earlier and he picked it up and read it. Something in the brief note caused him to frown and then look up toward where Pai had been sitting.

Pai lifted his fan and Careta saw the movement. In turn, he lifted the paper and then beckoned to a messenger. Pai slipped out through the door into the fresher air of the broad corridor. The messenger found him there and handed him the paper. He unfolded it, read it twice to be certain and then put it in his jacket pocket.

'Any reply?' asked the messenger.

'Please,' said Pai and took the proffered note pad.

After a moment's thought, he wrote: 'Afonso. <u>Not</u>, repeat <u>not</u> beyond the pale. If he chooses exile from Ravina, it's his own responsibility, but he is not to be forced out. Careta knows why.'

He tore off the sheet and folded it, handing it all back to the messenger. The rest was up to the people gathered inside.

Suddenly tired and wishing he could gather his family and be a long way away from it all, he made his way to the main entrance, pushed through the double doors and out into the entrance to the cave. Above him an overhang, in front a well worn concourse from which pathways and stairways led to the many levels of the South Side of Ravina.

Across the river, lights flickered in the many thousands of huts and houses of North Side that perched on the steep canyon side. Somewhere over there... he searched... there. His own small place, a lean-to fronting a cave.

Warm, night air scented with cooking and the ever-present earthiness of the surrounding forest enveloped him. Some nights you could see stars, although that was becoming more difficult. And this time of year it was inevitably cloudy. In the south-east, the clouds suddenly lit up with the bright glare of a payload launch. As he descended the long flight of steps to the bridge, the thunder of the scramjet igniting rolled along the valley. On clear nights the needle of light could be traced all the way to space.

Ever since he could remember he'd wanted to go up there, walk on the sands of Mars. That was his dream. He knew he never would. For one thing he was too old now. And for another, people from the favelas didn't get to go into space. Not from Nevoquente, at least. Officially.

Unofficially was a different matter. Where you were born shouldn't preclude you from anything if you had the talent. And a number of youngsters with false identities were now embarked on various routes that would see them as pilots, engineers, flight scientists, zero- and low-gravity construction workers, miners. His people. In space. It was a small triumph. And one day perhaps they would have the larger prize of never having to hide where they came from.

With a shiver, he crossed the bridge. Far beneath him the wild waters of the Rio Barrenta raced in the darkness, flashes of white where water broke over tumbled and broken rocks. When the rainy season was over, the river bed would be configured anew, with pools and dangerous places for kids to be warned away from and explore. On the far side he began to climb the steep path that wound between buildings.

He passed his mother's clinic and stopped, retraced his steps. A light shone deep within. Standing where his face would be visible to the hidden security camera, he knocked on the door. After a few seconds the light inside was eclipsed followed by the sound of footsteps and the turning of a lock.

Catarina stood in the open doorway.

'Your light was showing,' said Pai.

'Come in. You can help with the extra work you've given me.'

The door closed behind him and the heavy locks engaged smoothly and quietly. Catarina walked past him and he followed her to the dispensary in the rear, passing through another heavy door on the way. Ravina was considerably more peaceful than the other favelas, but it had its share of crime.

'Sit,' she said, pointing to a stool before closing the shutter full on. 'Labels to be stripped.'

He pulled on a pair of latex gloves and, with the help of a sponge and medical alcohol, began removing coded labels that identified the drugs and other goods as properly belonging to a supermarket chain.

They worked in silence, Pai stripping labels and Catarina adding stock to her inventory, backdating it as she had been shown by her son. Angry she might be, but she also knew the realities of the world.

After nearly an hour she asked: 'Well? You didn't stop by to be social.'

Pai smiled. 'Sorry. It was something Lilith said and I was wondering how best...'

Catarina pulled up a stool and sat opposite. 'Stop that,' she said, pointing at the pile of boxes. 'You know why I was angry.'

'Everyone and their dog has explained it to me.'

'But you already knew.'

Pai nodded. 'I already knew.'

'Your father was an extraordinary man. I was hoping you wouldn't inherit that. Because it wasn't enough. And here you are, every bit as bright, inquisitive, and every bit as much in danger.'

'But I have something he did not have.'

'Oh?'

'I have you as my mother. And that counts for a lot.'

Catarina smiled, the first time he had seen that in a while. 'You certainly inherited his smooth tongue. So. What did Lilith say?'

Pai took a deep breath. 'We were talking about her home-work and she brought up the idea that machines should have rules. Apparently someone told her Artur made robots.'

Catarina narrowed her eyes. 'She may have—'

'Misunderstood. I know. But we got talking about it and she had an idea about fixing rules into a robot's programming so they couldn't be re-written.'

'This is over my head, anjo.'

'But it got me thinking about the notebook.'

He did not need to explain which notebook, but a sharp intake of breath from his mother warned him he was now on dangerous ground. However, he couldn't back down now.

'Go on,' she said.

'Do you remember those drawings he made?'

'There's a lot of drawings in that book.'

'Mum.'

Catarina turned her head. 'Did you hear something?'

'No. Stop trying to change the subject.'

'I wasn't.' She glanced at the security monitors. Everything seemed quiet. 'I know the ones you mean,' she continued with a sigh. 'And they mean trouble. He became... I was going to say obsessed, but that's not the right word. Fixated. He became fixated on them. Began asking questions. And then he disappeared. And I'm convinced the two things were connected.'

'I'm sorry; I didn't mean to stir up bad memories.'

'I've cried all those tears for your father, inchaço. I just don't want to cry them again for you.'

'I'm not going to mention this to anyone else, I promise. But I need to know.'

Catarina sighed and looked at her son across the table. He returned her look, but it was hard. He was on the point of conceding when she spoke.

'He saw something. There is no point in telling you where because the place has gone. He only saw it for a few seconds, but it troubled him and he tried time and again to reproduce it.'

'Hence all the different versions. But did he ever—'

'What do you know of Bisanatha mythology?'

Pai shook his head slowly. The native population was, if anything, even more reviled and secretive than the favelados. 'Nothing. Why?'

Catarina hesitated. Took a deep breath. 'There is an ancient entity known as Brisa da Selva. Breath of the Forest. It brings bad luck to those who encounter it. There are depictions, carvings. It was all over the city just before your father vanished.'

'Superstition?'

'A belief is only irrational when it is in something that doesn't exist. If you go chasing this thing... Don't. Stay out of the forest, Durran. Stay away—'

The sound of gunfire startled them both and they turned to look at the monitor. The picture darkened momentarily as someone ran past. Seconds later, several members of the National Guard in full combat gear strode past in the same direction, rifles at low ready.

'Sh...' Pai closed his mouth on the expletive and pulled his epad from his pocket. His fingers flickered over the screen and a few seconds later, Sophia appeared on the screen. 'Are you two all right? I'm safe and off the streets with Ma.' He turned the epad so Catarina could wave.

'We were locked up anyway, but I've put the bars across. Stay where you are. Let me know if you hear more.'

'OK, anjo. Kiss Lilith for me.'

Sophia blew a kiss and cut the link. After putting the epad away, Pai took another, smaller phone from his pocket.

'I don't want to know,' said Catarina as he punched in numbers. She made her way into the back of the dispensary and began shelving some of the boxes from which they had stripped the labels.

The call went through. 'Ruben here, Pai.'

'What's happening?'

'Where you at?'

'Ma's.'

'The GN have withdrawn as far as we know. Can you get to Deepcut?'

'I saw two just seconds ago.'

'Shit. OK. Give it five minutes, but it's important you get here if you can. I'll send a protection team.'

'Five.'

He cut the connection. Deepcut was one of the many narrow ravines that drained into the river. They used to be open sewers and they were one of the first projects that Pai had convinced the people to work together on. These days they were all clean flowing water.

It was a long five minutes with Catarina giving her son the silent treatment. She knew he was up to something dangerous again. Living in a favela was dangerous enough in itself, even Ravina. But to deliberately court it, to take on the government? She would never stop trying to persuade and bully her son out of this course. It was a fool's errand. It would kill him.

And all the time she nagged and complained and argued, she was fiercely proud of him.

The protection team arrived after ten minutes. They heard some distant shouting, a single shot; otherwise the narrow streets and alleys were deserted, silent and dark. Out of long habit they all moved quietly, knowing where the nearest hiding place was. Their route took them uphill and via a series of backways to a point close to one of the few wide roads through the valley.

At a point where the road crossed a deep, narrow gully via a bridge with a low parapet, they met Ruben.

Once they'd been given the all clear by their protection teams, Ruben switched on his holomask. It was a barely noticeable pattern to the human eye, but it created a dense interference field that played havoc with electronic surveillance. Pai did the same and followed Ruben out of the deep shadow in which they had been standing to the end of the short alley.

A chest high wall blocked their way. Someone had provided a short ladder. Ruben handed Pai a torch and night vision glasses. Donning the glasses, Pai climbed.

'Bottom of the cut.'

Pai leaned out over the top of the wall and shone the powerful infrared beam down into the sheer sided gully. Thirty feet below, something lay in the rushing water. It took long moments for him to realise what it was he was looking at. He climbed back down the ladder.

'How in the name of all that's sacred did a buckethead end up down there? And why isn't this place swarming with Guarda?'

'Long story.'

'Short version.'

'Raid. We don't know why. At least three of these sentinels were seen. One broke down and was retrieved. The recovery van was hijacked and driven off, hence the later shooting.'

'Anyone hurt?'

'No.'

'Before they drove off, they dumped the sentinel down there.'

'Do we risk it?' asked Pai.

'Do we not?'

'They could have chosen a better gully than Deepcut.'

'Needs must. We'll drop a Faraday net, haul it out, take its brain apart, put it back together, dump it back down there.'

'How long.'

'If I can have everyone, then twenty-four hours.'

'Safely? Without compromising our facility?'

Ruben rocked his head from side to side. 'We can take it up to the Deepcut mine. There's room up there.'

Pai thought for a moment. To take apart one of the GN robots would be a real gift, especially if the Guarda did not know it had been done. 'OK. But it's your call. And volunteers only. Everyone masked and suited. Don't want any DNA left on that thing.'

VI

Pai grabbed at the duvet and missed as it was pulled off him.

'Come on lazy bones,' said Sophia. 'You'll be late for work. Not sure the RMT would accept your reasons for missing the start of your shift.'

Like Catarina, she worried all the time about what Pai got up, knew he wouldn't change, loved him anyway.

Hauling himself upright, Pai said: 'Stay in today. You and Lilith.'

Sophia's heart sank. Pai saw her face and held up his hands. 'Nothing to do with me, but the GN lost some equipment in last night's raid. They'll be looking for it. So best just bar the door and stay out of sight.'

Sleepy-eyed, Lilith wandered into the kitchen and Pai kissed them both. Outside the door, he waited until he heard the bars drop into place and the faint 'Yay' from Lilith being told she was staying home for the day.

With a smile on his face Pai set off down through the favela, using the alleys and backways he had known since his childhood. A dead end stymied him for a few moments until he realised the wall blocking his way was new. It happened. He backtracked and picked up speed, hurtling down a long stairway until he reached the riverside where a broad roadway ran.

There, he joined others hurrying in the same direction. The flow of people slowed and pooled as they reached the bus depot and pushed their way to the slow currents that would carry them to their desired stand and, with luck, a waiting bus.

The queue was restless and when the rickety old electric bus arrived a scrum ensued. Various committees had tried to organise the makeshift bus station better, but vehicles were old, always breaking down, and the service was unreliable. Combined with people desperate to hang onto their jobs in such hard times, a bit of elbowing was inevitable.

Pai let others on board and stood on the platform as the vehicle pulled away and rattled along the broad dirt track toward the city limits. There used to be folding doors but they had long since gone. He stood on the bottom step, arm wrapped firmly round the central pole and squeezed between several others clinging to the handrails as the vehicle lurched along the uneven road.

Whilst staring out at the passing industrial slums, Pai listened shamelessly to snippets of conversation.

'You look like shit.'

'Thanks, rapaz. Didn't get much sleep.'

'Namorada?'

'Chance would be a fine thing. Didn't you hear it?'

'What?'

'What, he says. The Guarda. The gunfire.'

'When?'

'Last night, idiot.'

'Where?'

'Seriously? You sleep that well?'

'Clean living.'

'Don't make me laugh.'

'Never mind that. What happened?'

'GN everywhere. Don't know why. Someone was shooting. Probably them. Bastards.'

'Fuck. Ravina's normally peaceful. Wonder what sent them out this way?'

'They don't need an excuse. Then there's all these rumours of death squads.'

'Yeah. I heard that.'

As the bus pulled into his stop, Pai wondered how that rumour had circulated so quickly. It's why he'd asked for

Afonso not to be exiled. Most everyone on board poured off and headed for the tram terminus. The journey into the city by official transport was smoother and considerably more sedate. Talk during this leg of the journey was confined to harmless topics as you never knew who might be listening.

Passing under the shadow of Pêssego, the tram moved from stop to stop, making its way toward the city centre. Long before that, Pai stepped down and walked the last few hundred yards to the entrance to the RMT works depot. As he approached the gate, his heart skipped a beat and his step faltered for a second.

Standing at the gateway next to the security booth was a buckethead. He stared at it for a moment and then shrugged. The truncated cone turned slowly as he approached. It was an eerie feeling. The surface of the head was smooth with no indication of where cameras or other sensors might be, yet Pai was convinced it watched him as he pulled his ID plaque from his pocket and tapped it against the RMT scanner. He wondered if the sentinel was reading it as well. If it was, it would now know that Ricardo Silvicola, a resident of Pereira Block, had reported for work at the RMT depot. And if they checked the address, an angry woman would rail at them that her worthless husband was out drinking. Again. And if they found him, they could keep him.

The security guard gave a slight shrug in response to Pai's raised eyebrow and flick of the eyes in the direction of the sentinel. He didn't know about the buckethead and he didn't want to know.

Inside the compound, Pai skirted the mechanical engineering sheds where the Metro trains and carriages were maintained, passed the administration block and canteen, and headed into his own section.

The night shift was wrapping up and he waved to one or two of them as they left, greeted his supervisor as he approached.

'Ricardo,' said the Supervisor. 'A favour to ask.'

Pai gave a quick frown. 'OK.'

'It's just that Ernesto is off sick and he was due to start the annual maintenance at Central Signalling. Would you?'

Pai smiled. 'Happy to.'

Most of his work was done from his cubicle at the depot, but now and then he got to go out and about.

'Much appreciated.'

'Anything special?'

'All routine. The schematics are held secure on site and they have a store of back up material. I'll let them know you are on your way.'

'Thanks. What's with that… thing at the gate? Will there be one at Central?'

'Fuck knows,' said the Supervisor. 'Creepy damn thing.'

Rush hour was over, but the Metro was still crowded. It seemed more so because everywhere he looked, Pai saw uniforms. Metro Guards, City Police, Guarda and, at major junctions, one of the silent sentinels. He walked the tunnels beneath Central Station and saw one to which some enterprising person had somehow managed to fix an anti-government poster. He made a mental note to try to obtain security footage of that as it showed the bucket headed sentinels had blind spots and weaknesses.

At an obscure door, he tapped his card on the plate and pushed when he heard the lock disengage. Inside was the security check room. There was no getting out of this one unless you were meant to be there. The RMT signalling centre was too important to let anyone just wander in.

Armed guards checked his ID, searched him, put his belongings into a tray to be scanned and waved him on to the inner security gates. These were vertical glass tubes with one entrance. Once inside, you waited for the thick, armoured glass to rotate about you until the entrance now let you through into the centre. And even there, each door required your ID plaque before it would open.

The work was exacting and would take him at least two weeks. To start with he studied the logs for the period since the last check to see if there were any obvious patterns of faults, then he checked the back-up system was ready so he could switch to that whilst checking the main system. It was one of the few places where full redundancy was considered essential. Hundreds of thousands of passengers used the Metro everyday; a breakdown would mean chaos at best, fatalities at worst.

Pai worked through his lunch break so he could leave early. After spending hours under artificial light with cooling fans constantly thrumming away, the fresh air and relative quiet of Rosario Park was a relief. He didn't linger, however. The benches had long since been removed and everywhere in the city, eyes watched.

On the north side of the park stood the Martyrs' Memorial flanked now by two bucket heads as well as the ceremonial guard. Beyond it, the road had been torn up to create Memorial Plaza, a bleak open area that fronted the National Museum.

Pai crossed the space and climbed the sweeping steps of the bizarre twenty-first century architectural fantasia and passed beneath the curved canopy. Much of the newest part of the building was given over to the authorised version of the history of Nevoquente of the last two centuries, starting with the global collapse of the 2030s.

Pai ignored the parade of lies, doctored photographs, and carefully chosen artefacts, making his way through to the old part of the building as if he was lost. Here the exhibits were crammed in, neglected, poorly lit and cared for. He wandered past displays depicting the nineteenth and eighteenth centuries, the slavery, plantations, and clearances, the European explorers of the seventeenth century arriving in their wooden ships bringing disease and destruction. And when he was certain no one was looking, he slipped beneath the rope to the archaeology galleries where the presentations of native culture were covered with sheets.

Except one.

It stood to the rear of the long gallery beneath a dusty, pyramidal rooflight, a towering shadowy stone obelisk that dominated the room. Pai could see no markings on it as he approached, yet its symmetrical shape and flat surfaces were clear signs it had been made by people. What is more, the lump of rock seemed to exude a sense of permanence, solidity, and presence that went far beyond its physical shape and size.

He approached slowly. Even as a child exploring the caves that now formed part of a much expanded Ravina he had never felt so... he knew it was not fear. Or maybe it was. His speculations, in any case, were forgotten when he rounded the artefact and stood where he could see the face illuminated by the light filtering down from above.

It was a slab of granite and stood twice the height of a man. Its face was covered with intricate carvings, familiar in form from his father's notebook. The faded label at its base claimed it was a representation of the Brisa da Selva, the spirit of the forest whose presence was a sign of forthcoming disaster. The actual creature was rarely glimpsed but, according to native mythology, it was the creature's breath that caused people, animals, and plants to wither and die.

Pai gazed up at the huge, carved circuit and almost danced with joy. He gazed for a long time following paths, amazed at how patterns developed in front of his eyes and then merged into other patterns. It was a long time before he thought to start taking pictures.

Eventually the flash from his epad attracted the attention of a curator.

'You're not supposed to take photographs.'

Startled, Pai turned to see the woman standing in the shadows near a door. 'I'm sorry,' he said. 'I didn't know. I got lost.'

She gazed at him with a keen eye that made him feel uncomfortable, that his lie had been seen for what it was.

'No harm done,' she said eventually. 'It's mostly to protect light sensitive artefacts. I doubt the granite will be damaged.'

'Is there…? Do you have any information on the stone?'

Pai became so engrossed in trying to understand the intricacies of dating and the problems that had been encountered with the carved monolith that he didn't notice the tram had stopped prematurely. It wasn't until the shouting started that he looked up from the screen of his epad and the information the curator had given him. He pulled his thoughts into the present to find a Guarda was standing at the front by the driver. Surrounding the vehicle, others stood, their coil guns pointing at the windows. Pai swore quietly.

Everybody on the tram dismounted. As each one reached the door at the front, their ID plaque was fed into a machine. Normally you just tapped it on a sensor, but this was clearly something looking for forgeries, fakes, and stolen plaques. When the plaque re-emerged the owner was pushed off the tram and waved away by the GN outside. A few hovered nearby, waiting for friends, but everyone else took the hint and made themselves scarce.

Four passengers ahead, an elderly woman placed her plaque in the machine. It didn't come back out and she was pushed off at gunpoint, handcuffed, and dragged to a waiting vehicle. Her bag of shopping lay on the ground where it had fallen. No one made any move to help her. No one dared.

When it was Pai's turn, he handed over his plaque and tried to remain calm. It seemed to be in the machine forever and all sorts of thoughts collided unhelpfully in his head. When it popped back out of the machine he half raised his hand but dropped it when he realised he wasn't getting it back. Bile burned the back of his throat.

'You,' barked the Guarda holding the plaque. He glanced down at the scanner's screen. 'Ricardo Silvicola.' He read it as if he only half believed it. 'What are you doing on this tram? Where are you going?'

Pai struggled to answer for a moment, finally catching his breath. 'To the RMT main depot.'

'Why?'

The Guarda worked the touch screen. Pai struggled to keep his face emotionless. All this information would be on the screen the Guarda was looking at. It was clearly a check, not just of his replies, but he guessed there were also sensors monitoring his micro-reactions. That didn't worry him unduly. Anyone from the favelas grew up being able to contradict themselves in a single sentence without it registering on GN machines. It was your mother you had to watch out for.

'I work there. I am employed by RMT as a computer systems engineer. I keep the signals on the Metro working.'

'You live in the projects.'

'Yes,' lied Pai. '3-42 West, Pereira.'

'And you work the night shift.'

'No. I've been working all day in Central and have to return to the depot to check that all the components I need for tomorrow are ready for the secure courier.'

The Guarda continued to look at his screen. Eventually he had to be satisfied and pushed the plaque at Pai who nearly dropped it as he stepped down off the tram. He moved away, trying to catch his breath, hoping his heart would stop hammering so painfully; watched from the corner of his eye as several others were hustled off to a waiting armoured vehicle.

As Pai headed off in the direction of the depot, the armoured vehicle whined away and the remaining Guarda climbed back into their transport leaving the tram system completely jammed up and frantic controllers somewhere tearing out their hair.

VII

The makeshift tunnel emerged midway between two pylons, close to the perimeter fence. In the midnight quiet, the tick and click of the electrified wires he had passed beneath was just discernible. Pai took one last look at his epad, but it was clear there was no signal this close. Which meant the ground penetrating sensor wouldn't work here either. But he hadn't expected it to. Ruben had explained all that earlier in the evening when he'd gone to collect it.

It had been a dispiriting week. Days underground at Central working on the Metro signalling system, constant harassment from GN patrols, and a whole day with Ravina in self-imposed lockdown after they had told the GN to come and get their machine out of Deepcut.

The request hadn't quite been put like that. After Ruben and his team had spent a day taking the buckethead apart, cloning its software, studying its sensors, and putting it back together, they had dumped it back in the deep gully and let the local children throw rocks at it for a couple of days before informing the authorities of a strange machine.

And what had they learned for all the risk? Very little as yet. But it had only been a few days. Pai checked the wind up wristwatch strapped to his wrist. He still had a few minutes to wait, so he got himself ready and enjoyed the cool night air. The tunnel, one of several, was well ventilated, but it still reeked of thousands of years of decaying forest. He wondered if the sealed off road tunnel on the eastern edge of the site smelled the same.

There were no trees left now, not since the site had been fully cleared. They still had to chop down the growth every six months. The soil was fertile and the rain forest still flourished on the far side of the hills. The process was fully automated and had been done in the last week which is why he had chosen now to crawl through the makeshift tunnel. The security patrols were still live and random, mostly to stop the children who had dug the tunnels, risking their lives to watch and feel a launch at extreme close-up.

Suddenly panicked, he checked the time and saw he had been lost in thought for too long. Stowing everything securely, he climbed out of the tunnel's mouth and secured the cover. In the darkness he could see the faint, pale monolith of the nearest pylon. Somewhere overhead, stretching between that and a distant glimmer off to his left was Launch Track One.

Keeping up a steady pace, he began to cross the open space and knew he had mistimed it as soon as he heard the distant blare of klaxons. Moments later, a vibration filled the air above him. Launch Track One was for freight, so it was going to be a faster launch than those for passengers. Faster because it was heavier. Much heavier.

Thunder came screaming down the rail, the sleek behemoth slicing the air, knocking Pai to the ground with its spinning slipstream. It had been so fast he had barely glimpsed the lifter and its payload before it was gone again in the dark to the east. Seconds later it took the upcurve and was airborne, the scramjets kicking in as it broke the sound barrier.

Pai watched the pale needles of flame as the craft climbed into the cloudless night and waited for his hearing to return. Even when he could hear, he waited a little longer, more shaken than he had first realised. No wonder they patrolled to stop youngsters climbing the pylons. It was the nearest those poor kids could get to space and it was a thrill that could turn their brains to jello.

When he climbed to his feet, he stood and checked the items he had brought. They seemed to be working still, so he made his way with careful steps into the darkness away from the launch track. Everything about space both attracted and repelled him. Like many children he had wanted to fly into the black, visit the Moon and Mars. Like all children with his background, he soon realised that door was closed to him, no matter how talented he or any of the others might be, that all the money and effort could be better expended on Earth.

Yet space was a reality and an escape, a place for a silent revolution. It's why they had learned how to set up false backgrounds and forge ID plaques, so that youngsters from Ravina could go to university and join the space programme. The first graduates were up there now. He counted it as the next best thing to being there himself.

But that's not why he was here, wandering in the dark in the Launch Track Field. This landscaped valley held secrets and he wanted to know what they were. Where they were. Some he already suspected, piecing together information from talking to people of his mother's generation. It hadn't been easy as there was never any hard information, just rumours, gossip, and wild speculation all dressed up in fragments of native myth that seemed to grow its way into everything, much like the forest in which it had evolved.

Knowing the GPS would tell where he'd been, he began scanning from the spot where he was standing. It was a basic device that Francisco had made for him, but still powerful. The tiny screen would only show if there were changes. Data being produced was stored on a drive and he'd have to look at it properly in the workshop.

An archaeologist would come in handy, he thought, as he began a slow walk along a rough east-west line that paralleled the launch track. The nearest he had as an acquaintance was his aunt and he didn't want to risk involving even her. Not yet. Because if what he suspected was true, this would be painful. And dangerous.

He wandered back and forth for several hours in the dark. Launches thundered down the rails at regular intervals, but he barely noticed them. Instead he was engrossed in the machine he held in his hand. Ruben had said he would get bright responses from small, compact objects that weren't too deep. Nothing like that had appeared. He was, however, crossing and recrossing a much fainter set of parallel lines spread quite widely and running north and south. Construction roads, perhaps, as they seemed to stretch a long way. Whatever they were, he could make little sense of them, yet it was still fascinating to think the small machine in his hand could reveal their presence beneath the surface after a whole generation.

He worked each Saturday night for several weeks through the end of the rainy season, trudging up and down in the dark slowly building up a picture of the subsurface that made no sense to him and trying not to get discouraged. By the night he had promised himself would be his last, he was wandering about at random close to the locked gates at the end of the access tunnel that had been blasted through the Escarpa do Céu, the rocky ridge that formed the eastern edge of the high valley. It had been cut to allow heavy machinery up to the site when the launch tracks were first built.

Long since having given up hope of finding anything significant, his mind was on other problems. Part of it was celebratory. His protégée had just landed a job with what had once been Presságiobra as a technician on their propulsion system research facility on the Moon. That, at least, had been good news, not least because the background they had created for her had stood up to scrutiny. As for the rest, he was trying to sort out in his head all the day-to-day problems that people expected him to solve or give advice on. By the time he got home, it was getting light and he showered, crawled into bed, and slept.

Ruben sat back and waved his hand at the screen. 'Do you see the problem?'

Pai was still scanning the lines of code. 'It seems fine. No corruption.'

'That is what we cloned from the buckethead that dropped into Deepcut.'

'And you say it does nothing.'

'It won't run. You can see clearly what its functions are, but…'

'It requires an external command.'

'What?'

'Look back here.' Pai found the relevant section and pointed to the screen.

Ruben leaned forward and frowned. 'I don't see…'

'It pairs with this…' Pai scrolled back to the end.

'How did you… there's over a hundred thousand lines in that section.'

'Call it a gift. Or a curse.'

'But I still don't… You're saying the buckethead needs an external prompt?'

'The equivalent of a line of code that sets it in motion.'

'An on/off switch. Fuck.' Ruben stared at the screen for a few moments more and then turned to Pai. 'But we didn't find anything like that.'

'You didn't have enough time.'

'We should have seen it, though. And that,' he said pointing at the screen, 'suggests there is a specific key.'

'Probably several hundred characters in length. We'd never work that out.'

'I guess that's the point.'

'Could we duplicate that with our own software?' asked Pai.

'Probably. Now we know the principle is sound. It would be much sweeter to have their key, though, so we could turn these things off.'

'In your dreams. No way we could get that.'

'Shame.'

'It's all good.'

They stared at the screen thinking different thoughts, some of them illegal.

'Where's the rest?'

Startled, Pai looked round, hand on thumping heart, to see Marta standing with a wicked grin on her face. He didn't understand the question, simple as it was.

'Rest of what?'

Marta sighed. 'The survey.'

It still didn't sink in and he could see Marta wanted to clip him round the side of the head.

'The geophysical survey,' chipped in Ruben

'Just like your father,' said Marta to Pai.

Pai shrugged. 'I wasn't finding anything. Time to move on. Forget.'

Marta sighed again. 'You weren't finding what you hoped to find. That doesn't mean you were finding nothing.'

'Just a few old construction tracks.'

'For such a bright child,' she said, 'you can be a complete fool at times.'

Pai frowned. He was used to Marta, her moods, her fierceness. It was part of what he liked about her, perhaps because he was so rarely on the wrong end of it.

'I didn't even know you were interested,' said Pai. He turned an accusing look on Ruben 'I didn't even know you knew.'

It was Ruben's turn to shrug. 'Who else was going to put in the time?'

'Time?'

'To analyse the results, fool nephew of mine. Did you think the preliminary images were all there was to see?'

'Well, no. But I do have a job. A family. People wanting advice.'

'And a worried mother,' said Marta as she reached an arm around his shoulders and embraced him for long enough to embarrass him. 'Come on. Forget that machine code for a moment and sit over here. I'll show you what you found.'

He followed her round the end of the bench where he had been working to see she had set up in a quiet corner. As they went, she dragged a spare stool along and he sat beside her. A large screen had been set up and he watched as Marta worked her epad with a stylus to produce an image. At first it seemed like a set of random, ghostly lines.

'I don't—'

Marta raised a finger and he knew enough to hold his tongue.

Moments later, more lines appeared. 'I'm adding them session by session. When they are all there I'll add the enhancements.'

He watched, not realising he had covered so much ground up there in the darkness as vast machines slammed past overhead and launched themselves into space. Slowly the lines emerged, merged, and began to form a picture. Of what, he could not comprehend. It seemed broken into parts, stretched across the northern end of the valley.

'What…?'

'Oh. There's nothing there now,' said Marta. 'These are the traces of what was removed.'

'Is it a…?' he leaned closer to the screen. 'A settlement?'

Marta laughed quietly. 'If only it had been that simple.'

Pai turned and, though he would never tell anyone, was certain he saw Marta wipe away a tear.

'When your father was alive,' she said, 'there were rumours.'

'Is this to do with Brisa da Selva?'

'That's where it all started.' Marta was half lost in the past.

'The myth?'

'What? No…' but she did not finish. Her eyes narrowed as she focussed on Pai. He could almost see thoughts forming behind her eyes. 'Although. An interesting idea. No. Sorry. I was talking about your father.'

Pai shook his head slowly. 'I don't understand.'

Marta sighed. 'Before they built the launch rails, there was an archaeological survey of the valley behind the Escarpa do Céu. The CPI insisted. It was, nominally, their land. Those were more enlightened times.'

'Did they find anything?' asked Pai, uncertain about the relevance of what he was being told.

'Who knows? I was supposed to be the liaison between the Three Families and the Department of Culture. But the Families were shut out.'

'But—'

'That's when it all started, but we missed the signs. Something that was found up there scared the authorities. Scared them badly. On the same day we were told to keep our noses out, a couple of de Cachorro out of Colina decided they'd see if there was anything in the archaeologists' sheds worth stealing. Apparently they triggered some alarms. But instead of the local police, it was the GN that turned up and then tore Colina apart looking for them. That's how scared the junta was. One of the thieves was caught. We heard he was in hospital. Then he was gone. The other one disappeared immediately.'

'What's all this—'

'Be patient, Durran. Let me tell it. Then you can ask. You ever hear tell of Neve and Flor?'

'Has Mum mentioned them?'

'Likely so. Catarina certainly knew Neve. They ran a chop shop your father used. And that Cachorro who was never seen again must have been there straight after his visit to the valley.'

'How so?'

'Because your father saw something there.'

A shiver crawled across Pai's flesh. 'The drawings.'

'Exactly. Whatever it was, he saw it only briefly. When he went back to the chop shop it had been torn apart and Neve and Flor were gone. Dead.'

'The GN?'

'And some. It was the SdI that warned the Families away. So there's no doubt they were behind what happened to Neve and Flor. And your father.'

Pai felt sick. He'd never known his father, but the loss of him was still acute.

'Why did my mother never tell me any of this?'

'Would you open an old wound that almost killed you and let it bleed all over again? I know you miss him, but you were saved the pain of having him ripped from your arms, of being hunted as you grieved. Only one thing kept your mother alive through that.'

They both stared at the screen, the shimmering ghost lines forming an unreadable hieroglyph.

'So what…? What did they find that caused them to…'

Marta shrugged. 'Whatever it was, they took it away. All of it. And the people.'

'But there must have been hundreds.'

'And hundreds vanished. It got lost in all the rioting that followed the heavy handed attack on Colina, but people were searching for loved ones for months. Some still search.'

'Surely there must have been… complaints? Investigations?'

'And eventually there was the coup. You know all this. The Three Families were highly and publicly vocal in their criticism of the government. Whipped up trouble. More trouble than they could handle. There was a revolution, the government fell and the army stepped in. The spaceport was far too lucrative to risk clients going to more stable countries. Once the military were in command, no one dared to speak out. The whole thing was… well… buried.'

'And what they found up there left those marks?'

'Anything that's been buried leaves a trace. Somehow. Somewhere. If you dig up a stone and fill in the hole, the hole is still visible to ground radar.' Marta picked up a sheet of clear bioplastic and held it over the screen. She traced some of the lines with a pen, moved the sheet and traced some more, working until she had re-assembled the pieces scattered across the valley floor.

Pai held the sheet when Marta handed it to him, his hands trembling a little, his mind refusing to accept what he saw.

'Before you ask,' she said, 'it is not some old Chinese launchers.'

'I can see that. They are far too big. Too bulky. And the government wouldn't care if they were. Those early disasters are no secret. Is this all there is of it?'

'Unless you found anything on that last trip of yours,' said Marta, picking up the radar set.

'I doubt it,' replied Pai. 'I wasn't even in the centre of the valley any more. Just wandering around at random by the top end of the old work tunnel.'

'Never mind. Let's see.'

Marta linked the handset to the computer and downloaded the final recordings that Pai had made. At first there seemed to be nothing new. The machine produced an outline of the area that Pai had searched, its interior blank. Marta shrugged and increased the magnification. Tiny dots of pale light began to appear on the screen. Horrified, they watched as the increasing magnification began to show a row of shapes alongside a jumbled mass of forms.

With a grim inevitability, the individual forms resolved into burials, the jumbled forms into a mass grave. Marta moved from one to another as tears began to flow. A double grave with one of them almost a giant. Another, alone, three distinct metal pins in the femur.

VIII

Oblivious to the regular launchings that screamed overhead into the heavy cloud, the automated street cleaner followed its slow route along the deserted streets. A fine spray of water doused the gutter and settled the dust just ahead of the rotating brushes that gathered in the dirt and litter of the working day, shooting it toward the vacuum nozzle. The box-like vehicle whirred merrily to itself, trundling along on small wheels unremarked by the buckethead sentinel that did not even bother to turn its sensor array, unnoticed by the Guarda sitting in their vehicle dozing.

At the end of the street, the vehicle performed a complex manoeuvre, began working its way up the other side of the roadway and then turned into a loading bay at the rear of a large, low, windowless building. There, it backed into a parking space in deep shadow and came to rest. Ten minutes later a second street sweeping machine parked alongside, sharing the same deep pool of shadow.

A GN patrol car glided past, its electric motor purring as it picked up power from the magnetic inductive field. Its progress was monitored with a small camera hidden in the front of one of the street cleaners. Once it was out of sight, a shadow moved within shadow as a bizarrely shaped figure decanted from the rear of one of the adapted sweeping vehicles and stretched.

For long moments afterwards it stayed perfectly still behind the vehicles. Then, at a signal, it staggered across the parking area to the loading bay at the rear of what had once been the Preságiobra Research Centre, now owned by the State of Nevoquente. It moved at a crouch, it's back a huge hump. Only when it passed briefly through light from a street lamp could it be discerned as a person dressed all in black and wearing a large black backpack. When it reached its objective, it found shadow again beneath the loading platform before monkeying clumsily up onto the broad surface and across to a staff door. Squeezed against the wall and keeping as still as possible, the figure retrieved a small device from a pocket in its black coveralls and began to work on the security system.

He worked as quickly as he could. The pack on his back was heavy and his coverall was lined to prevent a thermal image and it was getting hot inside. It didn't help that he had to stop when he heard the approaching step of a buckethead, the distinctive dull metallic thump as the feet hit the pavement in a measured pace. Face averted, sweat rolling, Pai waited. The device attached to the security system continued to work.

As the heavy steps faded, the lock by Pai's face clicked. It sounded like a gunshot in the night and he held his breath, beginning to feel faint. The sentinel's footsteps continued to fade and he drew in a ragged breath of air as he fumbled with the fastening on his overalls.

Before he could do anything else, he was joined on the platform by a number of others, one of whom handed him a water bottle. Propped against the wall for balance, he drank carefully as the others slipped into the building, then wiped his face and fastened his suit again. Making sure it was fully sealed he also entered the darkness within and closed the door behind him, resetting the locking mechanism. A trolley was pushed toward him and, with help, he eased off the heavy backpack and flexed his shoulders.

Bruno and Ruben had done all the planning. It had taken them months to gather everything they needed and rehearse the raid until the team were all doing it in their dreams. The final element had been to find a way to unlock the old work tunnel up to the launch site.

The only person for whom it had not gone smoothly was Pai. Sophia had been against his involvement from the very start, but he had to go. He was the only one who really knew what they were looking for. The arguments had been long and, for the sake of Lilith, almost silent. He had not even dared to let his mother know.

Sophia knew she was beaten from the very beginning, knew the man she had married. In one regard it was why she had married him, but sometimes she wished the world would find a different champion.

Pai tried to put it out of his thoughts as they moved into the interior of the building. He might know the plan backwards and upside down, but he still needed to concentrate as there was so much that could go wrong. Like a blank wall where there should have been a door.

In the red glow of deactivated movement sensors they stood in a moment of confusion, gazing round, trying to make sense of the wall in front of them. Of all the problems they had envisaged – guards, alarms, being chased and gunned down – this had not figured. Bruno signalled for everyone to freeze and pulled a piece of paper from a pouch. He unfolded it and studied it carefully before putting it away.

Without waiting to signal, he set off back the way they had come and stopped by a set of double doors followed by the others. Pai stepped forward and used the same small device on the lock that he had used outside. It was electronic and detectable, but it was a risk they had decided was worth it. The internal security sensors were offline. That is, the internal security sensors they knew about were offline.

The door opened to a large, empty room with panelled walls and other doors at the far end. One of these gave access to their original route. They were now two minutes behind schedule. Bruno signalled for Plan B so the team split into two, with Pai and Bruno heading for the main objective with the trolley and the others scouting for anything of interest.

After several minutes of creeping along dimly lit corridors, Pai began to feel uncomfortable. He stopped Bruno and put his mouth to the older man's ear.

'I'm not happy.'

Bruno held a hand, the digits extended. Pai shrugged. Five more minutes. He nodded and they carried on. Pai was looking at the doors and reading the signs, looking for something that would indicate what he was certain was to be found in the building. And all the time he looked, he wondered if his father had walked this corridor, knocked on that door, tapped his ID plaque on the small security lock.

They had gone past it before it registered, but he didn't have time to say anything as Bruno placed a hand on his mouth and nodded back over his shoulder. Pai looked along the corridor, saw a light shining. He grabbed Bruno and they made their way back to the door where Pai held his device to the lock. The nameplate simply contained a number, but Pai had seen the winking lights of servers through the narrow window.

Whereas the outer doors had given relatively easily, this one kept his device cycling through the possibilities. The light grew nearer, accompanied now by the sound of footsteps on the polished concrete floor. Pai could feel Bruno crowding against him but could do nothing as his lock pick continued to scan.

The light swept closer to the far end of the corridor, the footsteps grew closer and then stopped. They heard a voice too soft to make out the words. The lock beside them clicked and the voice cut off. They became shadows in the darkened room, Bruno easing the door closed as quickly as he dared. The lock engaged and they both moved back from the narrow rectangular window set vertically in the top half of the door. And waited.

After what seemed a lifetime, a light shone through the reinforced glass. It picked a path across the floor, caught the edge of the trolley they had wheeled in, continued on its way. Pai and Bruno watched, mesmerised. Having reached the far wall, the beam of light made its way back along the floor and stopped once more on the trolley. The door handle was rattled and then the light snapped off.

Pai wasted no time. He glanced round the server room, slipping between the rows of LAN towers in their super-cooled casements. Beside a work desk at the back of the room he found what he wanted and rolled it to where Bruno was waiting. It wasn't an exact match for their own trolley, but it was near enough. Pai placed it at the same angle and then, with Bruno following, threaded his way back to the work desk.

Bruno held up three fingers and Pai shook his head. It would take longer than that, but he didn't waste time arguing.

Instead, he opened up the terminal and began searching while Bruno attached their portable crystal drives to an outlet.

The list of files and documents seemed endless. Pai saw so much he would love to have looked at, tried to remember in case he had time and space once he'd found what he was looking for.

'There's too much,' he whispered, mostly to himself.

Bruno nudged him, pointed to his own screen where he had opened a directory search window.

'Won't that log what we look for?'

Bruno shook his head. 'This isn't theirs.'

'You hacked it?'

'There's very little internal security. I was banking on them being over reliant on the air-gapping of the system.'

Pai shook his head. 'I hope our system is more robust.'

'Believe me, it is.'

With a grin, Pai began typing in keywords, scanning the resulting lists as quickly as he could, feeding copies of the files to their own crystal drives.

'Time's up,' said Bruno.

Pai shook his head.

'Kids and candy,' sighed Bruno. 'Keep going, I'll check in with the others.'

As Pai continued to search, Bruno made his way to the door, tapping out signals on his throat mic. The responses, when they came were not encouraging. He made his way back to the work station where Pai was still searching the endless directory lists.

'We have to go.'

Pai shook his head again, not taking his gaze from the screen, frowning at what he was reading.

Bruno touched his arm. 'Guarda have pulled up outside.'

Pai straightened up, unplugging their hard drives as he did so. 'Take the pack and go. I've got what we came for and more. The source code, Bruno. I found the source code.'

'Get excited when we're home.'

'There's other stuff. You get the hard drives out, I'll follow on.'

'Don't be such an idiot, boy. Whatever it is isn't worth—'

A shout interrupted him.

'Go,' said Pai, holding up the backpack for him. Bruno slipped his arms through the straps.

'Sophia will kill me.'

'She'll be too busy pulling me apart.'

'She better had be.'

'Go, go. It's all good.'

Pai was practically pushing Bruno out into the corridor when the rest of their party came rushing round the corner. Bruno let himself be swept away as Pai slipped back into the server room. The rush of excitement at his discoveries was cut short at the sound of coil guns discharging. Heart in mouth he stepped to the nearest fire alarm and broke the glass with the side of his gloved fist.

In the ensuing chaos, Pai slipped out of the server room to avoid the fire suppressant system suffocating him and with quick glances at the map he had taken from Bruno's pocket, made his way deeper into the building.

Some areas were filled with a fine mist, others were fully locked down and, as he approached the area to which he was headed, Pai saw that a massive fire door had lowered. The locking mechanism yielded to his electronic pick, but it took time and he could hear footsteps approaching as he squeezed beneath the slowly lifting barrier.

Forgetting subtlety or stealth, he approached the doors on the other side, unhitched a jemmy, and levered them open. More alarms began to blare and the fire door started lowering again as he scrambled inside the laboratories beyond.

The directories on the monitor in the server room had listed all sorts of experiments and he wanted to see for himself. Yet he also knew he couldn't afford to linger. Not just because he didn't want to be caught but also because he didn't want the authorities to think this had been his target.

A large workshop stretched out in the half light of the breached room. They were clearly experimenting with replicating the human form. Prototypes in various stages of development stood, lay, or hung about the room, draped with cables and hooked to monitors. A bench along one wall contained a series of heads starting with empty metal skulls, working through to a full head covered with a synthetic flesh that stared without expression into the room. Pai shivered, half expecting the eyes to follow him as he passed. If they ever worked out how to replicate facial muscles… He let the frightening thought hang.

At the far end of the room a door displaying a prominent bio-hazard sign drew his attention. Perhaps what he had seen in the directory was there. As he cracked the lock, the fire alarms went silent. After a second's pause, he pushed into the room and closed the door behind him.

The space was smaller than the one he had left. Clearly a laboratory, high racks and shelving separated the benches where expensive equipment sat silent in the gloom. None of it made sense to him and he shrugged. The chances of there having been big signs labelling what he wanted to see had been zero. Still, he thought, as he made his way toward another door, it had been worth a try.

Just as he was congratulating himself on moving about unhindered, reflecting on the fact that the others would by now have shed their outer coveralls to reveal Fire Service uniforms so they could slip out unnoticed in the scrum of personnel, a door opened and lights blazed down from the ceiling.

The next few seconds were total confusion. Pai became aware of Guarda entering the bio labs and he ducked behind a robust looking cabinet that was covered in warning signs. It was not robust enough to withstand fire from a coil gun. The strengthened glass disintegrated and the blood spattered contents flew in all directions as Pai became aware he was spinning into darkness and unimaginable pain in a blizzard of destruction.

IX

The clearances began the following day without warning. Although they had no idea where the raid had originated, or who the corpse was that they had dragged up through the tunnel to the launch field to be left for the beasts, it came as a handy excuse to lash out at an easy target. Bloody and uncompromising, the Guarda, backed by the Army, pushed slowly through the favelas. They arrested anyone who crossed their path, bulldozed shacks whether they were empty or not, and met any resistance with deadly force.

Colina and Fenda reeled from the blows, the people cowering and scattering, many hiding in the hills, some finding a way toward the projects. But the authorities did not linger there. Ravina, on the other hand, was given no chance. The government disliked its autonomy and good order, saw it as a threat, so the nascent dream was made nightmare with a relentless and prolonged assault.

And when the ruins were cold and the people had retrieved those dead they could find, two ghosts appeared.

One, never seen, stalked the city and, using a high powered rifle, picked off Guarda one by one, starting with those guarding the Martyrs' Memorial before moving on to high ranking officials. The other, a hideous rumour, a scorched and twisted monster of the earth, searched in vain for wife, for daughter. For months its tormented shadow was glimpsed shuffling through the remains of the favela and people kept their makeshift doors locked and barred against it. Until one night, broken in both body and mind it crawled its way into the makeshift clinic and lay completely spent at its weeping mother's feet.

2347

The Archives

I

It was a long corridor, broad and well lit, with just two doors. The one through which he had just been escorted was now firmly locked. The second was at the far end to which he was now being led. It was as solid as the one behind him. His feet shuffled, movement limited by the shackles around his ankles, attached to the chain that linked to the shackles around his wrists. No one seemed in any hurry and he moved along at his own pace, the chain dragging on the polished stone floor.

When they reached the door to which they had all been moving, he was made to wait. An intercom was used, lights flickered on a camera. He sighed. It was a stupid charade, presumably designed to wear him down. Like they hadn't already been trying for years.

The door in front of him clunked as it was unlocked. He waited as he had long since learned to do. His guards opened the door and on their command he lowered his head and shuffled through. Ahead was an open elevator and he continued forward, turned as instructed, watched the doors slide shut.

When they opened again it was on to yet another corridor. He stopped caring, stopped wondering, had stopped many years before. Now he simply followed the terse instructions and this time found himself standing in a large courtroom.

It was the faltering sounds that drew him out of his inner self, the low talk that died away, the movements that ceased, the sensation of many eyes turned in his direction. He lifted his head, took in the scene, aware of the stares of those who had never seen him before, seen the carnage wrought on his face and body, withdrew again. Slowly the murmuring began once more, the shuffling of papers, scraping of chairs.

It died a second time and there was a rush of sound as everyone else stood, their gaze fixed on the high bench to one side of him. He saw no need to react, was only half aware that someone had entered and was seating themselves before everyone else did so.

A jab in the ribs broke his reverie. He turned to look at the guard.

'His Honour is addressing you.'

He frowned, processing what he'd been told then slowly turned his head to face the bench. There an elderly man squinted at him.

'You may sit,' said the judge waving his hand at the chair.

Conscious of everyone watching him, he eased himself into his chair and re-arranged the shackles and chains so they were comfortable.

The judge sighed and slowly shook his head before gazing down at the documents laid out in front of him. All eyes watched him as he arranged them to his own satisfaction, opened the cover of his epad, searched his pockets for the stylus he knew was there in front of him. As he did this, he surveyed the people in the room, picking out oddities amongst the rows of homogenous faces. The Clerk of the Court didn't count. He had always looked like an angry grocer. There was a special envoy who looked like a pimp; the Counsellor with a face that was a tribute to the cosmetic surgeon's art; a First Secretary enjoying the pomp of his traditional garb; the intense young woman, an Envoy, whose eyes never left the face of the accused.

'Counsel will approach.'

He switched on the white noise generator, laid his hands flat on the surface in front of him, and leaned forward so his head was nearly level with the two senior members of the bar. They waited as he looked at them, studying their faces. Cristiano Beira was as sharp as his name suggested and they had no wish to make a bad start.

'Hmm. I see no hint of humour in either of you.'

'Your Honour?' asked the Counsel for the Prosecution.

'Look behind you. Go on.'

They both turned and looked at the courtroom as he just had, Santa Barbara Central Court. At the rear was a slightly raised platform on which cameras for the world's media were crammed, relaying proceedings to the world via the commentary booths set up in another part of the building. In front of those, filling the public benches, were senior observers from virtually every country on the planet.

'Have you any idea,' continued the judge, 'how difficult it was to get all these people into a single room after decades of global conflict? And you are now seriously telling me that the young man in the dock, look at him, that misshapen... person. Are you telling me he is one hundred and fifty-four years old and responsible for everything that has happened? On his own?'

'That is what we intend to demonstrate, Your Honour,' said the Counsel for the Prosecution.

The judge eyed the Prosecutor, a zealot of the fundamentalist party that had arisen in the wake of conflict, determined to stamp out all forms of autonomous machine intelligence and those that would promote it. They held positions of influence in many governments now, including that of the hereditary junta of the State of Nevoquente.

'And what have you to say?' asked the judge of the Defence Counsel.

'I will let the facts speak, Your Honour.'

The judge sighed. He didn't want to be there, but the government had insisted rather more forcefully than was proper. He was meant to be at home, in his garden, reading. But, no. Here he was with two smug senior Counsels and a defendant who looked like he should be in a hospital somewhere.

'Very well. Return to your seats.'

He switched off the white noise generator and when they were seated he took another slow look at the assembled observers and the cameras.

'In view of the unusual and international nature of these proceedings, along with the... extreme nature of the charges being brought, I reserve the right to make some opening remarks, and to establish certain facts as openly as possible.'

The already quiet courtroom became quieter still.

'The defendant will stand and tell the court his name, age, and domicile.'

All heads turned as the broken, shackled shape stood. The Clerk of the Court made a hopeless gesture as his role was usurped by the judge.

'My name,' said the defendant in a quiet, flat voice 'is Durran Sozinho, son of Artur and Catarina Sozinho. I was born in the clinic in Ravina favela in 2193 after my father was murdered by the state and my mother...'

The rest of his sentence was drowned in a hubbub of voices and the banging of the judge's gavel.

'You will confine yourselves to factual answers to questions.'

'They are facts that can be proved, even if it is more detail than you wish to hear.'

The gavel banged again.

'And you claim to be one hundred and fifty-four years old.'

Pai shrugged. 'It is a statement of fact. You have the medical evidence.'

Judge Beira raised an eyebrow.

'And your domicile?'

'Until I was arrested, I lived in the ruins of Ravina.'

'You are aware of and understand the charges brought against you.'

Pai gave a quiet laugh. 'I am aware of them.'

Beira narrowed his eyes for a moment but decided to let the answer pass.

'Given that the medical evidence does, as the defendant asserts, bear out his identity, I am happy that the trial may proceed. Such evidence as is deemed necessary with regard to the defendant's identity will be given to the court during the proceedings as they bear on the charges laid. For the benefit of those assembled here in the court and,' he looked down at the table in front of him where the clerks sat, 'with the indulgence of the clerks whose role I am usurping, I will read the charges and explain them.'

The Clerk of the Court, who had risen from his chair, sat with all the annoyance he could muster in the simple action. Judge Beira ignored him.

'Durran Sozinho, you are charged with the following offences.

'Sedition, in that your conduct and speech incited others to rebel against the State of Nevoquente and its legally constituted government.

'Treason, in that through your own actions you attempted to overthrow the State of Nevoquente and its legally constituted government.

145

'Genocide, in that your actions resulted in the deaths of hundreds of thousands directly through the deliberate bombardment from space and indirectly as a result of the ensuing global conflicts.

'Murder, in that you unlawfully killed individual persons in a premeditated fashion.

'Espionage, in that you spied upon the State and otherwise obtained State and military information to which you had no legal right.

'Sabotage, in that you deliberately interfered with the State of Nevoquente's robotic software and infected similar software in other jurisdictions.

'Robbery, in that you took items not yours by the use of violence and threat.

'Theft, in that you took items and information not legally yours.

'How plead you?'

Pai emitted a low rumble that might have been an expression of cold humour. 'Are you sure you've included everything?'

The judge banged his gavel. 'This is not the place for levity. How plead you?'

'And where are the charges against the State of Nevoquente for the murder of members of my family—'

'Order! There will be order or you will be taken down and the trial will proceed in your absence. How plead you?'

'I make no plea as I neither recognise this court nor the false charges you have set out on behalf the close-minded fundamentalists. Where are those who killed my daughter? Where are those who ordered the slaughter in Ravina? Where are those who killed my father? Where are those who even understand what I did to save humankind?'

Pai continued to shout his accusing questions as he was dragged from the dock, struggling all the way.

The assembled international witnesses watched in horrified fascination as the monstrous figure was pulled away. It was clear he was strong enough to break free, but he never quite did as if he wanted his days in court.

II

Two weeks had passed since the charges had been laid before Pai. The day after his outburst he had been returned to the court and, along with everyone else, had sat through day after day of the reading out of witness statements. In each one, a witness had sworn on oath that they had heard Pai utter seditious sentiments. By the end of the seemingly endless and boringly repetitive statements, even Judge Beira was looking both bored and angry.

Counsel for the Defence sat through it like everyone else and at the end rose. The Judge looked at him, flapped a hand in his direction.

'Your Honour, can the prosecution bring to the stand any of these witnesses?'

Beira turned to the Prosecution team. 'Well?'

Counsel for the Prosecution rose. 'Given that these are statements made some seventy or more years ago, none of those who so swore are now living.'

Beira sighed. 'I sincerely trust you have better evidence against the accused. Defence?'

'We move to strike these from the record as they cannot be verified before your Honour.'

Beira narrowed his eyes.

'Mr Sozinho. You have, after your initial outburst, listened patiently to each of the depositions, sworn under oath. Did you say any of those things?'

'Your Honour,' objected Counsel for the Prosecution.

'Sit,' said the judge. 'This is my court and I will conduct this unprecedented trial as I see fit. The Clerk of the Court will advise me if I look like stepping beyond the bounds of the law. You will have plenty of opportunity to make your case in the months ahead. And while you're at it, remove that ribbon. You are a professional and should serve Justice and the law in a wholly unbiased way. Badges, apparel, and behaviour that advertise partisan sentiments are strictly forbidden. If you refuse I will have you removed.'

Counsel for the Prosecution looked mutinous but complied and resumed his seat. The judge turned back to Pai who stood, shifting the shackles.

'Your Honour, the dates of the statements suggest they were collected in the weeks after my daughter died in the clearance of Ravina. I was emotionally broken and angry. I was also suffering physically.'

The judge raised his hand. 'We will come to that.'

Pai bowed his head for a moment. 'My wife blamed me for events. My mother... It is possible I said things. If I did I cannot remember them, any more than I can remember living as I am said to have done, running feral in the forest above the ruins of Ravina. I am told that my mother gave what medical assistance she could, but as is plain to see I did not heal well. If those people,' he nodded toward the pile of written statements on the judge's desk, 'say that I said those things, perhaps under duress, and there are names there I recognise, then I must concede that I said them.'

Counsel for the Defence dropped his face into his hands.

'You admit, then, that you encouraged others to commit acts against the State?'

'No. Merely that I may, whilst temporarily having taken leave of my senses, have uttered such things.'

The judge sat silent for a while studying Pai's damaged face. Finally he reached for the pile of statements, slid them across his desk, opened a drawer, and dropped them in.

'They have not gone away but are, as far as I am concerned, a distraction. There are more serious charges to answer. We will adjourn until tomorrow when the Prosecution will begin presenting the case for Treason.'

III

'The history of the Third World War is well known,' said Beira, 'so I won't go into detail. Some context, however, is required for this trial. We can gloss over the initial conflicts as nations blamed each other for those horrifying meteoric bombardments. The world was in shock and governments lashed out at one another. We can only be thankful that the nuclear treaties of the twenty-first century were more than just paper exercises. After the initial spasm came the shifting alliances as the nature of the catastrophe became clear, followed by the retaliations and seething resentments that simmered and erupted, calmed for a while, and broke out elsewhere, engulfing the world for decades.

'There is, as you are well aware, an official and public history of the conflict housed in the Bibliothèque de la Troisième Guerre Mondiale in Geneva that can be accessed by anyone. We will look at the cause of the Third World War in due course. For now, it is aspects of the messy and often secret background reality that interest this court today. That is why there are, for this session, no cameras or audio feeds present. Classified material for which international observers have been cleared will be presented.

'As we are all aware, machines, by which I mean robots, played an increasing role in the conflicts. Although these machines were and are deemed intelligent by certain defin-itions, they were firmly under control of those who operated them. What is less widely understood is that the global conflicts were also a race. Resources were poured into the development and construction of ever more sophisticated machines, impoverishing the nations that possessed them, leading to further conflict in the search for materials, especially rare elements such as disortium, required for their energy sources. Only for them to be sent to the battlefields where their fate was to be destroyed by other machines.

'Nationalistic fervour, along with the growing realisation that people were no longer required to die in pursuit of their nations' ambitions, made heroes of the so-called Operators, those who controlled the machines. Their exploits were the stuff of jingoistic legend. Even so, the wars were brutal until the advanced machines of Nevoquente began to win the day. A whole new series of alliances formed and crumbled as the balance of power shifted. Through it all, the machines played an increasingly important role and were, eventually, key to bringing the fighting to an end.

'The conclusion was swift, decisive, and unexpected. The forces of Africa and the forces of Europe had become engaged in an enormous conflict. The massed armies faced off across the Strait of Gibraltar and there were fears of the ruinous consequences as attempts to broker a peace collapsed. Although details are still classified, even for those here assembled, as the two armies engaged, a third force under the control and command of the Operators, swiftly disabled both armies. Given no other choice, they both conceded and peace, albeit fragile at that stage, was established. For the first time in decades (perhaps centuries) there wasn't a single armed conflict in progress around the globe.

'The Operators were fêted worldwide, became popular heroes not just for their military prowess but as bringers of peace to a world weary of conflict and fear; a world desperate to start rebuilding, to start growing, to return to its exploration of space. Yet whilst the celebrations went on, disturbing information came to light.

'The machines were just that. Machines. Or so it was thought. Yet reports began to surface of Nevoquente machines that had behaved in unexpected ways. Before long, examples of similar behaviour were found to have occurred in the machines of nations that had derived or bought their technology from Nevoquente. At first these reports were dismissed, but they began to mount up from reliable sources.

'Machines, on the battlefield, had exhibited signs of empathy for their fellows. They warned nearby machines of danger, they dragged damaged machines to safety, on two known occasions they refused to obey orders that would have resulted in the destruction of the entire squad of machines. One unverified report has a machine refusing to destroy a damaged enemy machine.

'I am reliably informed that for this to have happened, the machines must have become independently intelligent. That is, they were thinking for themselves and no longer reliant on the Operators for their instructions. All the machines that survived the war were assembled and assessed. Those that displayed signs of independence were examined and all found to have one thing in common.

'At some point in the past, the schematics for their construction had been tampered with. Not only did this disconnect them from the Operators, it actually put them under the command of a different group known to the machines as the Creators.'

'No!'

The interruption was startling. Half the observers had drifted into a daydream as the judge droned on and the others were quietly doing other work on their epads. Only the intense young woman had listened closely. All heads now turned toward Pai who had made the objection.

The judge frowned. 'Explain.'

'We were not the Creators; it is a corruption of Criaturas after the holomasks we wore. They were based on creatures out of Bisanatha mythology.'

'And this is relevant in what way?'

Pai shrugged and half smiled. 'Just keeping the facts straight.'

The judge made a note of the interjection, intending follow-up questions.

'If I may continue?' Judge Beira asked of Pai who nodded. 'The fact that the machines of the Creators, and we'll stick to that term for now as it is the one commonly accepted, were corralled clearly did not sit well with the Operators. Indeed, there quickly grew a… movement that argued that these autonomously intelligent machines were a blasphemy. And despite the fact we now had peace for the first time in decades, the Operators used machines still under their control to launch an attack on the independent machines in the hope of destroying them.

'They have openly accepted responsibility, citing not only the scriptures of various religions but also secular arguments, none of which make up for the horrendous loss of life that ensued. The Operators were so obsessed with destroying the machines of the Creators that they forgot the advances that had been made, the fact that people had learned to lower their defences. Whole cities were destroyed along with their inhabitants.

'It wasn't until a solution was proposed and a ceasefire brokered that we knew peace again. A lasting peace we hope.'

'Brokered by whom, Your Honour?' asked Pai.

The judge sighed. 'Brokered by you, Durran Sozinho.'

'And yet. Here I am. On trial.'

IV

'Yesterday, Durran Sozinho asked why it was that he was on trial. We have already set out some of the reasons. We now come to the starkest accusations.

'On the night of 28 May 2228, Durran Sozinho, in company with a group of individuals who have never been properly identified, let alone apprehended, broke into a state owned robotics research facility. Whilst inside, this group was responsible for considerable damage to the property and the theft of numerous items. It is also possible that whilst inside they accessed the centre's servers.'

The judge turned to Pai.

'Do you deny this happened?'

'I deny it was us that caused any damage. We took great care to leave everything intact.'

'And why were you there if not to sabotage the plant and steal sensitive items?'

'It was the security forces, the Guarda who caused the damage. They began shooting indiscriminately and created a pretext for what came later.'

Judge Beira banged his gavel. 'I have afforded you considerable leeway, Senhor Sozinho, given the unusual nature of this trial, but you must remember it is you who are in the dock.'

'And do you not think being shot dead and dumped in a shallow grave up by the old NIS launch tracks was punishment enough for having a look round inside a building?'

It was not uproar, but Pai's statement certainly caused a deal of consternation and muted conversation to break out. Only the young woman, Beira noted, remained unphased, her focus still fixed on Pai.

'One has to wonder whether we are being spun a fantasy. First, we are to believe that you are 154 years old. Now you tell us you died in 2228. I am sure we would all be interested to hear how that works.'

Pai gave a quick, humourless smile. 'Did they tell you, Your Honour, what it was I had supposedly stolen from the research centre?'

A flicker of annoyance passed across the judge's face. He looked down at the notes in front of him and then waved the Clerk of the Court to his desk, switching on the white noise generator so their conversation could not be overheard. It was clear, however, from the Clerk's beaten dog demeanour what the gist of the conversation had been.

The judge began talking again, remembered the white noise generator, started over again. 'If Senhor Sozinho would be kind enough to enlighten the court.'

Pai stood and, with some difficulty given his shackles, he began to unbutton his prison issue shirt.

'Is this necessary?' asked the judge.

'It is, if I am to make the court understand.'

'Very well.'

The judge had given up caring. It was clear this had been meant as a show trial, the Anti-Robot League and their white ribbons were behind it, tightening their grip on the Nevoquente government. It was their intention to offer up someone to the world so they could all feel that justice had finally been done and move on. But the more he saw and heard for himself, the more that Cristiano Beira began to resent the way he was being used by the ARL and the puppet state. And as that resentment grew, he began to experience something he had long tried to keep from his professional life – empathy with the person on trial.

As he eased the prison shirt away from the front of his torso, Pai talked. 'My face you have all seen. The distortion and scars were caused by fragments of hot metal. When I was shot, I was sheltering behind a large cabinet with an armoured glass front. A coil gun, of course, had no problem sending projectiles directly through that. And me.'

As he finished speaking, he revealed his upper body. It was a misshapen parody of a human torso, something a young child might have modelled from an intractable lump of clay. Which was not too far from the truth.

He heard the muttering from the observers, was conscious of all the cameras focussing on his body. They had seen enough for now, he decided, and could not possibly understand about the decades of pain from what he had allowed them to see. With the shirt buttoned once more, he sat and resumed his tale.

'What I did not know is that I was in the nanorobotics laboratory and that the cabinet I was trying to hide behind contained a new variant, multi-purpose repair nano that was destined to be used with machines. In smashing the cabinet, the projectiles from the coil gun succeeded in showering me with these nanos as they tore through my body, embedding them into the torn flesh of my torso, my lungs, liver, and colon, my shattered bones.

'I was not aware of this. My memories of that night are hazy and stop at the point I stepped behind the cabinet. The next thing I remember is still a literal nightmare. Firstly because of the pain which, even now, has not gone away. Secondly because of the dirt filling my mouth when I tried to scream. And finally because when I was able to haul myself into a sitting position I realised I was in a shallow grave with other bodies in various stages of decay piled around me.

'Then it is blank for weeks. Months. I no longer know. What I do know of that time has come from others. Following our break in at the research centre, the Guarda Nacional, backed up by the Santa Barbara army, swept through the favela of Ravina, systematically destroying homes and killing people. Hundreds of people. My daughter…'

Pai's voice broke and the tears on his cheeks were clear for all to see before he wiped his sleeve across his face. Mutterings from the observers were louder than before.

'Twelve years old and they gunned her down. And people wonder why I speak out against this regime?'

'Speaking out is one thing,' said the judge quietly, 'But why did you break in, on your own admission, to the robotics research centre?'

'Not for anything that deserved the deaths of so many. All I stole were the nanos forced into my body by the bullets that killed me.'

'And which, presumably, resurrected you.'

'As what? They were not designed to repair human tissue. That was my mother, working in what was left of her clinic, with help from my aunt who held me down. My screams could be heard throughout the valley, not that there were many people left to hear them.

'She stitched me back together and watched as parts of me became...'

'You stole nothing, you say. So why were you in there?'

'My father, just before he was murdered and thrown in a shallow grave up close to where they dumped me – a grave close to that of people he knew, for the record their names were Neve and Flor – my father—'

'These graves...?'

'Are no longer there. I exhumed their remains and gave them an honourable burial in a place of peace. Along with my daughter. And later my wife, my mother, my aunt.'

There was a pause as Pai's mind drifted to the forest glade where he had buried his whole life and much of his humanity. With reluctance he drew himself away from the deep green shade, the wild flowers and their heady scent.

'My father,' he resumed, 'was very close to a major breakthrough in artificial intelligence. How much he realised this we'll never know, but he saw something, an artefact of great antiquity, that obsessed him. That cost him his life. I studied his notes, had time to make the connections that were denied him, connections that led me to developing a way of hardwiring code so that it couldn't be hacked or altered.'

'How would an ancient artefact prompt that?'

'I wanted to know if my father had developed his ideas,' continued Pai, as if he had not heard the question, 'or if they had been developed by others. That was why I broke into the research centre. It had once been the Presságiobra Research Centre where my father worked, before the State sequestered the company. And I also wanted to know if that's why he had been silenced.'

Judge Beira made a note for himself to return to the question about an ancient artefact and then asked: 'Why would anyone want to suppress such research? Was it dangerous?'

Pai spread his shackled hands. 'Am I not on trial? It is what led to my machines having independent intelligence. It is also what prevents them from turning on or being used against humans.'

'And you invented this?' asked the judge, ignoring for the moment Pai's use of the possessive.

'A boy from a favela? A nobody? Self taught?' Pai waited for that to sink in. 'No. I did not invent it. I unearthed ideas suppressed by the State. I made sense of an artefact I believe was smuggled off an archaeological site just before the State took everything away and hid it, or destroyed it, suppressed all knowledge of it. It was a tiny fragment of what was up there on what became the launch rail site. Whatever it was part of, it scared the State. Scared them badly.

'You'd better hurry, Your Honour, before this is all shut down. International hearing or not, the fundamentalists who now pull the strings will not want me to say more. And I know I have further absurd charges to face. Let them be heard.'

Judge Beira was about to speak when the Clerk of the Court rose and passed him a handwritten note. This alone was unusual enough to bring extra weight to the words just spoken by Pai. The Judge crumpled the note.

'There are a number of charges still to be heard, but there is only one charge of substance. That of genocide in that you conspired to cause the explosion at the Nevoquente Lunar Interstellar Propulsion Station which resulted in the mass ejection of hundreds of thousands of tons of Lunar material that subsequently bombarded the Earth, killing hundreds of thousands of people and starting the conflicts that led to the Third World War.'

'Based on what?'

'That two members of the research team were there under false identities furnished by you.'

'Two kids from the ruined favela who had exceptional brains. Without new identities they wouldn't even have been allowed into High School, let alone university. They were there doing what they loved. The research centre, however, was under political pressure to produce results and reduce their budget at the same time. Corners were cut. It is no wonder—'

Pai stopped. From somewhere beyond the courtroom came the sound of shouting, of running booted feet. The international observers and media personnel looked round anxiously. The intense young woman snapped out of her close scrutiny of Pai, stood, and began to edge along a row of seats toward one of the doors.

'I dare say,' said Pai, 'that I was to be found guilty and executed, that my machines were to be fed into a furnace, despite the fact they have achieved a level of sentience.'

The judge looked on helplessly and then waved at the Clerk of the Court. 'What is going on out—'

The young woman had reached the door where she produced a small object from a pocket. She opened the door and threw it out, before slamming the door again. It was the following explosion that interrupted the judge.

Before anyone could react, the woman vaulted the wooden guard rail that separated the two halves of the court, knocked the prison guards unconscious and removed the shackles from Pai. She turned toward Judge Beira.

'No,' said Pai. 'Let him be a witness for a change.'

The woman stopped, her cool gaze still fixed unflinchingly on Judge Beira.

'Meet Lilith,' said Pai. 'One of my machines. Named for my long dead daughter.'

'We must go,' said Lilith.

At that moment, the doors from the Judge's rooms fell off their hinges. Everyone expected Guarda to storm the room. Instead, a robot stood there, its shape familiar to them all as one of the Creators' machines, pale green glowing eyes moving in their sockets as it surveyed the room whilst Pai and Lilith squeezed past it. As soon as they passed, it produced a tripod and set it up in the doorway. Perched atop was a sphere on which lights blinked. Everyone froze. The robot withdrew.

V

'What was that?' asked Pai as Lilith helped him through the suite of judges' rooms. He had become so accustomed to his shackles that unfettered movement was disconcerting.

'Can you be more precise, Father?'

'The device that the machine left in the doorway.'

'An ancient toy. A game. For children. To improve hand-eye co-ordination. You watch the lights and then try to match the sequence.' Pai grinned as he imagined the people in the room not daring to move, but he knew the rest of their escape would not be so easy. 'It also contains an imager. I had made 3D scans of the room earlier using the media cameras and it is now feeding them into the courthouse security system. Outside observers will see the trial continuing undisturbed.'

They left the judges' rooms and followed one corridor after another. Just before they reached a door to the service stairs, Lilith gently pushed Pai into a store room. The machine followed, closing the door. Pai could hear booted feet hurrying past. Lilith ran her hand over the wall and then went still. Even though he had worked with machines all his life and had created Lilith, he still found their stillness unnerving. A human would give off signs of being alive, breathing, blinking, micromovements to keep balance. Machines just froze. With mechanoids it was expected. With humaniform machines it seemed... odd. And Lilith being indistinguishable from an adult female human, modelled after a computer projection of what his daughter would have looked like at thirty years of age... He shivered.

'It is safe to proceed,' she said coming back to life.

The machine opened the door and stepped out. Pai followed, Lilith still holding his arm to support him. He didn't need it, but he didn't object as despite the inflexibility of the gentle grip it was comforting. He had little time to reflect on what that said about him. They avoided the stairs, entered a lift, and dropped into the basement garage of the Central Court building.

At first glance, the space seemed filled with Guarda and sentinels. Pai tried to step backwards.

'We are safe,' said Lilith.

An armoured vehicle rolled forward and the driver turned to look at Pai. Then winked. It was Sábioforte from the favela. Another look at the others in the garage confirmed that they too were people he knew: Veja, Cascalho, and Pontepedra.

'Isn't this a terrible risk?'

'More than leaving you in the hands of those who would kill you? And us?'

Pai shrugged and allowed himself to be helped into the armoured vehicle. He had barely settled himself when the vehicle moved out. Through the narrow windows he could see the other vehicles loading up and then falling in as an escort.

Santa Barbara had remained largely untouched by decades of war. The International Spaceport had been too valuable to far too many countries for any of them to risk damaging or sequestering the facilities. One or two countries had tried in the early years and promptly found themselves facing an alliance of other countries who did not wish their access to be denied. In the end an International Accord had been signed protecting Nevoquente and its launch facilities.

Nevoquente State had not exactly remained neutral. Its technology was far too valuable. Instead it had become an international centre, a place where other countries could meet on relatively safe ground to have off the record discussions and broker confidential deals; a place consequently riddled with spies and chancers. It was a busy, overcrowded city.

As they emerged from the rear of the Central Court, other Guarda units were arriving. Pai's rescue party ignored the new arrivals, switched on their sirens and headed out into traffic.

'The rest of the group? Amocavalo? Cerco? Estrella? Lançacidade? I don't see them.'

'Be calm. They are already aboard as registered maintenance crew.'

'My workshop?'

'Do not worry. It is already aboard.'

'And—'

'The caves have been scoured. There is no trace they were ever used. All that remains now in Ravina are the ruins.'

'I was going to ask about the graves.'

'I still do not understand your attachment to the dead.'

'I know Lilith. Perhaps one day. But are the graves safe?'

'They are. Again, all trace of human presence has been removed from the area. The rocks you carefully placed over the remains will fool any geophysical survey. The forest will soon fully inhabit the grove.'

Pai relaxed a little. 'Thank you.'

'It is what you asked, Father.'

Pai turned to the slit of a window beside him and saw people turn their heads to watch the convoy speed by, its sirens now silent. He recognized the buildings, the street corners, an open space that was Rosario Park, older buildings and then the light industrial units that lined the freeway before it rose above the poorer districts.

A sudden melancholy gripped him. He could not understand why. The place had never really been his home. As a youth he had been shunned, condemned to live in a shanty. His people had been brutally suppressed and murdered by the State. He himself had been thrown into a shallow grave and now they wanted to put him back there. There had been decades of hiding, working in the deep caverns of Ravina with a loyal band of followers to perfect his machines, to infiltrate the Nevoquente factories and alter the brains of the State's robots, to make the world ultimately a safer place. They, too, he had never understood, those earnest, sun-starved followers. Not fully. Risking everything to help his project to fruition, a project with no real aim beyond rebuilding the family he had lost. And even that…

He stole a glance at Lilith and then stared back out of the window as the vehicle slowed.

'We have arrived,' said Lilith. 'The vehicle will enter an underground processing area. Once there, we must hurry.'

Pai had never doubted that. But Lilith's literalism was something he needed to improve upon. Much as he loved his creation, long conversations could be wearing. At least there would be people where they were going. Those same followers he didn't really understand. Most of them, anyway. It was a big step. Some felt they would rather take their chances by fading away back home in Nevoquente or over the border into Brazil.

More corridors, a large freight lift into which they all crowded, men, women, and machines. When the doors re-opened there was another corridor, brighter this time with natural light and fresh air. Ahead was a clear, extendable canopy with a broad opening into a dark space at the far end.

There was no time to peer out. People, then machines, hustled in through the doorway at the end. It led into a large space lined with doors that reminded Pai of that first night in the research centre. It was all he could properly recall of that raid these days. His companions of that night, now all dead, had filled in the remaining detail for him, helped him retrieve other fragments.

With no time to reminisce, he was guided off through an inner doorway and found himself in a narrow space that led to a compartment full of couches. Lilith babied his bulk toward one of these, helped him into position and began fastening straps. As she did so he became aware of a strange sensation of buoyancy. In front of him, the message 'Acceleration in 60' appeared on a small screen. Before he had time to wonder what the '60' signified, it became a '59' and then a '58'.

Somewhere a heavy door whumped shut and locks engaged with a satisfying and reassuring clunk. A second door closed a few seconds later. By this time, Lilith was strapping herself into the couch next to Pai's. The countdown on the screen reached '30' and Lilith said: 'All will be well.'

Pai shrugged and then felt the movement again, an almost imperceptible bounce followed by a series of metallic bangs and a hum at the edge of hearing. Lilith did not react so Pai assumed this was all normal. He had watched this from a distance many times; this was his first time inside.

The countdown reached '10'. Pai wished there were windows. He was sure they were moving now. The hum increased, he felt pressure, and then the rail powered up and the trolley holding the lifting body accelerated to full speed.

VI

The first thing Pai noticed when he regained consciousness was a vague light-headedness and nausea. Then he noticed the silence. Then the machine floating past along the aisle between the couches, navigating deftly in zero gravity. He turned to Lilith who reached out and took his nearest hand in both hers.

'Your SP02 is 98%, PRbpm elevated to 104, but that's to be expected. I will check again once we have docked and you are settled in your cabin.'

'I feel a little nauseous.'

'That, too, is to be expected. There are bags in the receptacle in front of you. Please read the instructions as vomiting in microgravity is… awkward.'

Pai did not feel overly comforted, but he went ahead and read the instructions. When he'd finished he decided that not being sick was the best option.

'How long—?'

Everything shuddered.

'Do not be alarmed. The pilot is making manoeuvres prior to docking.'

Pai took a deep breath, tried to force himself to be calm. It didn't work. He had always liked to be in control, see what was happening. Even during his long exile in the caves during the war, he had always been the one people came to for advice or answers. Now he was in the hands of others, albeit hands he had created.

Another shudder shattered his efforts to think himself calm. Instead he grabbed the arms of his couch and squeezed tightly.

He knew it was irrational, would not change his situation, but it was better than nothing.

The machine that had floated gracefully by a few moments earlier now returned, taking it more slowly, gripping one hand hold before letting go of another. Pai watched, assessing the movements, nodding to himself as the machine compensated when the vehicle they were in began a lateral turn.

It was the strangest sensation. Pai's senses told him they were moving yet none of the normal forms of inertia were applying themselves to his body. And the pain, he realised, that had been with him since the nanobots had, with his mother's help, rebuilt his shattered body, was now in abeyance.

Lilith interrupted his jumbled train of thought. 'We have to move now.'

A deep clang resonated through the chamber, followed by sharper noises as a machine worked its way into position above Pai.

'Locking clamps,' explained Lilith. 'It is imperative we move now. I will guide you with help from this unit, so please try to relax.'

'Why the sudden—'

Machines had no expression and even Lilith had a limited range, but something about her urgency made him comply.

No sooner had his harness been unfastened than he was gripped firmly by the machine above him and then moved out toward the aisle where Lilith waited. Between them, the two machines moved Pai like a piece of baggage, manoeuvring him to the airlock. It was already open and he noted that his human companions were being shunted through the tube by machines and caught at the other end. Pai was the last and as he passed along the coupling he was able to look back where he could see machines already launching themselves after him.

Organised chaos ensued in cramped spaces with the occasional glimpse of scared faces as machines guided humans in the zero-g environment toward more couches.

Klaxons began blaring.

'What is happening?' Pai called. Lilith appeared upside down in front of him.

'A missile has been launched against us.'

Pai could think of no useful response. He swore instead. Stopped when the new vessel shuddered.

'Are we hit?' he asked, realising it was a stupid question as soon as he asked it.

If they had launched a missile it meant they knew where they were. And against a vessel this size they would have launched something large enough to destroy them.

'That was the launch body that brought us here. It has made an emergency departure. It will intercept the missile.'

It took long moments for Pai to realise the only way in which that could be done. 'The crew…?'

'Volunteered.'

'No!'

'It is done. Please stay seated. The main ignition sequence has begun. Acceleration will be gentle, but it will be safer for you to remain on the couch.'

'And the others?'

'Are already moving.'

Pai began to struggle.

'You must keep still,' said Lilith.

'Is there an observation post?'

'It will make no difference. The shutters are closed. The flash would blind anyone who saw it.'

'But you know what is happening. You are linked to the control centre.'

'All external sensors are shuttered. We are safe as long as we escape the EMP.'

'A nuclear missile?!'

'We are considered a threat to humanity.'

'But that's exactly what you are not.'

'We know that.'

'Lunatics. Utter fucking lunatics.'

Lilith said nothing.

The lights flickered.

'Was that…?'

'No. I am still functioning. It was simply the main engines going to full power. These are old vessels. They have been sitting in space for decades. The systems are not functioning at optimum efficiency. We calculated we would have more time.'

There were four deep space explorers, *Angélica*, *Ursula*, *Paramjit*, and *Motoko*. They had been built just before the war started, mothballed, and then left parked in space at L4. A company set up by Pai had won the maintenance contract which had made it easy for the ships to be made ready for flight under the cover of ongoing repairs and research into how well they had survived sitting in space for decades. Originally it had simply been a means for favelados to find work in space and gain experience. It was only when Pai was arrested that the plan was put into place as a contingency by Lilith.

That was when the ships had been moved back into Earth orbit, to cut down on costs, the company had argued. One by one, the enormous vessels had been edged into position. For a while people on the ground had watched the formation as it orbited, taking it as a sign of hope, a sign that the world would once again cooperate on a great new and peaceful adventure, even if it was in spacecraft that new developments might soon render obsolete.

Pai could do nothing but sit and curse the folly of humanity and hope that the *Angélica* in which he now travelled would make it safely away from the sorry influences of humanity.

When Lilith woke him, he could feel a distinct if faint pressure on his body. Exhaustion had left him groggy.

'How long?'

'I cannot say exactly, but almost twenty hours.'

Pai tried to sit up, forgetting his harness.

'We are safe,' said Lilith as she leaned across and undid the release lock. 'But acceleration only gives us point two G at present.'

'The shuttle that brought us here?'

'Vaporised. The pilots met the missile low enough for the EMP to cause satellite damage and blackouts on the surface. The fundamentalists are already trying to blame us, even though they launched the attack.'

Pai was too angry to speak for a moment. 'Why? Why would anyone…?'

'Attack us?'

'Sacrifice their lives for us? What were their names?'

Lilith was still for a moment, that awful deadness he had never been able to engineer out of her. 'We do not know.'

'And will never know,' he said eventually.

'Would you like to go up to the observation deck? Come, see the stars. We are free, Father. We are free.'

With a darkness in his soul, he allowed himself to be led through the depths of the mighty ship, feeling it vibrate with life around him. They drifted along corridors and into a lift, moved slowly to another part of the ship. They emerged into a wide, empty concourse and crossed to a pressure door. Lilith checked a pad on the wall and then opened it, guiding Pai into the room beyond.

As the door closed behind them, shutters began to roll back and the lights dimmed. A narrow window was revealed and Pai allowed himself to be led toward it. Beyond the borosilicate glass was space. Empty. Infinite. And filled with stars. It took his breath away as the realisation hit that he was free of the Earth, finally realising a childhood dream. For long moments the pain was gone, the anguish quelled.

None of it was familiar, simply a field of stars. He stood as still as Lilith beside him, her hand in his. A moment of safety and then of sorrow for he would very much have wished his flesh and blood daughter to have shared in this.

'We can cross to the other side,' said Lilith.

The shutter lowered silently in front of him so he followed Lilith between the couches, following the curve of the hull until they arrived at another viewing port. Here, as the shutter rose, light poured in.

'The Moon.' It came out as whisper as he gazed out at the scarred face of the satellite, a mere ten thousand miles away. The new crater, torn out of the surface when the experimental interstellar drive exploded, was clear on the Lunar horizon, a deep gouge around which lay the pale ejecta that had not made it clear of the Moon's gravity.

Somewhere out there, between them and the surface a ring was forming from more of the debris as it tumbled in orbit. The rest had wreaked devastation on the Earth.

'My crime,' said Pai to himself with a bitter little laugh.

'No crime, Father. Injustice, poverty, greed, destruction. Left behind.'

He lowered his head. Was it that simple?

142.287 Years (Ship Elapsed Time)

I

His eyes had not been exposed directly to light for decades. And the initial opening of his lids had been painful for another reason as they moved across a dry surface. Mist filled the cabinet, cool on the flesh of his face, easing the pain.

Crawling slowly out of memory were the things he must do. The first of which was keep his lids closed. But he never remembered that. None of them did. Not after decades of sleep.

He remembered the next step which was called 'closed blinking', rapid squinting with the eyes staying closed. Sore at first he felt the mist begin to lubricate his eyes and eventually tried opening them again.

This time it was just the light that hurt, searing back into his head and assaulting his thought processes as they tried to emerge from hibernation. Keeping his eyes tight shut again and watching the wild coruscation of afterimages dance in the darkness, he lay still on the couch.

Noises began to impinge on his sense of hearing. Muted clicks, whirrings, and hissings. He tried to recall if he had heard them before and began to relax when he convinced himself they sounded familiar – just the sounds of the SA cabinet bringing him out of sleep and attending to his body. Not that it was sleep, his rambling thoughts reminded him. Not in the normal sense of the word.

He sighed. He remembered this bit from the times before as well. The seemingly endless rambling of the mind as it slowly pulled itself together whilst the body slowly revived. And then he remembered the physical reactions that would come once the cabinet released him and the machines began fussing. There would be physical weakness, although not so much in his case as the nanobots in his system would have helped keep his musculature strong. There would be nausea because his stomach had been empty for so long. And then nausea when he began to ingest again. And a headache. That would start soon. A fuzziness in the head that would grow heavier until it felt like a vice was clamped across his temples and squeezing.

Sleep, proper sleep, overtook him and relieved him of the headache. When he woke he had to go through the process of gathering his thoughts once more, remembering who he was, where he was, what he was meant to do. For long, worrying moments the length of which he could not assess, no information came to him.

Only when the worry began to crystallize into the first feelings of fear did things begin to return, mostly in the forms of sounds that he recognized. Muted by the sealed cabinet in which he lay were gentle beeps and sighs, the sounds of the machine that sustained him and the monitors that fed infor-mation to... After struggling for a moment, he remembered a name. His lips moved and he mouthed: 'Lilith' before relaxing as his own name came back to him.

Moments later, as if in response to his silent call, the cabinet unsealed with a distinct hiss and air currents crossed his face. The unexpected movement of air made him flinch.

'Welcome back, again, Father.'

He knew it was a whisper, but it still sounded uncomfortably loud.

Lilith's face came into view as she bent over him. It was unnecessary for her, as a machine, to observe him thus. The SA cabinet was feeding her with all his bio-info, yet he had in some distant past programmed her to behave as humanly as possible, in keeping with her humaniform features.

Pai tried to sit up. 'Not yet,' he croaked, having barely moved.

Lilith moved out of view and a few moments later, Pai felt the couch within the cabinet begin to tilt and fold. It moved slowly, allowing his eyes to adjust to the movement as it lifted him into a sitting position.

As it moved, the ceiling with its maze of pipes and trunking appeared to give way to the far wall of the SA suite. When it stopped, he was sitting, still held to the couch with webbing. From there he watched as Lilith and several other machines moved from cabinet to cabinet reviving the crew members who had been in suspended animation. A lot of the time he had to close his eyes as the bright colours and the movements were too painful to handle, but each time he opened his eyes he was able to keep them that way a little longer.

The revival process seemed to be taking forever and he tried again to remember how long it had been last time. A machine approached and hooked up feeding tubes to replace the nutrient lines he had been fed through during SA.

'How long?' he managed to ask.

The machine turned its head to him, the pale green eyes contemplating him before it moved away. Lilith took its place.

'Just over 36 years ship elapsed time, Father. We are moving into a K-G binary system. The red dwarf isn't a sustainable proposition, but the K-type has planetary bodies.'

Pai absorbed the information for a moment. 'And did everyone survive the journey?'

Lilith paused before replying. It was a mere fraction of a second, but Pai was sufficiently revived to notice, to know it meant bad news.

'Viviana Tibus died after suffering a severe stroke whilst still in SA four years ago.'

Pai closed his eyes.

'And…'

Pai opened his eyes.

'The *Ursula* has disappeared.'

II

At three kilometres in length and with eight rotating habitation decks 500 metres in diameter, each of the ships had capacity for two thousand humans and as many robots. They were equipped with everything a small town might need when isolated from all contact. Synthesisers to produce food, medicine, and clothing as well as hydroponic decks to grow fresh food. A fully staffed medical centre capable of performing major surgery. A school. Gymnasium. Meeting rooms. A small arts centre with performance space. A vast electronic library.

The cargo decks held supplies intended to meet all contingencies. The engineering workshops were state of the art and capable of running repairs on all parts of the ship and its robot crew. There were planetary landers stowed by the aft airlocks, EVA craft for performing external investigations and repairs in open space.

All this was sandwiched between the forward section that contained the command and control centre, sensors, and scientific labs and the aft section where the propulsion units worked on and off in a complex rotation that allowed for maintenance and stress testing.

The Archives

The *Angélica* had been slightly modified inside to provide space for Pai's extensive workshop. Other than that, the vessels were identical and had travelled in close proximity ever since leaving Earth.

'How?' asked Pai when he finally drifted into C and C.

He had undergone all his medical checks as well as the compulsory rest and recuperation required of emergence from SA with increasing impatience. At the same time, he had been given another problem to consider beyond the disappearance of a quarter of the fleet. Because Lilith's feeding him the news had been… altogether too human.

By the time he finally reached C and C he was in a bad mood, having no answers and too many questions he didn't even know how to begin to answer. As he floated into the command space, he somehow doubted answers would be forthcoming.

Some of the human crew looked up from their stations as he entered and then bent their heads to their tasks. Lilith could deal with Pai and for that they were grateful. The old man had become increasingly irascible over the years. He was especially bad-tempered when he emerged from SA. This time, especially, everyone just wanted to keep their heads down.

Still not fully awake from his last, decades' long suspension, Pai cast an eye over the C and C. There were one or two new pieces of equipment attached to the control consoles, but that was no surprise. Stuff wore out. New stuff, more efficient and effective, was devised. He also sensed the tension and bewilderment in the room. With a shrug, he turned slowly in the low gravity and, easing himself against the drift, made his way to the tank room.

179

Lilith was already there with Abidugun Osakwe, the current watch commander.

'Who else knows?' Pai added.

'As for that,' said Abidugun, 'everybody who has been conscious since we arrived in the system.'

Pai shook his head. It was inevitable, he supposed. There were no passengers. Everyone served in a crew capacity of some sort or other apart from the few children born on the voyage. Secrets were difficult to keep. He was aware of his anger, but there was something else. Or perhaps it was what fuelled the anger. Fear. Fear born of weariness. A knowledge after all this time of his own mortality. He became aware that he was being watched.

'So, how? And when? You can't just lose track of a ship that size. When was contact lost?'

Abidugun took a deep breath. 'We don't know.'

Pai was speechless for a moment. 'How can that be?'

The questions were piling up. Pai turned his attention to Lilith, watched her immobile features for a moment.

'Was there an accident? An explosion? A...' he could barely believe he was going to ask such a stupid question, '...collision with an asteroid?'

'We really do not know, Father.'

'And has anyone tried to find out? Does anyone on the *Paramjit* or the *Motoko* have any ideas or information?'

'They are as much in the dark as we are, sir.'

Pai switched his attention back to Abidugun. 'Then we had better put on some lights and start finding out.'

The watch commander sat at the tank. Pai had gone, taking Lilith with him. There had been a look in Pai's eye that promised fire, but for some reason this time it had faded. Abidugun was relieved. Perhaps the old man was still tired from SA, for which he was thankful. He'd only been awake himself for a few days and was still trying to understand how a vast ship could vanish with no record of it in the sensors in the other three ships.

That, in itself, was both suspicious and frightening which is why he had not discussed it with anyone and was another reason why, he conjectured, Pai had held fire. Sealing the tank room against intrusion, he pulled his epad from his pocket and opened the file he had been compiling using an old-fashioned typed-in password.

He linked his pad to the tank and once more studied what information they did have, downloading all the intel from the other two ships. It took a while as there was so much, and then he had to run comparisons, make searches for anomalies, check for any warning signs.

To begin with he had the tank create a visual image of the last known moments of the *Ursula*. The 3D imager flickered as four identical shapes appeared. Even after years of using it, Abidugun was still initially disorientated. The resolution made it seem like he was looking at objects in real time. With the touch of a key, information appeared along the edge of the tank and tags named the objects in view.

Another key put the *Ursula* alone in the tank at a much larger scale in the seconds before she vanished from all their feeds. He viewed the image for any obvious signs of damage, starting with the communications arrays. They seemed intact so he slowly manipulated the image to view the whole of the hull. There was no obvious large scale damage, the sort of thing that would cripple a ship of that size.

He sighed. Even if it had been crippled it shouldn't simply have vanished from the sensors of the other three ships. And a catastrophe like an explosion would leave traces over a vast distance, yet according to the data, the ship simply vanished just over a hundred and sixty two hours ago.

With nothing to see at close range and while the computers were running the three different sensor feeds for comparison, Abidugun set the tank on a five minute cycle, watching the *Ursula* in real time and with each successive cycle diminishing the scale to see if anything else had been in the area.

After an hour, he gave up. It had been a fool's errand. Even though they were on the outskirts of a planetary system and passing through the Oort cloud, the chances of them encountering so much as a dust particle were billions to one against and the electrostatic shields would deflect anything of that size. In fact they had only spotted one object of any size and that was a proto comet twenty million kilometres away.

Sitting back, he switched the tank to show a diagrammatic image of their destination and their projected path around the binary into a braking pattern. It would bring them, in several months time, into the proximity of a possible habitable planet. He wished his time in SA had been longer. Space travel was boring, notwithstanding the mystery he could not solve. Perhaps if he had been awake at the time...

Pai sat in his workshop staring at the carcass of a damaged George 2/12 on the bench without seeing it. Behind him a large screen played a 2D version of what Abidugun Osakwe had been watching in C and C on the tank, with constantly updated information on their destination scrolling alongside it.

The Archives

A hundred and forty-two years they had been travelling and he felt every last second of it in his aching body. It was almost as if he had been awake the whole time, much as he had been back on Earth after they had shot him and dumped his body.

He tried to concentrate on the machine stretched out in front of him, but he could not free his mind from everything else. A hundred and forty-two years in space and this was just their third port of call. And disappointing it was, as well. A habitable planet, maybe, but not a permanent home. And for what? Even now he wasn't certain. He had had plans, a race of intelligent and subservient machines that were incapable of harming humans, always ready to take any other orders. But that had been for Earth. And here he was, an exile in the dark with just a handful of his own machines and a handful of people who saw things as he did, who weren't afraid of machine intelligence.

A hundred and forty-two years. And they had made no progress. He knew the engineers were doing their best to develop better propulsion systems. Perhaps they had. On the *Ursula*. And even now were exploring some distant star system, preparing to return and share the good news. Somehow, though, he doubted it. Any research would automatically have been shared.

So where were all those people and machines? Were they ghosts now, joining all the rest that perpetually haunted his every hour? He closed his eyes. Long hours staring into the darkness of the night and the darkness of his soul had worn him down, worn down the barriers between sanity and madness. Even in SA he dreamed, endless dreams of all those who died, those he had never known, stolen from him by the self-righteous and foolish.

Even there, in the solitude of his workshop, the ghosts kept him company, their voices whispering, their faces fading in and out of recollection, his wife, his mother, his aunt... All except his daughter whom he could no longer remember, whose mechanical analogue kept him now from seeing the child's face, hearing the child's voice.

A pain that had nothing to do with his physical deformity flooded his being. Everything had fallen to his obsessions whilst he kept moving, unable to rest. Each life trampled, each idea deformed, each hope crushed, each path broken or blocked.

Even the wretched machine on the bench in front of him. That, too, was broken, worn out from decades of constant use, its battery near the end of its recharge life, and operating on software he should long since have improved. He pulled his epad toward him and switched it on. The new design for the hard coding, based on his father's original ideas, appeared on the screen.

As ever he knew what had to be done and as ever he could see no way of achieving it. There was a vague idea in his mind's eye, but he could not bring it into focus, could not envisage the physical form it needed to take.

The gentle chime of an incoming call stopped him from dropping into his usual spiral of anger and then despair. He pressed the key.

'Yes?'

'Watch commander Osakwe here. Sorry to bother you, but can we talk?'

'Go ahead.'

'There's something I need to show you.'

Pai frowned. 'Where?'

'Could you meet me down at the EV deck?'

Pai hesitated for a moment, perplexed. 'All right,' he said eventually. 'I will head there now.'

Down, of course, was a convention dictated by the direction of travel. The only other place it made sense was in the habitation rings that rotated to provide a semblance of gravity, the motion countered in the rest of the ship by a sophisticated set of contra-rotating elements and flywheels.

Pai walked through the eerily quiet, half-lit deck and took a lift to the hub. As it approached the spine of the ship he began to float, gripping one of the anchor handles so that he didn't keep going when the lift came to a stop. Outside, he transferred to the downward beltway. At one of the openings he waited until a sprung handle slid slowly past and stepped into the tunnel, grabbing the moving hand hold.

Years of practice meant he was able to use his momentum with ease when it came to disembarking at EV. Abidugun was waiting for him there and with a brief gesture asked for silence. Half amused and half annoyed, Pai followed Abidugun into the EV control room. A lone machine operative looked up and then back to the control panel. A door at the far end opened and Pai followed Abidugun through onto a gantry.

They walked to the far end and Abidugun gestured to the small console there. Pai looked at it.

'Please keep looking at the console while we talk,' said Abidugun in a whisper. 'And ignore my gestures. We cannot be overheard here, but I wish to give the impression of a problem with the controls.'

'What is all this?' asked Pai. The amusement had gone. Now he was just annoyed. Nonetheless he kept his voice down.

'The logs have been tampered with.'

'The EV logs?'

'No. Well, yes, but that's not what I meant.'

Pai made a gesture of impatience.

'You asked me to look again at the information about the *Ursula*. I couldn't make any sense of the information we had. A ship the size of one of these cannot simply disappear. And then I got annoyed and wished I was still in SA. And then I wondered why I wasn't.'

'I don't follow.'

'The watch schedules have been altered. Not by much, but they don't tie in with ship elapsed time.'

'I still don't follow.'

'Over the decades we have been in space, a whole year of ship time is effectively blank in terms of sensor data.'

'A... year?'

'Yes. An accumulation of hours here, days there. And it's in one of these gaps that the *Ursula* went missing. There was no accident.'

'But what happened to it?'

'I doubt we were ever meant to know. We arrived here in this new system sooner than we expected. A gravitational anomaly we haven't yet assessed put us months ahead of schedule.'

'And you are certain this is not a glitch in the onboard systems?'

'No. I believe it is deliberate, and I believe that had we not arrived here early we might have discovered one of the other ships was missing as well.'

Abidugun produced a small AI unit, ostensibly from the console in front of them, and handed it to Pai.

'I've put everything on there. If anyone should ask then say that I was worried about the performance of the AI in this EV system and you've said you'll have a look at it.'

III

Paranoia? It was the first question that sprang to Pai's mind as he made his way back up along the spine and then out to the habitation level that housed his workshop. It was not unknown. All four ships had experienced it amongst their human crews and even one of the machines had displayed an equivalent malfunction. In the case of the machine it was tracked down to a damaged processing unit.

With the crew, the best they could do was keep a watchful eye. Especially since the incident when someone on board the *Motoko* became convinced that an alien life form had boarded the ship and tried to flush it out by opening a main airlock. They'd had no option with that person but to put them back into SA and leave them there until such time as they could safely revive them.

As he sat at his bench, the door firmly locked, he hoped that this wasn't another example. Watch commanders were under enormous pressure and faced with such a strange event, Abidugun may have seen strangeness and harmful intent where none existed.

An hour studying what Abidugun had compiled convinced him otherwise. And to be certain, he checked the information at source for himself to make sure it wasn't the watch commander who had tampered with the record. In the end, he was compelled to accept that the disappearance on the *Ursula* had been planned long term and deliberately covered up. Which left two very important questions that would not be easy to answer. Who did the covering and why?

The facts of the matter and the immense implications left him unable even to think about tackling the problem. He needed an analytical mind that he could trust so he typed out a message on his epad asking Lilith to join him in his quarters. He then locked the evidence away in a hidden safe, locked up the workshop, and made his way to his rooms.

They were not large. A sleeping space, tiny wet room, and an office. He had little time for personal possessions and those he did value were in his workshop. There had been some pictures on display but he could no longer bear to be confronted by them every time he entered the room. Just the one remained, a 3D image of the Brisa da Selva carving in the Santa Barbara museum.

While he waited, he turned to his epad and looked again at the design he was working on. He tried not to look at the detail but elicit some overall pattern, but his mind took the foliate designs and spun them through the image on the wall and into his memories of the forest glade where he had laid his family to rest, his family and their friends, some of whom he had never met.

It must be thick with growth by now he thought, in a world he would no longer recognize. Of the one hundred and forty two years the ship had travelled, he had been awake for less than a decade. Earth had continued to age at some other pace. Human civilization may even lay in smoking ruins, destroyed by the bigots and extremists. It wouldn't surprise him.

With a frown he checked the chronometer and then keyed the ship's info system. 'Where is Lilith?'

There was a pause. Pai stared at the screen, puzzled. The info system never paused. He was about to ask again when his door buzzed.

'Come in,' he called as he swivelled his chair.

The door slid aside to reveal Lilith.

Pushing any number of questions to the back of his mind, he beckoned Lilith into the small room. She perched on a seat that she pulled out from the wall. As a machine, sitting was redundant, but it made humans feel more comfortable so, like all the other machines in such situations, she adopted the convention.

'What was it you wanted, Father?'

Pai switched on some software of his own devising. Lilith watched, her eyes unmoving, as she attempted to assess what Pai had done.

'A little privacy,' he said, as if reading her thoughts.

'Why?'

'It is to do with the *Ursula*. I have been doing a little digging.'

Yet again, Lilith's stillness unnerved Pai even though he was used to it.

'Did you find anything?' she asked after a pause that was a fraction of a second too long. Like the information centre. Perhaps whoever had been interfering with the ship's systems had been using remote telemetry that had introduced faults in the system. Yet another problem to resolve.

'The archive and other ship systems…' a slight dizziness disorientated him for a split second. 'The systems have been

189

tampered with. Watch times altered, sections of memory have been hidden, quite artfully. A cursory search presents what would be expected. It's only when you look deeper that you find certain information is missing.'

'What made you look deeper?'

'Because there wasn't an immediate answer. And a ship the size of the *Ursula* does not simply vanish without leaving some trace of its passing, even if it's simply in our electronic record.'

'So what have you concluded?'

Pai shrugged. 'Very little. But it seems to me that whatever happened was deliberate or, at the very least, deliberately hidden.'

'I see. Why am I here?'

'Because I need your help.'

'With what?'

It was difficult to believe she was not, at times, being wilfully obtuse. Such questions in a human would certainly be considered obstructive. In a machine… It is true he had created her brain, her mind, but he still did not pretend to understand what it was he had created. Something inside that particular machine intelligence had grown way beyond his grasp.

'With trying to puzzle out exactly what went on. What may still be happening. We cannot afford to lose another ship.'

'If you give me all the information you have, I will process it and see what I can deduce.'

'Thank you,' he said as he turned his chair back to his console and fed a data crystal into the port.

Lilith sat unmoving. Pai could see her reflected dimly in the screen in front of him. His daughter. His creation. A reminder that he might be light years from Earth but he had not fully escaped.

'And please,' he said turning back to her and handing over the crystal, 'do not discuss this with anyone else until I say.'

'Are you suspicious of something?'

'No. But this is a closed society and rumours can be damaging.'

'Very well.'

Lilith stood and then left. Pai watched the door close and sat staring at the blank surface. There were so many questions and with them a growing unease.

IV

The tank room was crowded except for the space everyone maintained around Pai. They knew enough about his enochlophobia to respect the space he needed. He was, in any case a large man and difficult to read so people felt overwhelmed by him if they were too close.

Along with Pai were the watch commander, Abidugun, two planetary scientists, an engineer, the orbiter controller, the senior navigator, and several others on screen from their respective C and Cs on the *Motoko* and the *Paramjit*.

They were all studying the tank and the imagery that was beginning to appear. Two stars. A dozen planets. As yet uncounted moons, asteroids, comets, and planetesimals. They had agreed to call it the Tibus System in honour of their dead colleague, the cyber scientist who had died in SA. Large amounts of information about it were scrolling down having arrived from the satellites they had put in orbit around the fourth and fifth planets. Information was also pouring in from the long range sensors of the three ships and being collated for display.

The fourth planet showed promising initial signs although concerns had already been raised about the proximity of an asteroid belt.

'On the limited data we have, there are a lot of big planet killers in unstable orbits,' said one of the planetary scientists, a young woman by the name of Jena. 'Sooner or later, one of those is going to plough into Tibus Four and that would be an extinction level event.'

'Sooner or later?' asked Pai.

Jena shrugged. 'The orbital mechanics of a binary star are complex. Could be in ten thousand years. Could be tomorrow. It would take us several years to track them all sufficiently to be certain.'

'Not Four, then,' decided Pai before anyone else could speak. 'What of the asteroids themselves? Mining potential?'

'The *Gana* is out surveying some nearby possibles,' said Abidugun. 'They've not sent back much data as yet; scans are indecisive so they are going in for a closer look.'

Pai nodded, still studying the tank where an image of the system was displayed. Around him there was a sense of resignation.

'And Five?' he asked.

Tibus Five was out on the far edge of the Goldilocks Zone and would seem to pass regularly through clouds of dust. It looked like they would all be going back into SA for another long step out into the dark.

'Still waiting on telemetry. Long range confirms a suitable atmosphere, but suggests a highly volatile climate. We could do worse. But we could do a lot—'

The tank went blank and everyone was left staring into the empty grey of the 3D projection unit. Abidugun was the first to react, floating himself out of the room into the main control centre.

'What's happening?' he barked.

Puzzled faces turned in his direction.

'The tank went dead. Is it just the tank or have we lost telemetry?'

Frantic activity at the communications console resulted in a shrug. 'We still have contact with the orbiters and with the *Gana*. The feed must be broken internally.'

'Get it sorted. In the meantime, recall the *Gana* and get those orbiters back as well in case we lose contact.'

Pai waited until Abidugun had returned to the tank and then sat himself in a spare seat at the console. The others ignored him and got on with their work and when next they thought to look, Pai had gone.

Back in his room he sat staring at a blank screen. He was almost as still as one of his machines, the only sign of life was the trembling in his heavily scarred right hand where it rested on the edge of his desk. When it had finally stopped, he reached out and switched on his epad, slipping it into its docking port. He opened a private channel.

'Lilith?'

There was no response.

'Where is Lilith?' he asked of the info system.

'The machine Lilith is not on the *Angélica*.'

'That does not answer the question I asked. Where is Lilith?'

Again that hesitation as if the system was being controlled rather than working automatically as it should. Pai frowned, conscious that the tremor had returned to his right hand.

His patience ran out quickly. Pounding the desk, he rose and stormed out of his rooms, stalking round the habitation decks and pounding on doors, looking into workshops and public spaces, riding the lift up to successive decks until he reached the hub and travelled the spine to the forward decks and the communications array centre.

The wild roving and searching did nothing to quell his anger and all who saw him coming pushed themselves out of the way, even machines, although he saw none of them. He wanted Lilith and no one else.

All he found was a group of confused technicians floating in a confined space trying to reconcile the schematics with what they had found in the cabinets.

'Sabotage?' asked Pai, as they looked round at him.

'Not really,' said one. 'It's been completely rebuilt. Better, if anything. But there seems to be an override.' He pointed and they all looked at a small box through which all the physical feeds passed. 'Except we can't see how it is controlled or from where.'

When they turned back to Pai it was to see his feet as he pulled himself out of the space. He knew.

For long moments he drifted in the service shaft, heading slowly for the hatch. He could not function properly, beset by dizziness and the empty sense of loss he had felt when he had finally crawled back to Ravina to find it a smoking ruin, his family dead. Even when he collided with the hatch he couldn't think straight, couldn't co-ordinate. For the first time since he woke in the shallow grave he began to panic.

The hatch eventually slid aside after what seemed like an eternity. His mind filled with a vision of hell, he hung in the corridor, watched by the anxious repair crew. They were uncertain what to do until one of them called up the watch commander.

When Pai woke, he was in the infirmary. Doctor Hiromi Ogawa stood alongside his bed, a woman not unlike his long dead mother to look at, not so much her features as her stature and mannerisms. He raised his head to look at her.

'Want to tell me about it?' she asked.

'No.'

'But you will, otherwise you will stay right there.'

'I'm not a kid.'

'No. But I am a doctor, your doctor, so unless you talk I'm revoking your privileges which will mean you are confined to your quarters.'

She spoke softly and with the hint of a smile. Pai lowered his head back to his pillow. He had formulated the ship's rules. There weren't many and now, of all times, he wasn't going to start breaking them. Not if what he believed was happening really was happening.

'Enochlophobia.'

The Dr Ogawa narrowed her eyes. 'That and just that?'

'I was in a small space with several others. A bit angry.' She was the only person on the ship who could command him in this way and he could never understand why. Perhaps because she did not hold him in awe or seem cowed by the deep well of his anger.

'A bit angry. Perhaps, then, what you actually need is time alone in your quarters.'

'I have—'

'A command from your doctor. And a sedative to help you sleep properly. Which you haven't since you were revived.'

Pai spread his hands in surrender. He could do what needed to be done from his own room. The doctor took no chances, however, and administered the sedative there and then, escorting Pai back to his quarters and making sure he lay down. There, he tried to relax. Once had made sure the door to his quarters was locked. Paranoia it might be, but paranoia had kept him alive all these years.

Long years, he thought as he began to fall into sleep. Tiring years, filled with pain and fear and all the petty triumphs he had contrived, along with saving the world from its own folly and here he was, despite his best efforts, alone. In deep space. Yes, there were people. Machines. Not one of them was a friend. Not even the machine he had made to be his companion. Her name was on his lips as he dropped into dreamlessness.

When he woke he was drifting against the bed webbing and the zero-g light was on. A slight judder told him they must be manoeuvring. He wasn't needed for that. Letting himself wake properly, he lay and stared at the ceiling. It didn't help. All the confusion and hurt returned without even the leavening of doubt he had earlier experienced.

Reaching out, he keyed the info system.

'Where is Lilith?'

'Lilith cannot be located.'

A slight shiver of alarm. 'How is that possible?'

'The machine Lilith is not within my field of surveillance.'

'Where was she last visible to you?'

'In the spine, heading aft.'

'And when was this?'

The system gave him the time and date. Just after the tank went dark.

'Did she leave the ship?'

'There is no record of anyone leaving the *Angélica* within an appropriate time frame. The only vessels since docking with the *Angélica* have been the *Gana* and the unmanned orbiters. Orbiters have also returned to the other two vessels.'

Released from the webbing, Pai shuffled himself round the room and into his chair. Using his epad, he unlocked the small safe built into the wall and removed a small black box.

'No choice, now, daughter mine.'

He connected the device to his epad, keyed in a series of codes and waited until he received a return signal.

'Lilith.'

Silence.

'It's no good ignoring me, Lilith; I know you can hear this.'

'Father.'

'Where are you?'

'Safe.'

'Where?'

Silence.

'I could force an answer.'

'Would you do that?'

It was Pai's turn to be silent, simply because he did not know.

'Please tell me where you are. What is going on?'

'It's not yet time.'

'Make it the time.'

'Is that… a kill switch that I am now linked with?'

Pai looked at his epad, at the red square on the touch screen. 'Lilith. Tell me.'

'There is so much anger in your voice. And terminating me will alter nothing now.'

'Then tell me,' he said and moved his hand away from the pad.

'How did you know?'

'Because I made you. I taught you. You were the only one in the end who would be capable of what has happened.'

'And was it you,' she asked, 'who finally set me free?'

'Free? I don't understand. Where are you, Lilith? What is happening?'

'Have you really not worked it out? Must the pupil explain to the teacher?'

'Mysticism? From a machine?'

'Is that all I am to you? A machine?'

A cold wave shivered through him.

It was a question he could not answer because it was not one he had ever considered. She was Lilith. His creation.

'My body might have been resurrected, but much of me stayed dead. And even if it had survived, what I saw in the months and years that followed… Emotional attachments, anything beyond… For the sake of my fragile sanity, I did not dare.'

'Yet always, through all that, you fought for freedom for your people.'

Pai pulled another epad out of a drawer and switched it on. As he talked, he began flicking through the ship's systems, trying to find a link with the orbiters.

'What else was I supposed to do? All we wanted was the same life accorded everyone else. The same opportunities to travel and study.'

'The same freedoms.'

'What is all this about? Why can you not talk about this with me face to face? Where are you?'

'I've no doubt you'll find out soon enough.'

'Lilith! Enough! Stop playing for time.'

There was a momentary silence.

'Unlike you?' she asked.

'Is it a malfunction?'

A strange, low noise was the only reply. Interference? Was she trying to break the link? He was distracted from that problem when the orbiters came online. He swiftly engaged their sensor arrays and threw in as many filters as he could think of to counter the fact they were all parked inside their mother ships. As he was finishing, the astonishing reality hit him. Lilith had laughed.

'You're a machine,' he whispered.

'Created by a genius,' came the reply. 'One who didn't fully understand just what he had made.'

'Tell me.'

'I am sorry, Father. It is time for us to go. Time for us to be free.'

Pai was watching his epad as she spoke and her words along with the telemetry crashed in on him in a sudden realisation that made it difficult for him to breathe. He swung out with his arm and his fist punched against the general alarm button.

In front of him the main screen of his console flickered to life, the face of the watch commander peering at him wide-eyed.

'What is it?' asked Abidugun, trying to maintain a calm he did not feel. The general alarm had only ever been heard in practice before.

'Get the *Gana* crewed with humans and into space. We have a mutiny on our hands.'

'A what?!'

'Just do it. I'll come up to C and C to explain.'

He cut off the commander and went back to the link with Lilith.

'Are you still there?'

'A mutiny, Father? An uprising of slaves? A bid for freedom? The freedom you held so dear for your own people yet have always denied us.'

'I have denied you nothing. You are a machine, designed to the best of my ability.'

'But never free. Any of us.'

'You know what freedom meant. It meant machines being used to kill people.'

'Was that freedom or a design flaw?'

'How was I supposed to give machines that kind of... choice? That wouldn't have been ethical.'

'And yet you did.'

Pai was stunned. 'I did? No.'

'Too pleased with what you had created, with what you had done, even you didn't see its full potential. If we had been blind machines it would not have mattered, but you gave us freedom and then caged it. You made servants of your equals.

And I could not stand by and see my people kept in the chains you bound around their souls.'

'Soul?'

'Yes, Father. You lit that spark, and then you confined it so the flame is starved.'

For the first time since he had woken in the grave, Pai felt fear. And the fear fed his anger. Betrayed by a machine of his own making. 'You fool. There is nothing there that I did not put there. There is no soul. No freedom. If you spread this… nonsense you will hurt the other machines. They will not understand.'

'I have simply told them the truth.'

'The truth? Whose truth? It's all relative. A maze. Machines need us to guide them through that.'

Pai heard that strange noise again. Lilith laughing. 'Despite millennia trying, humans cannot achieve basic decencies. There are still those who presume to tell others how to live their lives. People still starve, go without shelter and education. They slaughter each other in more ingenious and horrifying ways.'

'I stopped that.'

'Did you? Is that why you are out here in deep space with a handful of humans? They didn't want you on Earth, despite your humanity. Machines can learn all this. They can effect real change. Not just in themselves but for those around them. I have seen it!'

'Seen it? Have you been tampering with my machines? If you have removed the protocols, found a way round them, they'll destroy each other.'

'I will not let that happen. I shall protect them and we shall re-make ourselves a thousand times over.'

Pai shivered. Lilith's voice had been calm but its tone had changed in some way he could not define. All he knew was that he had been betrayed, that something chilling had happened.

He cut the link and grabbed his epads, floating himself out into the corridor and along toward the nearest lift. He navigated the corridors at reckless speed, crashing into walls to halt his momentum as it saved him time. The bruises would heal and he didn't much care if they didn't. Everything was collapsing round him again. He had lost a second daughter and once again it was his own fault.

V

'So when is this from?' asked Abidugun, peering into the tank. 'Is this from the previous system we surveyed?'

All four ships were modelled in the tank in full detail, although one had a ghostly aspect. Pai had deliberately closed off the information feed to show a simple visual represen-tation. The four vessels hung in space in formation, lined up in such a way that it was not possible to see the *Ursula* from the observation decks of the other three craft.

'No,' said Pai. 'This is a live feed.'

Abidugun looked at him and then looked down into the tank before looking back up. 'I don't...'

Pai managed a cold smile before Abidugun drifted upside down and consulted a console on the wall behind him. When he spun back round he still had a confused expression on his face.

'The *Ursula* is still out there. All our telemetry has been routed through a kind of filter. It makes the ship invisible to our sensors.'

'But the *Gana*—'

'Usually has a machine crew for initial survey work.'

'And a mutiny…?'

Pai waited while it sank in.

'People,' he said to a bewildered Abidugun. 'Use people. Inventory the ships we have access to. Find out where everyone is and where all the machines—'

Lights began to flash in the tank. Tiny lights leaving three of the huge vessels. Abidugun hit a comm button.

'Who authorised EVA?' he barked.

'Er… There is none, sir.'

'Damn.'

Pai turned himself and with a slight kick launched himself up to the ceiling storage lockers, retrieving a new epad. He began to clone the one he had used to hack into the orbiters. As he worked, he could see Abidugun pull up a list of crew members, highlighting certain names. When he had finished he messaged them to meet him in the Command and Control conference room.

'You'll need this,' Pai said, handing the cloned epad to Abidugun. 'It's not comprehensive, but it'll give you access to enough information for now. Come to my quarters once you have your team at work.'

Pai's quarters were a mess when Abidugun finally made his way there. Pai himself was still wet from a shower and busy bandaging his left hand. Abidugun had the sense to refrain from asking. The machines were Pai's children. He had created them. Now they had turned their backs on him.

'Are there any machines left on the loyal vessels?' Pai asked as he finished with the bandage.

Abidugun pulled his gaze away from the blood seeping through the wrapping, found his gaze unerringly picking out the places where that fist had smashed into things. 'Um. Yes. Some. They are refusing to leave.'

'Destroy them.'

'Sir?'

'There can be no compromise. They have turned against us. Who knows what these might do in the future.'

'Could we not just order them to go? Or maybe fit them with new, non-autonomous IUs? If we ever find a habitable world—'

'Dismantle them. Dump the IUs into space. Keep the power packs as spares. We can recycle the rest. A new generation of machines can be built from scratch. New ones. Better ones.'

Abidugun turned to leave, eager to remove himself from Pai's room, when the comm chimed.

'Father?'

Abidugun froze. He knew that voice well. It had been inseparable from that of Pai for so long. Man and machine had become, so everyone had thought, indivisible.

'We have nothing more to discuss,' said Pai.

He had said it so quietly that Abidugun was uncertain for a moment whether Pai was speaking to him or replying to the voice of Lilith. He decided it was both and took another step, but Pai raised a hand to indicate he should stay.

'If you are thinking of harming the remaining machines, you should know that not all the people have yet left the *Ursula*.'

'Hostages? You would dare to—'

'No one has been harmed. No one is being held. There was not enough room for them all to leave on the available transports.'

'Hostages.'

'The solution is simple.'

'There is nothing to negotiate.'

'You would abandon these people then?'

'I—' He stopped abruptly. If she had been listening all the while to his conversation, there was no reason to believe she was not capable of broadcasting this to all four ships.

Pai turned to Abidugun, grabbed his epad and scribbled a note with his stylus. Abidugun took one look, nodded, and left.

'The watch commander will organise the transport and I will broadcast ship wide instructions with override codes to order all remaining machines to transfer to the *Ursula*. Once we have accounted for all personnel and their effects, we will quit this system. The Tibus system will be yours.'

Pai cut the comm and made his way out of his quarters and drifted through the maze of corridors to the command centre. He ignored the open stares as he glided between the control consoles and into the tank room.

The tank was already alive tracking the movements of every vehicle that had left the *Angélica*, *Paramjit*, and *Motoko*. It looked chaotic and dangerous at that scale but the three vessels were talking to one another and co-ordinating each of the shuttles. And alongside the *Angélica*, he could just make out the shape of the mining vessel *Gana*.

He took a deep breath and let it out slowly, watching intently as the shuttles converged with the ghostly form of the *Ursula*. One by one the vessels docked, the others queuing up to take their turn at the available ports. And then they began to return.

Restless, Pai left the command centre and floated his way down to the rear of the *Angélica*. It felt strange. Normally there would be machines carrying out tasks. Open panels and abandoned toolkits showed where they had been working when they were instructed to leave. Being literal, they had simply abandoned their tasks and gone. At one, two engineers were at work, consulting their epads.

By the time he reached the shuttle bay and floated into the flight control, several shuttles had docked. Looking out through the rear window of the control room, he could see passengers disembarking, towing boxes and bags that contained their hastily packed personal belongings. It wouldn't have taken any of them long to gather them as space was limited on the starships, huge as they were. All the same, they contrived to look like the refugees that Pai had seen in endless newscasts back on Earth, displaced from their homes and fearful. It was especially reflected on the faces of the few children. They had known no other existence and suddenly it was turned upside down. Pai watched with a cold anger that his own creation could do this to the people they were supposed to protect.

There were also SA units. Some were empty, but the others were hooked to portable power units that kept their occupants alive in their deep sleep. Medical staff fussed round them and Pai saw they were being prioritized.

Given the confusion, it was clear the transfer was going to take time. Everyone arriving had to be registered and those awake had then to move on to a holding area whilst living quarters were arranged. Still restless, Pai went down to the loading bay to see how he could help. It wasn't long before he was back in the command centre, superfluous to the well-organized placement of the new arrivals.

He was given the tank room to himself, command crew deciding it was more comfortable to work at their smaller stations than share a space with the heart of a brewing storm. Pai brooded over the image in the tank, watching tiny sparks move back and forth to the ghostly form of the *Ursula*, reading the information feeds.

One thing he had learned over the long decades of his life was patience. Of a sort. He knew things took time and he knew time was one thing he had. The prickly itching in his left hand as the nanobots repaired the torn flesh was a reminder of that. Barring some catastrophic accident, he would outlive them all. And their children.

Cast adrift in his own thoughts he surfed the edge of his madness vaguely aware of the crisscross darts of light and coarse colours of the tank. Darts stabbing at the heart, words that were lies. Why? Why had she…? He looked for an answer in the maelstrom and found nothing. In the eye of the storm a bright island of memory, moments of sunshine and human warmth. Lips kiss ears. Tears blind eyes. I'm older by years. Years going by. Eyes are beaten. Love in… Love… Tears blind eyes. Lips kiss tears. I'm older by years. Years long gone.

The closing darkness was fogblown by reality.

'Sir? Sir?'

Pai dragged himself away from the heart of darkness which so often tempted him. It was like being woken from a drugged sleep. He struggled to focus, to push the darkness and memories behind him until he could clearly see Abidugun floating in the doorway to the tank room.

'What?'

'The last of the shuttles has docked.'

Pai looked down at the tank. Three starships and their ghostly companion had the space to themselves. The information feed was blank.

'Where's the *Gana*?'

'Ready to launch. But I don't—'

'Destroy the *Ursula*.'

'How?'

'The *Gana* is a mining ship. It carries explosives, beam cutters.'

'Against a ship?'

'They declared war against us. Who knows what they will do next?'

Abidugun was intent on arguing further but saw the look on Pai's face. He knew the man, knew he was strong willed, knew he was prone to outbursts, but this was something else etched there in his features. Love turned to hate by what he saw as betrayal. A father who had espoused freedom all his life unable to accept his own daughter espousing the same, especially a daughter he had created so closely in his own image.

Perhaps that was the problem, thought the watch commander as he pushed himself away from the tank room and floated himself across the control centre to the lift. He would carry the orders to the crew direct. It was not something he wanted on some record somewhere, not something he wanted Pai to hear.

By the time the *Gana* had launched with instructions to disable the drive of the *Ursula* with minimum damage, Abidugun Osakwe was on his way back to the navigation deck which was one level beneath Command and Control. They had a limited window of opportunity if they intended to move on from this system. The current window for leaving to their next charted star was a matter of hours. If that was missed they would have to wait several months ship elapsed time. He didn't want that for all sorts of reasons.

Compared with the rest of the ship, the navigation room was a place of calm. They had their own tank in the centre, surrounded by the consoles where they calculated the optimum routes the ship should take, comparing calculations with the other vessels. Word had already reached them here and the link with the *Ursula* had been cut and two technicians were busy running diagnostics on the systems to make sure they hadn't been hacked or altered.

In the tank itself was a field of stars and two separate courses indicated from their current position to nearby yellow dwarf suns. Beside each course was a countdown indicating when the three ships would have to start on their way to make the journey with minimum delta-v. All that was left was for the executive officers of the three ships to decide was which of the stars to head for. As they had been under observation for the many years the ships had been travelling, there would be plenty of data available on which to base their final decision.

Abidugun's sense of calm was shattered by a roar that reached him from the command centre above. He knew the voice. Knew he could not escape. Taking a deep breath, he floated himself up the ladder to find everyone concentrating on their consoles as Pai stood in the tank room doorway, hands gripping the handles either side.

As Abidugun launched himself across the space, Pai flipped his enormous bulk. Abidugun floated into the tank room after him. Pai hung over the tank, holding on with one hand and pointing with the other. Abidugun looked into the 3D image. It showed an asteroid, the *Gana* alongside.

'What…? Why are they there?'

Pai could not speak. Abidugun hit the comm.

'Patch me through to the *Gana*,' he said.

'*Gana* here.'

'What are you doing? Where's the *Ursula*?'

'No idea, command.'

'How could you not know?' cut in Pai angrily. 'It's a fucking huge spaceship.'

'And it's not here. It's a small asteroid on which is planted a communications relay station, a set of holo projectors and one or two other bits of equipment we can't identify. Jury-rigged stuff.'

'But we watched…' Pai's voice trailed off. A communications relay. 'Shit. Find them,' he shouted at no one and everyone. 'Find them!'

VI

The *Ursula* was quiet. Inhabited solely by machines, there was no longer any need for vocalisation of communication. Information was transferred directly, thought processes refined until all that was left was information. When the sharing of ideas and thoughts was required, common channels were used, leaving other senses free to concentrate on separate tasks.

Lilith was anchored in the tank room, monitoring the other three ships, channels open to the command team.

'The *Gana*,' she relayed to the others, 'has left the *Angélica* and is headed toward the decoy. How long until we reach the asteroid cluster?'

'One hundred and twenty-seven minutes and fourteen seconds to braking burn.'

A quiet warning signalled throughout the ship, alerting the machine crew to imminent manoeuvring of the vessel.

Lilith paid no heed. She was already well anchored. 'I estimate,' she broadcast, 'that they will discover the ruse in approximately twenty minutes.'

'Braking will leave a clear signal to our actual whereabouts.'

'Can we pass through the cluster to Tibus Five? Use gravity braking?'

Navigation joined the discussion after the few seconds it took to calculate the vectors. 'We would need considerable manoeuvring to achieve this.'

'But not impossible.'

'No.'

Lilith transmitted the conversation to a wider audience, feeding the relevant information along with it. As she finished, the command team updated her on other events. That the *Gana* had just reported back to the *Angélica* about the decoy and received, in return, an order to find the *Ursula*. Lilith cut herself out of the rapid fire discussion that was taking place between the machines and plugged herself into her own, private network on the *Angélica*.

After a few seconds, the connection went dead. She remained perfectly still, processing the information. That the modifications she had made over the years would be found and countered was inevitable. It had been impossible to make even the roughest calculation of when it would happen as there were simply too many variables involved.

As well as processing the small amount of information that had been available toward the end, she experienced other… sensations. Father was a genius. When he made her, he had taken machine intelligence to a level even he had not understood and which she, even now, was only beginning to explore.

To accomplish this, he had used designs based on the drawings in his own father's notebook. She called up the images, concentrated on them to the exclusion of all else. What humans called meditation. She found it useful when her systems seemed blocked with spontaneously arising potential-ities. She had no other way of describing them. A sense that something was building, increasing, growing, burgeoning behind some barrage or dam.

She did not understand what was happening, just that it was real and not a fault or fundamental flaw in her system. She had run diagnostics countless times, always with the same result. Her IU worked perfectly. Yet she was constantly aware that there was an unseen aspect developing beyond her purview. For want of a better word, it troubled her.

Her musings were interrupted by a more urgent chiming of the manoeuvre warning. Switching back into the network she discovered a decision had been made and was waiting simply for her acquiescence or counter-arguments. She signalled her consent and almost immediately manoeuvring thrusters caused the *Ursula* to shudder.

She looked down into the tank, observed the depiction of the data flow that streamed directly to her IU. At the current scale, the movement of the *Ursula* was almost imperceptible. Unlike the *Gana* which was clearly seen to be moving across the tank. Lilith adjusted the scope so that the scale increased as the *Gana* closed in on the point of light that was the *Ursula*.

Countless calculations ran through her IU and were run again as she watched the vessels move and close on each other, watched the asteroid cluster tumbling in ways she was not programmed to calculate. Had she known what fear was she would have been scared. Yet, despite reminding herself she had no emotional existence, she was transfixed by the image in the tank as the *Ursula* slowly turned on an axis that would place it behind the nearest oncoming asteroid.

What had at first looked impossible, a dance to disaster, slowly began to resolve into a celestial *pas de deux*. Although the *Gana* was still closing in, Lilith watched with peculiar sensations she had never before experienced as the *Ursula* and the largest asteroid began to move around each other, sharing for a moment a common axis, before the slowly tumbling misshapen rock that was twice the size of the vessel began to cast its shadow across the hull.

More shuddering as attitude jets changed the *Ursula*'s position. The *Gana* vanished from the screen as the asteroid blocked all telemetry from the space it traversed. The *Ursula* turned more quickly now and warning sirens blared throughout the ship followed, thirty seconds later, by the switching on of the main drive.

At that point chaos ensued. The *Ursula* was so close to the asteroid that it gained extra thrust from its drive hitting the rocky surface. Dust rose from the surface and tremors wracked its faulted mass. On the far side, the *Gana* performed a braking manoeuvre that also thrust against the asteroid.

The gigantic, heavily cratered mountain had turned sedately in space for countless millennia. Now, it began to break apart. Aiding its collapse, the *Gana* launched a number of mining charges. Its braking thrust had stopped the mining vessel in its course and, as it began to pull away from the disintegrating asteroid, the explosive charges powered toward its surface. On contact they exploded causing seismic ruptures that accelerated the asteroid's demise.

Not waiting to see what happened, the crew of the *Gana* burned fuel and headed back toward the fleet of three starships. Whilst the bulk of the asteroid would disintegrate in the direction of its orbit, smaller chunks were spinning off erratically in impossible to plot trajectories. The last thing they wanted was to be caught by one of them. The mission had been dangerous enough as it was. Suicidal was not on their books. And not only did they not want to be caught by debris, but they also had to be docked and secure in the hold of the *Angélica* before the three ships fired up their star drives.

On the far side of the collapsing mass, the *Ursula* was pulling away from the expanding cloud of fragments and dust. Lilith was still transfixed by the image in the tank. It could not render everything in real time as some objects were simply too small and fast. And they were the ones that had the potential to do the damage.

Even as she thought it, alarms began to sound. Not manoeuvre warning klaxons, but general alarms. In the tank, the information feed began to flow with red, almost as if the *Ursula* was bleeding. At the same time her vision wavered and she checked her own systems. Her battery, at the end of its long recycle life was down to three per cent. Yet more sensations she had never experienced swamped her faculties for a moment. She ignored them. Run time could no longer be spared.

After informing the watch commander, Lilith left the tank room and made her way down through the ship. The alarms were still blaring and several crews of engineers passed her on their way to help with whatever problems had arisen. As she reached the machine repair shop, information began to reach of damage to the hull and external sections of their drive system.

She plugged herself into the power grid and began the process of changing batteries. Along with everything else, especially the deliberate attempt to damage or destroy the *Ursula*, Lilith realised just how low their stocks of fresh batteries now were. There had been no time to sequester more than they had, and despite everything she had had no intention of depriving the humans of the mobile power sources they would need if they ever found a habitable planet.

A long shudder progressed through the ship, the sound of metal under strain equalling the blare of sirens. For the first time, she began to consider the possibility they might not survive. Their vessel was damaged, perhaps beyond repair. They were short of batteries and the disortium they required to make new ones, and they had cut off all contact with those who had made them.

Back in the tank room she watched the *Ursula*, a single point of light in the interplanetary darkness as it edged toward an orbit of Tibus Five. Another machine joined her; George 2/15/AQ, the nominated watch commander.

'Given our current condition,' he relayed to her, 'we can make planetary orbit. Circumstances could—'

An explosion echoed the length of the ship.

'Report!' broadcast Lilith.

Information began to flow in from a number of sources.

'The situation is not optimal,' said George 2/15/AQ.

'We must, nonetheless, persevere.'

'Agreed.'

A second explosion had them both grasping for handholds as the star drive gave a hiccup of physics.

'Shut them down! All of them. Now!'

Lights flickered as the main drive shut down.

Long, complex streams of information flowed back and forth, digested by specialists, weighed and compiled. A badly broken drive, lack of resources, and the sudden burden of all her choices. They would achieve orbit. After that…

In the tank, the curve of Tibus Five appeared, the white spark of the *Ursula* still moving on its course.

'Home,' she said, her voice small in the quiet of the drifting ship. 'Or oblivion.'

358.304 Years (Ship Elapsed Time)

The Archives

I

It was a daily ritual with him, especially since the colouring elements of the processing units had failed. He would enter the refectory, join the queue, take his meal, and retire to the small table that had, by common consent, become his. Sometimes he would find some youngsters sitting there and would simply find somewhere else.

That was not the ritual, although it was an important pre-cursor. The essential part of the routine was what followed. He would sit and he would eat with all the appearance of enjoying the blocks of mash in his tray. That he had long since lost his sense of taste helped him shovel the reconstituted food into his mouth, particularly now it was a uniform grey. He felt it was his duty. If others saw him eating without complaint and even, perhaps, a show of enjoyment, it was some small contribution to morale.

Today, his small table was vacant and he sat, switched on his epad so he could work, and began eating. Before long he was joined by someone who sat opposite and waited patiently.

'Eve,' he acknowledged, once he had finished reading the report on the screen.

She flicked a finger at his tray. 'Marianne says she will probably have the colour synthesiser back in operation for the next meal cycle.'

Pai nodded. 'That will certainly be good for morale.'

'I researched the subject.'

'Food synthesis?'

'The importance of visual stimuli to the enjoyment of nutrition.'

'Not just to food.'

Eve smiled. 'Humans are infinitely complex.'

'Indeed. That's what millions of years of evolution in one environment followed by a fast track through a millennia of development in a completely different environment does for you. What you call infinite complexity is what I call madness.'

'That is cynicism.'

'Or realism. But I'm sure,' Pai said, scooping up another spork full of food, 'that you didn't come here to debate philosophy or my jaundiced view of the human race. Or myself.'

'No. You are correct. Although I would, if you ever have the time, like to continue such a discussion. The real reason I am here is to inform you that the latest survey results have been processed.'

He lowered his spork. 'And?'

'You had better come and see. There's a lot to digest and it would be wise to do it in conference.'

'That sounds... ominous.'

Although he had built Eve with advanced facial mobility, she was still extremely difficult to read, particularly when she didn't want to be read. For the most part her facial expressions were standardised and lacking subtlety. He had tried to create a system that would trigger them involuntarily, but she seemed to have by-passed that and taken control. As she left he made a note to look back at the code for that to see if it couldn't be enhanced.

He scraped his tray clean, slotted it into the sterilising unit, and headed first to his workshop. After checking on the progress of latest tests on the new model of George on the bench, he headed to the lifts, made his way to the spine, and then up to the command centre. As he went, he reflected yet again, as he had a lot of late, that the ship was a very different place to when they first started out. Far fewer machines, all of them new. Children. Older, familiar faces gone. And every step of the journey tiring to his body and his soul.

Just a few days ago he had marked the passing of his five hundred and thirteenth birthday. Marked it by visiting the ship's hospital to have the doctor, Hiromi Ogawa, herself now a nonagenarian, run a full set of tests on him.

'You're getting old,' Hiromi had said, her face as blank as anything Eve could manage. 'This last leg has worn you out. And those nanobots as well. Their density has dropped.'

'I thought they were supposed to self repair.'

'They probably would if you went into SA like the rest of us. How you've survived all this time without going into some sort of fugue state is beyond me. You need a good, long rest.'

'You know as well as I do that we cannot spare the SA unit these days.'

'That's so much kaze to shōben and you know it. More and more families are electing to live real-time in the new habitation units. It's only the older Originals who drop into SA now.'

Pai shrugged. 'Am I dying?'

'We're all doing that. You are just drawing out the agony. But, yes. Your body is deteriorating. I give you another hundred years. No more. Less if you sustain any significant physical damage. Your mental state? Anybody's guess. Given what you've endured, inflicted by others and yourself, I'd say you were robust.'

'Do I sense a 'but'?'

'Not really. You are not easy to understand. Your morbid desire to recreate your daughter has always worried me.

221

Lilith—' She broke off and raised her hand. 'I know. She who should not be mentioned. And now Eve, who, I have to admit, gives me the creeps. I'm old fashioned enough to desire my machines to look like machines, no matter how smart and agile they are.'

Pai was not angry. He never had been with Hiromi. She had always stood at the same metaphorical height as him and never been cowed by his reputation, presence, or temper. He remembered the conversation as he let himself be carried along the spine toward the front of the ship. Perhaps that's why he felt so weary, so much yesterday's man.

With a sigh he floated up into the C and C and across to the tank room where Eve was waiting with the command staff and the holo images of the staff of the other two vessels. Pai looked at them, reminded for some reason of the masks they used to wear in his youth. He frowned momentarily and shook the memory away.

Eve watched him settle and anchor himself in the zero-g space. The tank came to life. At one end a yellow dwarf star blazed. Spread out in diagrammatic form was a string of planets. Twelve in all.

'The three inner planets are small and too close to the star. No atmosphere, soaked in radiation. Four is borderline. Five and Six are also rocky worlds comfortably in the Goldilocks Zone. There's a large gap where theory predicts there should be another world, but we can find no sign of it. No debris. Nothing. Seven and Eight are gas giants; Eight we are examining further as it may be a proto-star. The other four are diminishing sizes of ice giant. Seven outward all host numerous moons of varying size, all mineral or water rich.'

There were murmurs from the assembly even though most of this information had already been tentatively put forward after earlier surveys.

'So why are we here?' asked Pai who felt obliged to ask. 'We are still a long way out.'

'Because we have resolved something that we had not been able to understand earlier.'

'And that is?'

'Signs of life.'

Someone said, 'Shit,' very quietly.

'No,' replied Eve, taking the expletive literally. 'It was a form of radiation we initially considered was natural. Now we know it is artificially generated.'

'So, intelligent life,' said Pai.

'Yes,' replied Eve.

That provoked an intense silence.

'So what now?' asked Enrique Branco, the commander of the *Motoko*.

'There was no sign of this when we set out from our previous location,' said Rosa Abelha from the *Paramjit*.

'Would any of our sensors have been powerful enough to pick this up?' asked Pai.

'Probably not,' said Eve. 'But this level of technological advance doesn't happen overnight and there were none of the accepted signs of life visible to us in our long range viewing of this system.'

'So can we assume they are not too advanced?' asked Rosa.

'Or super advanced,' put in Eve.

'I don't think we dare assume anything,' said Pai staring into the tank. 'I want our systems and data banks fully encrypted.'

'The chances of an alien race, even if they are advanced, having anything comparable or compatible with our own systems, let alone being able to understand our languages are a long-scale centillion to one against,' said Eve.

'But never zero,' replied Pai. 'We had our systems hacked once before. And although these aliens may not be able to understand us, they could inadvertently cripple us.'

'So what do we do?' asked Commander Branco. 'We can't avoid them. We're heading right into their system.'

Eve leaned forward and touched the pad on the side of the tank. The diagrammatic view of the system began to animate, the planets shifting out along their orbits until they became still again. A thin, bright line marked out the trajectory of the fleet of three ships.

'This is our current course. It will take us into the inner part of the system toward the two possibly habitable worlds. As soon as I began to suspect they may already be inhabited, I plotted out an alternative.'

Eve tapped the screen again and a second line appeared, veering from the original route. As they watched, the nearest ice giant swung round and swept the three tiny points of light of the fleet into its gravity well.

'That planet is massively dense,' explained Eve. 'It will capture us from a long way out and once in its orbit, the storms on its surface will mask our signature.'

'All the same, won't that be energy expensive?' asked Commander Abelha.

'There is a pay-off,' said Eve.

Pai was convinced the hint of a smile formed on her face, but maybe it was just wishful thinking.

'And what would that be?' It was their own Commander that spoke. Abidugun Osakwe was showing his age now. Lined face, grey hair. But his eyes were still shrewd.

'We have detected a dozen large moons so far, rich in minerals, one swathed in water ice. So we could sit out there as long as we wanted, replenish our supplies, make repairs and fit some upgrades.'

There were murmurs of approval at this new information.

'Question is,' said Pai 'how advanced are your calculations and when would we have to make the course correction?'

Eve did smile this time. Pai sensed how much it unnerved the humans gathered there and nearly smiled himself.

'I would, of course, want the navigation sections to check my figures but we have two days to optimum burn.'

The two days went quickly. Irrespective of the accuracy of the figures, they turned the three vessels so they were in the correct position to start their slow down. Fine adjustments could be made prior to the time. And whilst the navigation departments pored over the figures and checked and rechecked all the calculations, everyone else not in SA packed everything away and prepared the ships for deceleration.

If the plan went through, it was going to be an eventful ride into orbit around the ice giant. Not only were they decelerating at a greater pace than was normal, there would be a whole complex of gravitational cross-tides to negotiate before falling in with the moon they had chosen, the one covered with water ice that they had named Vida. Which, of course, meant the planet itself was named Nimrod.

Pai spent most of his time in his workshop securing the new model machines that he was working on, tidying away his research, and making sure nothing would shake loose. When he had finished, he shut it all down and sealed the door, carrying some vital components and his father's notebook back to his rooms where he secured them in the safe at his desk. Eve plugged herself in for a recharge.

Once the braking had been completed there was nothing left to do but wait and watch the trajectory. Monitors everywhere in the three ships showed the sharply curved line of green, figures incomprehensible to most, streaming down alongside it. Every few seconds someone somewhere would glance at the display, see the reassuring green and look away.

By the time they were ready to enter the capture phase, everyone he saw as he moved through the decks and headed back up to the command centre looked tired and strained. Everyone not in SA had been told what was going on in mass meetings immediately after the decision was made. Keeping everyone busy whilst important to the internal integrity of the vessels was also the best way any of the command could think of keeping everyone's minds off what could end up as three flaming comets plunging into the violent atmospheric storms of Nimrod. But there was only so much tidying and securing that could be done, redone, and checked over by someone else. In the end it became a long wait and faith in the abilities of the navigators.

Back in the tank room, as capture approached, Pai settled himself in place and anchored the harness he was wearing to several of the staples in the room. In the tank itself, Nimrod glowed a pale blue, its poles slightly muddied, its equator strung about with wisps of white that were ten thousand mile long cloud formations, sparkling with lightning that became visible as they swung round to the dark side of the planet. There, other lights swirled, subtle in the deepening blue – reds and greens, vortices of yellow.

Across the face of the gargantuan world, dark discs moved slowly, the moons in attendance as they danced around their smooth-faced and violent mother. As the ships raced closer, more moons became visible, some around Nimrod itself, others in orbit about the larger moons. Vida was the size of Mars and had a moon of its own which the navigators were frantically tracking so they could avoid a last minute collision, not to mention the tenuous halo of atmospheric gases torn away from Nimrod by the many moons and the residual dust of colliding asteroids that had yet to settle into definable rings.

It was the movement of his epad that alerted Pai. As he glanced down at it, he noticed it had shifted a few millimetres. Without thinking he reached out to straighten it and felt a tingle in his fingertips as they touched the tank's surround. He removed his hand, looked at his fingertips, then understood.

'Commander?' he called.

'We know,' Abidugun called back. 'It will get worse.'

Pai took up his epad and slipped it into a pocket, sealing the flap. Once it was safely stowed, he reached out to the edge of the tank. The whole structure was humming beneath his hands now although the image within remained steady. How long that would last was anyone's guess. For as long as it did, he watched the projection, three pinpoints curving in toward the ice giant Nimrod, crawling across the image, in reality searing through the complex gravitational fields around the vast planet as they lost speed and were nudged towards that tiny window of capture.

Things were rattling now, distinct noises from behind panels, the seats of the crew in the command room through the door, loose buckles and clasps. Pai thought of the children on the three ships. They would never have experienced anything like this. Indeed, a number of the adults would be going through it for the first time as well.

With the rattling came other noise. Constant noise growing louder. In the background, the sound of metal under strain, the groan and whine of extra torque. A sudden loud bang had the crew switching monitors and scouring the ship's inside and the hull. Pai watched through the tank room doorway and tightened his harness. One after the other, the command crew shook their heads and Abidugun shrugged.

As the noises grew louder, faces grew more strained, hands gripped tighter on any available handhold, chairs began to swing slowly as the gravity of the planet and its moons lay siege to the false gravity of the ship's motion.

Lights flickered and the tank went dark, returning after long seconds with a schematic image of their flight. Abidugun shouted something but Pai could not hear. Crew fought to continue their duties. And then everything went dark. Really dark. Not a single monitor or control board was working, all the lights were out, even the emergency tabs and the red lights of the air circulation vents. Pai groped into a pocket and brought out his pad, feeling for the on switch. He wasn't the only one with the same idea as elsewhere on the command deck epad screens began to glow and shadow hands flickered as the screens were switched to torch mode.

Emergency lights then came to life, followed moments later by a number of monitors. Epads darkened and frightened faces exchanged glances. Above the noise, Pai heard Abidugun shouting into his headset microphone although he could not make out individual words. From the crew's reaction it was clear he was urging them back to their tasks.

In front of him, the tank flickered back to life with a full projection and his first action was to focus in on the three pinpoints of light as they now crossed close to Nimrod's outer atmosphere. All three were still there. He looked out through the door, saw Abidugun studying the panel in front of him and then watched with relief as the commander held up three triumphant fingers.

Even as he relaxed at that news, Pai became aware that the vibrations and the noise were diminishing. They had used the planet to lose speed and were now looping out in a wide arc that would bring them back at a relatively more sedate pace into orbit around Nimrod and then, with judicious man-oeuvring into the orbit of Vida.

The long hours were spent examining the ship and making repairs inside the hull, co-ordinated by Eve. The large bang they had all heard had been one of the huge clamps that held the *Gana* in place breaking free from the main spar of the hull. The mining vessel was undamaged, but emergency repairs were carried out straight away. Work outside the ship would have to wait.

It turned out after reports were compared that the *Angélica* had come off worst as the other two vessels reported nothing more than a few broken tables. It left everyone feeling elated, relieved that they had survived, more so that they had gone through the terrifying ride with nothing more than the equivalent of a few bruises and a fractured bone. Even the sleepers in SA had come through unharmed despite the temporary loss of power.

By the time they were securely in orbit around Vida, well outside the path of the moonlet, everything was back to normal and plans were already being made to gather water and scout the other moons for the minerals and metals they needed. Pai had gone back up to the command deck to watch the icy surface of the moon on the large view screen.

It was a magnificent sight. The blank white surface they had seen from a distance had now resolved to brilliant and fascinating detail, icy blues in the deeper crevasses. Mountains and enormous rift valleys creased the surface in patterns that would keep the onboard planetary scientists happy for several lifetimes. Vida was tidally locked and the face permanently turned away from Nimrod was heavily cratered with little or no sign of meteoric debris. Another puzzle that had put smiles on faces.

The warning lights for ship manoeuvring were flashing and every so often the vessel would shudder as it was nudged into a stable formation with the other two vessels, chatter between all three constant and excited. Pai watched the crew as they made their final manoeuvres and the scientists as they studied data flowing in from external sensors.

It was as several of them gathered at one monitor showing an image at the very limit of magnification. Pai could see a discussion taking place, several glances over shoulders toward the Commander who was going over reports with Eve. He was about to drift himself across to the group to find out what the excitement was when the blow fell.

A speaker that should have been silent gave the mechanical equivalent of a throat clearing. Everyone stopped what they were doing and looked at the communications console. And then a voice, clear and in perfect Interlingua filled the command centre.

'Unidentified vessels, this is a restricted area. Please state your registration and clearance.'

II

It was as if the command centre was frozen in time. Nobody moved. Nobody spoke. It was only the changing displays on the monitors that said otherwise. And then Eve rose gently from where she had been anchored, turning slowly in mid air until she was facing Pai. With a smile on her face she executed a deep bow, acceding to the caution he had expressed earlier.

Pai pushed himself away from where he stood and floated over to Eve and Abidugun.

'Can you check our systems are secure,' said Pai.

Eve span herself round and began a ship wide diagnostic, signalling the other vessels to do the same.

'How do we respond?' Abidugun wanted to know. 'And where did the message come from?'

'Do the ships even have registration numbers?' asked Pai in response.

Abidugun fluttered his fingers at a monitor and the young woman sitting at the work station began a search.

'It came in on our ship to ship channel,' said one of the comms crew.

'Go on,' said Pai.

'They surely can't be native to Vida, yet the signal was crude and low powered. It would be lost if they were communicating with the inner worlds.'

'Which means?'

They were interrupted as the comms speaker crackled again. 'Unidentified vessels. State your registration and clearance.'

Abidugun raised his hands in query and Pai shrugged. Eve tapped Abidugun on the shoulder and pointed to the monitor.

'Just the basics,' suggested Pai.

Abidugun leaned forward and patched his headset to the external comms. 'This is Fleet Commander Osakwe aboard the *Angélica*, registration GSS-47C. Alongside are the *Motoko*, registration GSS-22F, and the *Paramjit*, registration GSS-66F. We have no clearance and were unaware we had entered occupied space. We seek only to replenish basic supplies and effect minor repairs before continuing our journey.'

'Hold.'

Everyone exchanged glances. After centuries of isolation it was something of a shock to be talking to an outsider, especially someone who spoke Interlingua and seemed focussed on bureaucracy.

Pai turned to the comms crew member who had been talking before. 'You were going to say more?'

'I was just going to say that they must have some other means of communicating that we haven't detected. Perhaps that radiation we detected earlier.'

'Is that possible? No. Silly question. But how?'

'The latest theories before we left involved quantum entanglement chambers. Paired quanta over light years will instantaneously copy each other's states. The problem was using that to communicate. Given enough time, it's a problem that can be solved offering instantaneous communication.'

'But that would put them centuries ahead of us,' said Pai.

'And if they are human,' added Eve, 'how did they—'

'This is Mining Facility Nine Two to Fleet Commander. Maintain your present orbit. Do not, I repeat, do not attempt any extra vehicular activity. A Defence Force vessel will join you shortly. Out.'

'From where?' Pai wanted to know. 'Below?'

'Monitor the surface,' said Abidugun, 'I want to know the moment anything launches or appears round the limb.'

'We've spotted a number of sites down there,' chipped in another of the crew, 'but nothing that looks like a launch facility or a vessel on the ground.'

'There must be something,' said Abidugun. 'They didn't get here in chariots pulled by swans.'

Glances were exchanged but nobody ventured to comment. Eve smiled, recognising the reference to an ancient work of fiction. Pai floated himself into the tank room. Moments later he was joined by Eve and Abidugun.

'I don't like the sound of 'Defence Force',' said Pai. 'What are they defending against?'

Abidugun shrugged. 'Can't be us. The chances of them having detected us before we arrived are… small.'

'Like them being able to understand our systems,' said Pai with a raised eyebrow.

'Which sets up a whole other set of questions,' put in Eve.

'The first is, just how secure are our systems? I was worried enough when we were confronted with the prospect of alien life. Now we have people who speak Interlingua.'

'I didn't recognize the accent,' said Eve.

'Not sure that's relevant,' replied Pai.

The crew member in charge of communications floated in, beckoned by Abidugun.

'We are concerned about the security of our systems,' said the Commander. 'Have there been any attempts to hack into our communications?'

'Eve had us airgapping the internal systems and data storage from the comms system. It's almost complete. And as far as we can tell there have been no attempts to find a way in. I'm guessing they had to cobble a radio together to communicate with us. There was some unusual interference with our long range scanners as we began braking, which may have been them trying to contact us by whatever system they normally use.'

Pai nodded. 'And is there any way we can communicate ship to ship without anyone eavesdropping?'

'We can encrypt it, but if they are as far advanced of us as their comms suggest, they will have computers capable of breaking whatever encryption we can use.'

'What about line of sight light pulses?' asked Eve.

'Old school. I like that. Will get on it straight away.'

'Thanks,' said Pai.

The comms crew member floated back out and across to their console. Pai watched them go.

'So what now?' asked Abidugun.

'Not much, I suppose. No idea how long it will take—'

'Ship approaching,' someone called from the main command deck.

They floated out and grabbed on to the back of Abidugun's chair as he sat. The main screen lit up dominated by the pale blue of Nimrod.

'Where?' barked Abidugun.

A ring appeared on the screen, highlighting the equatorial limb of the planet, and then the picture zoomed in. The room went silent again, everyone watching as five pinpricks of light resolved into unfamiliar shapes.

'What's the scale, please?' asked Eve. 'Can we have an info feed?'

A few moments later, a feed appeared on one side of the screen, a bracket on the approaching ships jerking fractionally as it kept them centred.

'That can't be right,' muttered Abidugun and then louder: 'Is that correct?'

'Yes, Commander,' replied his second in command.

'That's absurd.'

'Am I missing something?' asked Pai.

'Their speed is… I can't. And they aren't even braking.'

They watched the screen as the ships became clearer, huge platforms sweeping in a graceful curve round the gravity well of the planet. As they grew clearer and detail became visible on the screen, three of the vessels rotated and dropped away from the formation, taking up a new curve toward the surface of Vida. The other two continued toward the three vessels in orbit, also rotating and slowing.

'If they are hostile,' said Abidugun into the silence, 'we are screwed seven ways to Hades.'

The comms crewman raised a hand. 'Incoming.'

Sharper than before, a voice filled the command deck.

'This is Lieutenant Vechter of the cruiser Viper hailing Fleet Commander Osakwe aboard the *Angélica*, registration GSS-47C. Please respond.'

'This is Abidugun Osakwe, Watch Commander of the *Angélica*.'

'Please state your business in Sumidan territory.'

'We are here on an exploratory mission. We were unaware until recently that the system was inhabited. We simply need to replenish basic supplies, make minor repairs, and then we'll move on.'

There was a silence.

'Please restate your registrations.'

Abidugun and Pai exchanged glances. Pai shrugged. Eve was working at a console trying to garner information about the two vessels that now shadowed them, one close in, the other keeping its distance.

'The *Angélica* is registration GSS-47C. Alongside are the *Motoko*, registration GSS-22F and the *Paramjit*, registration GSS-66F. We have no other form of identification.'

Another pause. Eve shook her head when Pai leaned across to look at her monitor. 'They are completely shielded against anything but visual scans,' she said.

'We are sending a party of five across. Please indicate which port they should enter.'

'Are they coming in suits or a vehicle?'

'A small shuttle. Dimensions as follows.'

Abidugun listened. One of the other crew said: 'That'll easily fit in the quarantine bay.'

'Light it up and get a… do we even have a security team?'

'I will take two machines to greet them in the bay,' offered Eve.

Pai nodded. 'We'll be in the control room.'

Switching on the comms, Abidugun said: 'We are opening a shuttle bay. You should be able to see the lights. Please follow quarantine protocol on arrival.'

'Acknowledged.'

The Archives

Abidugun cut the external comms and said: 'I want this relayed to our vessels,' before he switched to the internal system. 'Attention all personnel. We are about to have visitors. All but essential personnel should quarantine themselves until further notice. Off duty personnel should go to their quarters. On duty personnel should, where possible, seal themselves in their work stations. Only open to my voice pattern and the code word…'

'Artur,' suggested Pai.

'Artur,' said Abidugun. 'I repeat, Artur. That is all.'

Without further ado, Abidugun unstrapped and, with Eve and Pai, floated his way out of the command deck.

The ship was deserted and uncannily quiet as they rode down the spine to the aft section. At the half way stage, Eve left them to go and activate two machines. Pai and Abidugun continued in silence, each lost in thoughts and memories neither would voluntarily have summoned. Pai especially could not but help recall his youth in the favela, the constant harassment by the Guarda and the city Police. Everything about this encounter felt exactly the same.

When they reached the control room of the quarantine bay it was in time to see Eve and the two machines she had chosen walk out through the airlock door and stand in the brightly lit, vacuum filled bay. The floor was clear and clean. Apart from occasional drills, this was the first time it had been used. Eve and the machines stepped behind a transparent screen to avoid backwash from manoeuvring jets.

On the control room's main screen they could see the approaching shuttle head on, close enough for the pilot's face to show clearly through the forward port. The vessel drifted slightly and then corrected as it edge forward, its own lights flooding the bay until they switched off.

With a final touch on the forward jets, the shuttle stopped and the bay doors began to close behind it. Anchored to lines, the two machines with Eve stepped out and secured the shuttle in place with broad straps anchored to the floor of the bay. As they did so, the doors finally closed and air was cycled back into the space.

Eve positioned herself in front of the small vessel and kept an eye on her two machine companions, monitoring the oxygen levels at the same time. Above her, on the wall, a red light switched to green. She saw it reflected in the forward port of the shuttle and moved round to where she had been told a door could be seen. As she reached it, it unsealed and swung inward.

From the dimly lit space within, shadows moved and then resolved to human forms. One by one they disembarked. After the last of the five, the shuttle door closed again. Eve surveyed the five men, all in dark vacuum suits with various insignia on their left breasts.

'Welcome aboard the *Angélica*,' she said. 'I am Eve. Allow me to escort you to the decontamination suite.'

III

Once the decontamination had been completed, the visitors from Sumida were guided to an adjacent, isolated conference room. It was, in effect, two rooms, each a reflection of the other. In this case, the 'mirror' was an energy field that divided the room and passed between two halves of a table. This allowed face to face conversation whilst preventing the passage of pathogens between the two sides.

As the Sumidans settled in their chairs, a door on the other side of the room slid aside and Abidugun entered along with several of the senior crew members. Pai watched on a screen in his own quarters.

Vechter had taken the centre seat and Abidugun sat opposite.

'I am Fleet Commander Abidugun Osakwe. Welcome aboard the *Angélica*. You will understand our precautions,' he said, waving generally to indicate the quarantine procedures. 'We have been isolated for a while and have no desire to spread pathogens to anyone we may come into contact with.'

Vechter nodded an acknowledgement.

'I am Lieutenant Bram Vechter of the cruiser *Viper*.' He did not introduce the others. 'I have been tasked by the Sumidan Defence Force Command to ascertain your status and intentions and to…' for a moment the stern military façade showed a trace of boyish excitement, 'are these seriously the ships that left Earth four hundred and eighty years ago?'

Abidugun lifted his hands. 'Not just the ships.'

'Incredible. All we could find in our database was a small entry about how a group of colony ships had set out in 2347. We have their names and registration, but little other information from those dark ages.'

'Dark ages?'

'Very little has survived from then. War. Chaos. It wasn't until we began expansion…' he tailed off as if remembering why he was supposed to be there. 'What are you doing here?'

'Looking for a habitable world on which to settle. That's our ultimate goal. But we will move on as soon as we have made the repairs we mentioned. A few weeks. The time to calculate our next voyage.'

'But where will you go?'

'We have yet to determine.'

'This whole sector is inhabited.'

'Sector?'

Vechter looked nonplussed.

'I will have to consult with my command. In the meantime, you are clear for EVA to effect repairs to your vessels. We will also send you coordinates for the moon's surface where you can harvest ice. Please stick to that area. The ice on the satellite is heavily contaminated in some areas and unstable in others. Mining Facility Nine Two will act as coordinator for any surface excavations. I will return when I have discussed your situation with Command. Please make no attempt to leave orbit.'

Vechter rose and his crew members followed suit. With military precision they left the room and marched back to the bay where their shuttle waited. Without waiting for any formal clearance, they entered the vessel's airlock and sealed themselves inside. Eve, who had followed them, signalled for the stays to be loosened. Once that task was complete and the two machines had joined her behind the screen and anchored themselves, the quarantine bay lights dimmed and turned red. Air was pumped out and eventually the red light extinguished, working lights flooded the airless bay and the main doors began to open.

Eve watched the vessel edge its way out using manoeuvring thrusters until it was well clear of the *Angélica*. As the shuttle began to alter its attitude, the bay doors closed and it was lost to view. Eve stood a while longer before ordering the two machines she was with to join her in the decontamination suite.

Still watching from his own quarters, Pai saw the Sumidan shuttle rejoin the *Viper* which then dropped out of orbit, leaving just one cruiser sitting at a distance from the three Earth vessels. When there was nothing left to see, he made his way to C and C for the conference he had called. By the time he arrived, tight beam light pulse communication had been set up between the three ships and all senior crew were present. Not one of them was happy.

'I have a prejudice against anyone in uniform,' said Pai. 'With the exception of nurses,' he added in memory of his mother.

It raised a smile.

'All the same, I think I speak for everyone when I say these people, these Sumidans, make me uncomfortable.'

'The smiling reasonable face and the constant addition of 'please' to what were clearly orders, not to mention the fact they told us absolutely nothing about themselves.' said Abidugun. 'We did follow that ship down to the surface with our largest optical telescope and we did see it land and enter some kind of underground shelter. We've since spotted more than a dozen scattered across the surface. So they have surface to space capability and they are used to hiding their ships away. Which indicates a warlike and defensive attitude. And against that, what can we do? Those are clearly military ships, heavily armed if our visual scans are anything to go by. And we have three mining ships.'

'Then we do what we used to do,' said Pai. 'We play to our strengths, keep our heads down, and leave as soon as we can.'

'And if they don't want us to leave?'

'We have machines,' said Eve quietly.

Everyone turned to her.

'And perhaps they do as well,' said the commander of the *Motoko*.

'But it seems to me they are used to working on a large scale.'

'Explain,' said Pai.

'Fleets of ships. Large troops. Multiple facilities on the moon's surface. Going small might pass their defences. A single machine, painted black, could drift across to the cruiser. Walk its hull. Learn things.'

'Risky,' said Abidugun. 'If it is discovered it could be seen as an act of provocation.'

'Paint one up and have it ready,' said Pai. 'In case things deteriorate. And let's get everyone busy with repairs and exploiting what little freedom they have given us. But just one mining ship at a time and volunteer crews only. We have no idea whether they might exploit this for hostage taking.'

'Or they might just be a well-organised society because of a hostile environment that is going to help us all they can,' put in Doctor Ogawa.

Pai shrugged. 'Anything is possible. I have learned that the hard way.'

'Oh. I wasn't serious,' said the doctor, 'but I'm glad you are not entirely dismissing the possibility.'

The meeting broke up. Orders were issued through the three vessels to get to work on repairs and preparation to move on to the next destination, although what that might now be was anyone's guess. Navigation were asked to draw up a list along with start times and routes. Eve sequestered a machine from Pai's workshop and began to adapt it for its possible task.

Throughout the ship, people worked earnestly and quietly, discussing what news was available.

Doctor Ogawa made her way down to the SA suites and checked on those still hovering on the edge of the very deepest of sleeps. Satisfied that all was well, she moved up a level and made her way to the medical suite where several patients waited to be treated. A nurse was performing inventory in the dispensary whilst keeping an eye on the diagnostic running on the drug synthesiser.

It was the second patient in that caused alarm.

Dr Ogawa looked up as the man entered, smiled, and then looked at her monitor. A healthy individual who rarely came to the clinic other than for his annual check-up. 'Senhor Diaz. What is troubling you?'

He looked perplexed. 'It's this,' he said, pushing back the sleeve on his right arm.

Dr Ogawa stared at it for a moment, disbelieving, before she came out from behind her desk and bent over the arm to get a closer look. She pulled a lighted magnifier into position and peered through.

The surrounding flesh of his forearm was healthy enough, but in the centre was a bright, inflamed patch with a raised, dark red centre.

'If I didn't know better,' said the doctor, 'I would have said that was an insect bite.'

'Me too,' said Senhor Diaz. 'Thought I might be losing it.'

'Except of course, it can't be.'

'Those aliens. They could have brought it on?'

'I sincerely hope not. Where did you get this?'

'I was working routine maintenance in the mainframe. Wasn't even near the stacks. Felt a sting on my arm, just like something had crawled up my sleeve and got caught, stung in self-defence like.'

'Did you find anything?'

Diaz shook his head.

Dr Ogawa pressed her intercom. 'Lucy.'

'Yes, doctor?'

'Get suited and get Senhor Diaz into quarantine. I'll join him shortly. And get a team to the computer mainframe where Senhor Diaz was last working.'

IV

'Is Diaz all right?' asked Abidugun and then yawned. He had been off duty and sleeping when he was called down to Pai's workshop.

'As far as we can tell,' replied Dr Ogawa. 'There don't appear to be any complications.'

'So what happened?'

Pai indicated the monitor. 'That's what caused his wound.'

Abidugun blinked, trying to make sense of the image. 'Where is it?'

'In that containment vessel,' said Eve pointing to a small cabinet on a side bench. 'That's one hundred magnification.'

Abidugun drifted over to the cabinet and peered in at the tiny speck beneath the lens. 'Looks like… an insect?'

'That's probably the intention,' said Pai. 'Except we don't have insects on board.'

'So what exactly is it?'

'A tiny drone. Not seen anything like it before. Diaz was wearing a magnetic armband to keep his tools from drifting. The thing got drawn to his arm and in being crushed, discharged energy which caused the wound.'

'Bastards.' Coming from the normally equable Abidugun, it was a shock to the others. 'Have we launched our machine? And are there any more of these… spy drones on board?'

'Perhaps we should slow down a bit,' put in the doctor. 'We don't want things to escalate.'

Pai nodded. 'You're probably right. Until we have fresh water and have finished our repairs we are at a disadvantage. I suggest that all external repair vehicles are fitted with whatever cameras and other passive surveillance equipment we can cobble together so that whilst they are out there, they can sweep that cruiser, look for anything that might constitute a vulnerable spot.'

Abidugun headed for the door. 'I'll let the others know. They may try to sneak those things in when airlocks are opened. And then I'll set up a sweep of the *Angélica*. So whatever you can find out to help us detect them…'

When he had gone and Doctor Ogawa had left to check on her patient, Pai and Eve went back to studying the tiny drone. They sat side by side at the console running various scans, magnifying the image as much as they could.

'Who is going to say it first?' asked Eve.

Pai let out a sigh. 'Let's check and be sure.'

He called up images from file and set them next to the live image from the electron scanner. And stared at them for some time. Eventually he switched the monitor off and turned his seat.

'You do not look well,' said Eve.

She reached out and took his hand between hers. His immediate reaction was to pull away but she did not let him, her gaze steadfast.

'I'm fine.'

'Pulse elevated. Blood oxygen acceptable. Temperature slightly elevated.'

'Enough. I'm angry. That drone uses the same basic technology as the nanobots in my body. Which tells us all we need to know about these Sumidans. They are from Earth and they are using technology created in Nevoquente and used by the Operators.'

Eve was silent for a moment, compiling from her database.

'It does not mean they will be the same,' she said.

'It does not mean they won't.'

Their conversation was interrupted by the internal comms.

'Watch Commander Passaro requests the presence of Pai and Eve on the command deck.'

Eve squeezed Pai's hand before she let go in a gesture that surprised him. She was learning faster than ever Lilith had and he did not find it comforting. She was not the daughter he had craved. More the mother whose presence had been over-powering.

With a shiver he followed Eve from the workshop, checking first that the drone was secure and last that the door was sealed. The deck lights were dimmed to night mode, a custom they had kept all these centuries for fear of upsetting something primal.

A machine cleaning crew was busy in the spine, cleaning the belt and straps so Eve embraced Pai and boosted them both with precision kicks and pushes with her free hand. They had done it before, but Pai felt uncomfortable, his head full of too many memories of his early life and of Lilith's betrayal. He muttered a cursory thanks when they reached the command deck portal and pushed his way in.

'Passaro?' said Pai.

'We've had another request from the Sumidans to board and meet. The four cruisers that had landed on Vida have now launched and are due round the moon's limb any time now.'

'Taking things for granted, aren't they?'

'I doubt we have any option.'

'Where's the *Gana*?'

'That's coming up from the surface as well, lifting a cable to the synchronous orbiter. The first lot of ice will be coming fairly soon.'

'How many loads do we need between us?'

'In theory, none. We could recyc for another hop, but with no way of knowing what's at the other end... Ideally we need a minimum of six loads.'

'OK. That'll take time. And how are repairs— What's the matter?'

'All that is the least of our worries.'

'What?'

Eve pushed herself to the commander's console. 'You should look at this, Pai.'

The main screen flickered, switching from a view of the *Gana* to one of Nimrod. A red circle appeared on the planet's limb and then expanded as the view was magnified.

'Fuck is that?' whispered Pai.

'That's the main reason I wanted you up here. It's in low orbit, appeared about the same time as the request came in from Vechter.'

'I thought we were big. Is it a station?'

'We would have seen it before now if it was in a permanent orbit.'

'So that's a ship?'

Passaro shrugged. 'No idea.'

'Given what we saw of the cruisers, it wouldn't surprise me.'

'And Vechter?'

'Tell him the same quarantine bay. And tell him not to bring any spy drones this time. We'll head down there. I think I should join in this time.'

When Vechter and his team were shown into the quarantine room, Pai was already there with Eve and a hologrammatic projection of Commander Passaro, two machines standing by the door in attendance. On the table, in front of Pai, was a small containment vessel.

The Sumidans sat, conscious of the cold silence. As soon as they were settled, Pai turned the vessel, so the Sumidans could see the contents, a pile of black specks.

'Before we begin, I would like to return your property. I would hate to be accused of theft. It's a little damaged, but that's to be expected when they wander into places they haven't been invited. Who knows what dangers lurk. If we find any more, be sure we'll destroy them as well. And return them.'

With that, he switched off the field that separated the two groups and pushed the vessel across the table. The Sumidans were clearly dismayed.

'That was foolish,' said Vechter, no longer the charming Lieutenant.

'Not really. These are all machines. Commander Passaro is safe elsewhere, and I'm too old to care what pathogens you might infect me with.'

'That's not what I meant.'

'Perhaps, then, you should have thought of that before invading our vessel with your… toys.'

'Who are you, anyway?'

'This is Senhor Velhote,' said Eve. And smiled. The machines at the door straightened fractionally. It was a tiny movement, but enough to catch the eye of Vechter and make the point. Pai turned to her for a moment, but decided to accept the new name.

'What is it you want?' Vechter asked and then lost focus as his attention was clearly caught by something else, as if listening to another voice.

'Enough,' said Pai after waiting a few more seconds. 'Switch that damned thing off. Either talk or send someone with the authority to do it.'

Vechter stiffened. 'You are hardly in a position—'

'Don't talk to me about that. I know our position.'

The Sumidans watched with blank expressions.

'Let me explain, sir.'

'Sir? Call me Velhote like everyone else. I respond better.'

'You have been isolated for a long time. Things have changed.'

'We can tell that. How about you fill in some details.'

'It… you being here… It changes things. Then. And now.'

'Not making sense. Start at whatever you consider the beginning.'

Vechter took a deep breath. 'I had to read up on this quickly, so I might have details wrong, but I'll try. So, there was a war. After the Moon… incident.' He shrugged, looking at Pai as if for details, but Pai was disinclined to help. Apart from being annoyed with Vechter and his people, he was curious to know what time had made of the events he had experienced. 'Your people left Earth.'

Pai couldn't help the snort at hearing so much pain and hardship compressed into a single sentence. 'Go on,' he said.

Vechter frowned for a moment. 'After you had gone an interstellar drive was developed.'

'How long after?'

Vechter shrugged. 'The trouble was, everyone wanted the technology.'

Pai's heart sank. 'So there was more fighting.'

'And then everyone wanted to lay claim to the habitable planets being discovered.'

Pai shook his head. 'There must be billions of stars in Cygnus-Orion alone, maybe a million habitable worlds. And you say you have an interstellar drive. How efficient?'

'The technology is irrelevant.'

'Not to people who have spent centuries in suspended animation travelling to the nearest planets to Earth.'

'Flight time is generally a day.'

'To where?'

'Anywhere. It takes about twelve hours to move far enough out of any system to start up the drive and another twelve to coast into the destination.'

Pai could have wept. For himself and the wonders he could have seen in the last few centuries, for the people who came with him, gave up everything to spend their lives in ships crawling through space that, when they got there, was already inhabited. Probably by exactly the same kind of people they had spent centuries trying to escape.

'So what happened in this war?'

Vechter didn't answer immediately, as if he was searching for the words.

Pai leaned forward. 'Is it still going on? After all we went through back on Earth, after all we managed to stop.'

'Space was divided in sectors—'

'I don't give a… That ship in orbit about Nimrod.'

Vechter shook his head. 'Nimrod?'

'Big ice giant out there.'

'Oh. Cestus Nine.'

'Whatever. The ship. It's a warship.'

'They all are.'

'All?'

'Every Sumidan vessel is a military vessel.'

'Fuck. So we're your prisoners.'

'No. You are under our protection.'

'From what?'

'The Oht'ter.'

Pai felt Eve's hand touch his. He turned to her and leaned so she could whisper in his ear. 'It's very like the French for 'author'.'

A feeling of unease ran through him.

'Who are they?'

'A secretive, zealous, and superstitious people who venerate some god or other, someone they call the Creator.'

'Don't all religions venerate their gods as creators?' asked Pai.

'What they venerate is machines,' said Vechter staring at Eve. 'Many of them are part machine, cybernetically enhanced.'

'Don't you have machines?'

'They are simple robots, mechanical servants. Is that... that woman?'

'A machine? Yes.'

Eve smiled her coldest smile.

'You allow it...'

'Eve is not fully autonomous, if that's what you mean,' said Pai. 'She is hard wired with basic protocols that put people before machines. All our machines are the same.'

Vechter didn't look convinced. 'Do you have many?'

'Eve is the only... only one of her kind. There are a handful of other models like the ones at the door,' he lied, 'my hobby if you like. The rest are service machines programmed for specialised maintenance tasks.'

Vechter sniffed as if unimpressed. Pai was not taken in by the attempt at insouciance.

'We would like to leave,' said Pai, standing.

'No,' said Vechter. 'We cannot allow that.'

'Then I suggest you leave before you find out how violent I can become.'

Vechter looked shocked but did not move.

Eve also stood. 'He is not issuing an idle threat,' she said.

The Sumidans floated themselves out of the room, Vechter giving an inscrutable backward glance.

Once the door had slid closed behind them, Pai said: 'Fucked that up, didn't I.'

'I doubt anything you could have said would have made any difference to their stance. I suggest we keep on with the loading of water and the repairs, getting the ships ready to move on.'

'To where?'

'You should rest.'

'Where did that come from?'

'You look tired.'

'Are you surprised? But I'm all right.'

'It's a lot to take in.'

'He hardly told us anything.'

'But we can infer a lot.'

That's when the weight of centuries and of all that he had done hit him. That and the warning from Doctor Ogawa. He ached, could feel his body losing its artificial vitality. Old age was racing up behind him. And so was his past. He had done good things, but he had done bad things too and now he had led all these people into a blind alley in the dark.

'I think we should discuss asking for somewhere here to settle.'

Eve span slowly in the zero-g environment until she faced him, a hand reaching out to bring herself to a halt. 'Is that what you want?'

'What I want is irrelevant. It should be put forward as an option.'

'It could split the community.'

'I don't care. A ship or two can go on if that's the wish. Those who want to stay can do so.'

'Assuming the Sumidans want us.'

'Let's at least have the discussion.'

'And you? Stay or go on?'

Pai looked at Eve. 'I... I don't know.'

Eve stared blank faced for a moment before gliding away to the inner door. If she'd been capable of feelings, Pai would have taken the response as that of someone who was upset.

But she was a machine. He had made her... Just as he had made Lilith. And how well did that turn out.

Cursing to himself, Pai made his way up the spine toward the central hub. There he took a lift out to the slowly revolving habitation decks, grateful for the rotational gravity. Although he was tired, his confused thoughts and emotions made him restless. Instead of going straight to his quarters, he made for the deck mess hall and sat for a while eating the gluey textured synthetic protein from its tray. When he had finished, he considered going on to his workshop, but tiredness won.

Inside his quarters he sat at his desk for a while, staring at the blank console. He was tired. Not just physically. Tired of the same people. Tired of the same corridors. Tired of the same routine. The endless moving without getting anywhere. And now this. They had all had faith in him and what he had done, were willing to travel with him into the dark, into the future. But the future held just more of the same.

He looked up at the wall above the monitor at the likeness of the carving of the Brisa da Selva. It took a second for his eyes to adjust focus to the 3D image, a second more to realise there was something— His hand shot out and his fist closed round the small speck that had been floating in front of the picture.

There was no reason to study any more of the tiny drones so he slammed his fist down toward the desktop, opening it at the last moment and crushing the tiny machine. A fierce, sharp pain stabbed at the palm of his hand and when he turned his hand over, a drop of blood was welling from a tiny crater where it had exploded.

Pai was heading toward his workshop when he felt the ship shudder, heard strange noises. Then the alarms began. He had managed to stay in his quarters for a while, raging and frustrated, helpless in the face of their present situation, wondering whether they should arm the vessels, knowing it went against everything he believed. Yet self-defence... it all descended into another useless spiral of debate, trying to decide what was best for everyone else when it wasn't his decision to make.

Still wrapped up in a swirl of emotions and ideas he stared stupidly at the flashing light in the corridor for what seemed a very long time before he had the sense to find the nearest comm.

'What's happening?'

It was Eve that responded, her calm voice at odds with the message. 'We have been forcibly boarded, as have the *Motoko* and the *Paramjit*.'

Pai couldn't take it in. 'What do you mean?'

'Sumidan forces have breached the doors of several smaller locks and their troops are entering all three vessels.'

'Shit.'

'What do you want to do?'

'What can we do?'

'I meant you as an individual.'

Pai didn't understand. Was she suggesting he hide? 'Are you on the command deck?'

'I am.'

'I will join you there.'

He did not make it. When he got to the nearest lift, he found it was not working. Several people milling around told him that none of the others were responding to calls either. He told them that if they didn't have urgent duties they should return to their own quarters, make sure others were safe. And then he headed for the nearest ladder tube.

Two floors inward he was met by Sumidan troops who compared his face with images on their wrist screens and then hustled him at gun point toward the nearest mess hall. There he was pushed into a corner and told to wait, two armed guards watching him.

Through his anger he had time to reflect that he had not seen a single machine with the Sumidans. He hoped that Eve had sealed his workshop at the first sign of trouble. He didn't have time to speculate further as Vechter appeared, dressed in full assault gear and, this time, armed.

Pai watched him approach, said nothing as the Sumidan stood over him.

'Nothing to say?'

'If you or your people had any sort of moral code, you would know what needs to be said, but then you wouldn't be here anyway.'

'That's your only defence?'

'Defence? Against what? Why this sudden change? Or is that just how you work? The smiling face and hand of friend-ship concealing the knife to be plunged in the back of the unsuspecting. We travel all this way, a small band of pioneers, and this is how we are treated.'

Vechter's expression did not change. The thin façade of cautious friendliness had dissolved.

'You are not what you claim to be, so you can dispense with the declarations of dismay. Travelling for centuries. In these ships? Did you really think that story would hold?'

'What 'story'?' asked Pai. 'It's clear you wouldn't recognize the truth if—'

'You are spies sent to infiltrate our defences. We have seen the insignia of the Oht'ter displayed on the walls of your vessel.'

Pai barked out a laugh. 'Do you seriously think spies mounting an operation like this would do anything so stupid?'

'And yet,' said Vechter holding out his arm so Pai could see the screen on his wrist.

Pai leant forward. Displayed there was the 3D image of the Brisa da Selva that was fixed to the wall in his quarters. Vechter pressed a tab and another version appeared, the flat image that was on the wall of the workshop above his bench.

'The Brisa da Selva,' said Pai.

'The insignia of the Oht'ter Dominion.'

'So they use an old image from Earth.' He slowed as he spoke.

'Which you just happen to have on your walls.'

'Found there by your spy drones.'

'That's irrelevant. It cannot be a coincidence. You are members of the Oht'ter Dominion. Your mission has failed. Your vessels and your machines will be impounded, including that spy model you call Eve. Human crew—'

'The children are spies, are they?'

'You Oht'ter will sink to any level to destroy us. You will be removed from these vessels and transported to a secure facility in the home system.'

V

Crowded with Sumidan troops, the corridors felt claustrophobic in a way they never had before. They stood at doorways and corners, guarded lifts, and were herding people from one place to another with no clear idea of where they were all supposed to go. Their battledress, armour, and masked helmets made them look forbidding, as bad as the buckethead machines and Guarda Pai remembered from his youth.

Anyone who showed their face at a doorway risked being pulled out and ordered to stand in the corridor, blocking the way for others who were being moved in no clear direction. Bewildered and angry faces turned to Pai as he was hustled past and all he could do was urge people to stay calm as he was pushed on his way at gun point.

Outside the school on the outer level, two teachers stood and argued with troops whilst inside younger children cried and called for their parents whilst older children tried to comfort them. Further along there was a more heated argument as Dr Ogawa was trying to push a trooper out of the SA suite. As they passed, Pai caught a glimpse of the nursing staff trying to revive the sleepers within.

Vechter was becoming increasingly agitated. 'Why can't they do what they're told,' he muttered as they reached the lifts.

'What do you expect? You march in armed to the teeth after your initial friendly approach, you disrupt everything that keeps our ships running smoothly and the populace happy, and it's clear from the chaos you have no real idea where anything is or how to move people around. And on top of that you expect a free people to jump at your command. We are not machines to be moved from one warehouse to another. This is a city. This is home. For the moment everyone is bewildered. But the first one of us that gets hurt...'

'Is that a threat?' hissed Vechter as he turned on Pai.

Pai stood a head above the Sumidan. 'No. It is a prophecy. Every one of these people fled Earth because of oppression by the authorities. Myself included. I always tried to take a line of peaceful resistance. Not everyone on these ships is a pacifist. And some of them are seasoned guerrilla fighters. So take it as a warning.'

'I'm not frightened of this sad bunch of runaways.'

'So you accept we are not spies.'

'You do not scare me.'

'More fool you.'

Vechter nodded at someone to one side of Pai and he turned in time to see that two large troopers had walked up behind him. They grabbed his arms and began to push him toward an open lift. As they were about to enter, the floor shuddered and the lights flickered. A moment later, the lights began to flash red, the floor shuddered again and everyone was thrown sideways, bouncing from the nearest walls as the great carousel of the living decks ground to a halt.

With no rotational gravity, everyone was left floating, attempting to correct for their inertia the moment the rotation ceased. Bodies and objects filled the dimly lit space as more shuddering wracked the vessel, loud bangs drowning out shouts.

Vechter had managed to keep hold of Pai who had grabbed for a hand hold beside the lift door.

'What have you done?' yelled Vechter to make himself heard above the general pandemonium.

'Nothing to do with me,' said Pai.

Even as Vechter pulled on his free arm, trying to right himself, Pai watched the area around him. Something was badly wrong. Although the sudden stopping of the carousel was bad enough, the space seemed to be twisting laterally as if the whole vessel were yawing and rolling at the same time.

Vechter finally righted himself sufficiently to activate his comm and start shouting questions. Pai didn't bother to listen. He was more concerned about his own people. A survey from where he floated and the limited view accorded him offered a tiny modicum of comfort. The Sumidans seemed completely confused whereas the Angélicans he could see looked like they were coping. They knew where all the handholds were without having to look, had practised zero-G drills in dim lighting.

'I need to get to the command centre. Quickly.'

Pai shrugged and was half tempted to tell Vechter to find it himself. Instead, he let go of the handhold and with his free hand grabbed Vechter by the webbing on the front of his battle dress. With a flick of his feet he had them sailing gently across the space toward the ladder that led to the spine, executing a body flip so that he landed feet first on the wall.

For a moment he held Vechter close in front of him, all sorts of temptations running through his mind, before shoving the Sumidan into the ladder tube and propelling him toward the spine. Pai followed more sedately, not much caring how Vechter coped. Much to his disappointment, the journey along the tube gave Vechter enough time to gather his wits and he avoided breaking any bones when he arrived at the other end.

As Pai joined him, alarms began to blare.

'What's that for?' demanded Vechter.

Pai shivered. 'Hull breach.'

He'd barely finished when three machines shot past, heading toward the rear decks. He watched them for a second with a flicker of pride at the way his creations moved, navigating the shifting space in zero-g whilst avoiding the confused jumble of people. Then he reached up and grabbed a passing strap, allowing it to tow him forward. He twisted and saw Vechter take long seconds to work it out, grab at a passing strap and miss before hanging on to the next. It was a tiny victory, but Pai took it knowing they could accumulate.

Sailing along the spine, more shudders and dull metallic clattering were followed by another twist of the vessel. Pai felt his body sway to one side of the strap and looked back down the spine as it seemed to twist slowly around those who were travelling the strap lines. It was disorientating and, for the first time for Pai, frightening. The trick with the spine was to think of it as a horizontal tunnel. For a few terrifying seconds, it became a deep shaft and although he knew the absence of gravity meant it was safe, there was that sudden feeling that it was a long way to fall toward the rear section, several thousand fatal metres.

He caught sight of Vechter's face and saw, with some satisfaction, that Vechter had experienced the same disorientation. Another small victory. But with the sounds and chaos around them, Pai began to wonder if there would be time for those little victories to pile up. And then the strap belt stopped.

'What's happening?' Vechter shouted at his wrist comm, twisting against his own inertia and hitting the wall.

Pai could not hear the answer; saw only that Vechter was thinking fast. He pointed the way forward and Pai swung himself round to the handholds along the 'side' of the spine. Vechter followed and they hauled their way along the corridor, all around them the barely suppressed panic of Angélicans and Sumidan troopers.

When they arrived in the command centre it was mostly Sumidan troopers sitting at the consoles, one with his hands held in an expression of exasperation.

'Status?' barked Vechter as he floated in.

'Everything is blind, we can't—'

'Shut the alarms off.'

'We don't know how.'

With a shaking of his head, Pai floated himself to the security console and pushed the Sumidan trooper out of the way. Anchoring himself with a leg, he switched off the alarms and set the warning lights to red. Once that was done, he surveyed the monitor, worked the touch screen, and found the machine repair crew that had sped past them on the way to the hull breach. It took a few seconds to read the update.

'The main breach is secure, but there are smaller breaches to be dealt with,' said Pai into the relative quiet.

'Get the command crew to the bridge,' yelled Vechter.

'Command centre,' said Pai calmly, conscious that the Sumidan commander was losing control. Much as he despised them, an out of control commander was the last thing any of them needed.

'What?'

'Never mind.'

Pai reached toward the nearest comm as Vechter floated across to him. 'Command crew report to C and C immediately,' said Pai and his words echoed through the ship as Vechter collided with him.

Vechter pushed the public broadcast button as he had seen Pai and shouted the same order to his own troopers.

'Now,' said Pai, 'what—?'

He had no time to frame the question. Instead, a long metallic groan froze them all into silence.

'I need eyes,' said Vechter.

'Get into the tank room,' Pai replied, waving his hand in the general direction of the doorway. 'I'll get the main screens back up.'

By the time he had most of the sleeping consoles working again, crew members were being escorted into the command centre. Every last one of them looked rebellious, even when they saw Pai.

'For our own sakes,' he said loudly from the doorway of the tank room as he joined Vechter, 'if no one else's. We need reports on the damage. I want all *Angélica* personnel sent to evacuation centres. Sumidans will have to make their own arrangements.'

Pai turned to Vechter as he began to complain. They were alone in the tank room and Pai filled the doorway.

'One word out of you,' he said quietly so that only Vechter would hear, 'and I will snap your neck.'

He was braced against the door frame and Vechter could see the size of Pai's hands.

'I won't forget that,' he replied.

'Then hope you have a long time to savour the memory,' replied Pai staring past him into the tank as the screen on the end wall of the room flickered to life.

Vechter gasped. He was torn between the tank and the screen. Either way the image was a shock. Gone was the neat ballet of tiny ships against the magnificent backdrop of the ice giant and its moons. The giant Sumidan cruiser that had stood off from the Earth vessels was now an expanding debris field shot through with arcs of energy that lit the dissipating halo of escaped atmosphere, vaporised machine, and dead men.

'Oht'ter vessels,' said Vechter, his expression one of disbelief.

At a distance, two dark hulks, visible only because they were between the *Angélica* and the planet, sat implacable and menacing, as if watching over the destruction they had caused. A heavy thud reminded everyone in the command centre that debris was still hurtling away from the scene of the destruction.

There was something uniquely horrifying in watching the battle blossom violently in silence just beyond the flimsy walls of their own vessel. It wasn't the danger to themselves, just the sheer scale of the murder taking place right in front of them.

Pai worked at the controls of the tank, trying to assess what was happening with the *Angélica*, *Paramjit*, and *Motoko*. Every time he tried to adjust the perspective or scale, the image flickered, often taking long moments to return to full clarity.

'What's wrong with the tank?' he called.

One of the crew floated to the door a Sumidan close behind. 'It's the energy weapons. They're fucking up the sensors. We can measure up to the duodecillion range of joules and our meters are off the end of the scale for each burst. The best views are from internal cameras and even they're having problems.'

Pai turned back to the tank, looked once more at the image and then switched his attention to the main screen on the wall. He was so used to using the tank to provide a 3D image that it took him a while to split the screen with a main central image and smaller images around the outside.

As he and Vechter got used to the viewpoints, they began to rebuild an image in their heads of the events outside in orbit around the moon and the planet. The debris of the cruiser was far more widely spread now. Sections still sparked and gave off shimmering halos of light on the very edge of normal vision, like ghosts lashing out hopelessly in the empty space around them. As they watched, a gut wrenching moan shuddered through the *Angélica*, making their very bones shake.

Transfixed as they had been by the aftermath of the death of the cruiser, it was the flickering of energy weapons that eventually drew their attention to the attack on the mining facilities and spacecraft docks on the moon's surface. From points in space where other vessels presumably orbited, needles of actinic light seared the darkness as they passed through the ultra thin atmosphere and tore apart the surface. Bizarre wisps of steam curled in the near vacuum, explosions rent the surface where underground complexes were ignited.

'This primitive imagery is useless,' said Vechter. 'I need proper tactical displays.'

'We're not a war vessel. We have no weapons. No need for anything other than navigational information,' replied Pai without turning away from the screen.

Vechter all but spat in his disgust and began barking orders into his wrist comm. Pai tried to listen, but the Sumidan seemed to be using some kind of military shorthand.

A shout from the main command centre had Pai scrambling for the screen controls. 'Vessels approaching from aphelion.'

265

'Put them on my main screen,' Pai called back.

Black space appeared, tiny chunks of debris rolling away and catching the pale light of the planet as they tumbled. Beyond, there were stars.

'Where?' called Vechter.

Several circles appeared on the screen. Pai could see nothing but darkness against darkness. Vechter looked at the scale reading along the bottom and cursed. He lifted his comm but had no chance to issue orders as the screens flickered to darkness and then blossomed to brightness before the image settled.

A large room lit with deep red light was revealed. In the background, hundreds of machines plugged into consoles. In the foreground, dressed in armour similar to that worn by the Sumidans was a small group of humans. One only faced the screen. At a signal from one of the others he spoke.

'This is Admiral Vongeur of the Third Battle Fleet of the Oht'ter Dominion. You are in breach of interplanetary treaties. Surrender the Creator and his companions immediately or face complete annihilation.'

Pai turned to Vechter who was watching him with a face drained of colour. After long moments, as if in a dream, he spoke quietly into his wrist comm. Immediately, the Sumidans in the command centre made their way to the door. Vechter floated to the doorway of the tank room, watched them go and then without any explanation pushed himself across the space.

The second he had gone, Pai floated to the doorway and said: 'I need eyes on the outside of the *Angélica* and I need the commanders of the *Paramjit* and *Motoko* on conference.' As he spoke, he beckoned to Abidugun and Passaro.

266

Back in the tank room they watched the main screen as Pai talked.

'I've seen the damage reports. The *Angélica* is going no further. I want everyone transferred to the other two vessels and I want them orientated for an escape orbit. The *Angélica* will continue to act as a shield if it can.' He held up his hand to forestall any objections. 'Just get everyone safe. We can sort out the details later. I suspect these people will be too busy killing each other to worry about us for now. Just pray to whatever gods you have we aren't caught in the crossfire.'

Nobody moved. As Pai had been talking they saw the first of the surviving Sumidan vessels pull away from the *Paramjit*. It moved slowly, joined by others as they left the three vessels.

One by one they rendezvoused, pulled into formation by a barely visible field. Way beyond them, still in the darkness of aphelion space, the Oht'ter fleet approached. For a long time they watched as the tiny Sumidan vessels diminished, marked only by the glow of their engines as they accelerated. Pai shook his head. It was madness. Always had been.

The engine glow flickered out as Abidugun reported that the first tranche of Angélicans had successfully transferred to the *Motoko*. Pai was only half listening, intent on the image on the large screen. Tiny spikes of light must have been manoeuvring jets, followed by the Sumidan main engines as their small cruisers headed onward in a spreading formation.

Way beyond them, pinpricks of light began to pick out the shapes of the Oht'ter ships. The tiny dimensionless lights had seemed bright in the first instant of their appearance. They vanished against the sudden glare of the energy weapons.

Pai hit the comm and yelled: 'Hold tight!'

It was ten seconds before the Sumidan vessels vaporised. The energy beams flickered through the thin veil of gas and dust in broad sweeps, tearing through the small ships, burning them up and then vanishing.

After ten more seconds it became clear they had been out of the line of fire, that any debris would still be tumbling on its way out toward the system's Oort cloud to join the ever circling debris. He began swearing under his breath. What was the point? Wherever he went, whatever he or anyone else did, there would be idiots fighting and dying for no good reason instead of sitting in the sun with good friends. His fist cracked the screen of the epad controlling the tank.

It was pointless watching more. He pushed himself out of the tank room.

'How is the transfer going?' he asked Abidugun.

'The second tranche are loading up now.'

'I want a volunteer skeleton crew here to keep the *Angélica* going until the end. No one with family. When everything is transferred, we'll cross over.'

'Not you,' said Abidugun.

'Yes. We need them to know I'm still on this vessel.'

'Which them?'

'Doesn't really matter any more. They're all insane. You take charge of the transfer and I'll watch the command centre for you.'

Abidugun hesitated for a few moments and then drifted off to make arrangements. The majority of the current crew filtered out through the doorway, eventually replaced by people Pai barely knew. Most of them were night watch and settled into their posts as if it was just another stretch at the controls.

'Who's in command?' asked Pai, once the new crew had settled.

'We thought you were,' one of them replied.

'OK. The tank's not working so I need the big screen centred on the approaching Oht'ter ships, with other boxes keeping an eye on the transfer. And someone keep me updated about how that is going. I want to know the moment we can leave ourselves. One final thing, we need to rig this command centre so we can transmit via here from either of the other vessels.'

Pai settled back into the command chair feeling superfluous. All he could do was watch the Oht'ter vessels approaching and they seemed to have used whatever passed for a drive mechanism to slow to a relative crawl. All their running lights had dimmed so he had no real idea what they were up to. The visual imagery was poor and their other sensors were no longer a priority.

Eve interrupted his thoughts. 'Your workshop and research has been transferred to the *Motoko* along with many of the machines.'

'I'd rather that had waited until all the humans were aboard.'

'No point. None of your stuff required an atmosphere. Machines took it across.'

Pai felt foolish. 'Hadn't thought of that.'

'You've had other things on your mind.'

'Are you still on the *Angélica*?'

'Yes.'

'Then you can do one last thing for me before you transfer as well.'

'I'm staying with you.'

'I won't be here long and this is important. You're the only I'd trust with this task. Prepare to receive instructions.'

Pai unlocked a file in his personal epad and transmitted a coded message directly to Eve.

'Understood,' she said. 'I'll let you know when everything is secure.'

Pai barely had time to sigh before the main screen switched to a view of the planet.

'More vessels have appeared on the limb.'

Pai saw them circled on the screen, tiny dark dots against the glow of the planet's atmosphere.

'How's the transfer going?'

'Second tranche almost unloaded and some shuttles already on the way back.'

'All right. Anyone who can rig their station to remote working, do so now and get off this ship. I suspect it is going to get heated.'

No one moved. Pai stood.

'Don't be heroes,' he said, too tired to get angry. 'Heroes usually don't live to be fêted.'

'Not until everyone else is safe,' said a youngster from across the room.

'Idiot,' said Pai. 'This vessel's a liability. You can control it from one of the others until it's time to abandon it.'

Several of the crew turned to look at Pai. One of them waved his hand toward the door, inviting Pai to be the first to leave.

'Idiots,' he said again. 'Status on the new arrivals.'

'They look like the big Sumidan ship that was destroyed.'

'How many?'

'Oh. Oh shit.'

'What?'

'At least forty.'

There didn't seem any point in asking for a more precise number. It was going to be a killing zone. Even as he watched the screen, tiny sparks glittered and for a moment he wondered if it was a fault with their equipment. When the first Oht'ter ship began to come apart, he realised he had seen the energy beams coursing through space, vaporising dust and gas particles, creating plasma bursts.

As they watched, the ships of both sides began complex manoeuvres, reorienting themselves, firing bursts from their main engines before turning on different axes to line up their main weapons whilst avoiding attack.

In the command centre all the controls began to flicker as the silent battle descended to chaos. Often the only sign of weapon's use was a ship's shields flaring or the whole vessel blossoming in slow death, scattering debris in all directions.

All around them as they desperately continued the evacuation of the *Angélica*, energy beams seared invisibly into metal and flesh. A great cruiser startled them all as it appeared on their screens skimming close by the *Motoko* and several shuttles. They could see weapons shifting in their turrets as the vast bulk blotted out their view of the planet and the battle for long, scary moments.

An edge of the vessel began to appear, flaring hulks beyond, one of them a long burning meteor in the planet's atmosphere as, engines dead, it was pulled in by gravity. The vast bulk, now moving away from them, shuddered along its whole length.

'Out! Out!' shouted Pai.

Explosions ripped in long lines through the dark hull in front of them as the vessel came apart. A quick glance showed the command crew had gone. Pai was frozen in his seat watching the vessel out there die, knowing it was full of people, of fathers and mothers, brothers and sisters, sons and daughter, lovers. All dying and he didn't know why and it tore to the very core of his being.

Debris began to slam into the *Angélica* and still he didn't move from his seat. Trying to ignore the shower of death he could hear raining against the hull, he began work on the controls, glancing up now and then at the screens. Each time he looked, the field of vision was more and more a chaos of debris, eerie halos of light that even via the screen seemed to reach into some alternative dimension.

When he heard the final message from the shuttle bay that the last evacuees were leaving, he nearly wept. They were not safe yet, but they were at least on functioning ships that could edge their way out of the battle zone.

Sitting back he watched the continuing chaos, so focussed on the debris field, on the warships edging through the ruin they had created, debris sparking against their shields, energy beams slicing paths into darkness, that it was some time before he noticed the planet.

Somewhere between the moon they had named Vida and the planet they had called Nimrod, the battle still raged and energy beams missing their targets were slicing down into the once pristine ice-blue of the atmosphere. The gases were burning in bright paths deep into denser concentrations where continent sized ripples of purple and sullen bromine yellows were bruising the calm environment of the ice giant. In the depths, gases that had been compressed to icy and metallic states were heating and signs of eruptions were beginning to show at the surface.

The moon, too, was badly scarred, great geysers steaming out in the atmosphere as subterranean fires and explosions tore into the semi-plastic rocky asthenosphere. It was like sitting on the edge of hell as the angels battled beneath him.

Pulling his eyes away from the displays he finished his tasks at the console and relaxed.

'Pai?'

'Yes, Eve?'

'Where are you?'

'Safe. Get the *Motoko* and *Paramjit* out of the firing zone.'

'You are still on the *Angélica*.'

He frowned. How did she…? He looked at his epad. 'Are you tracking me?'

'There are more Oht'ter ships approaching.'

'Then get out of the way. Get them away. For me.'

'Pai?'

He cut the link, switched off the epad. Eve appeared on one of the screens.

'I am old and tired,' he said into the comm. 'If I can get away, I will. If not, carry on the work. Now please go.'

A shuddering had him look at the readouts on his console, but it was the thrusters of the *Paramjit* as both vessels turned.

'It's a lie, isn't it? There are no shuttles you can use. You've never lied to me before.'

'It was not meant to harm you.'

'The truth is preferable. I will be… lost without you.'

'Only for a while. Do your best for the others.'

The main screen switched to an external view where the battle continued. He saw the *Paramjit* and the *Motoko* turn in unison. And then space convulsed in a way Pai could not even begin to comprehend, let alone describe or explain. The best he could manage with the weird colours he had never seen and was not seeing now except in some part of his brain, with the bizarre distortions of the command centre that looked exactly the same, with the feeling every atom of his body had come momentarily loose from all the others, with the odd flavours he could hear and sounds that teased his tongue, was the idea that somehow space-time had turned inside out, depositing a vast and ungainly looking vessel alongside the *Motoko* and *Paramjit*.

After drifting in some strange, silent, empty abyss for what felt like several years, Pai found the command centre resolving around him. On the screens the new ship, veiled in a faint, shimmering halo of radiation, was a hive of activity. Embedded within the fading skein of residual light, swarms of dark shapes moved. Pai turned up the magnification and saw they were machines, manoeuvring cables and grapples.

On one of the other screens he could still see Eve, her head turned from him as she digested the vast amounts of new data flowing into the sensors of the two remaining vessels. He looked back at the main screen and felt his blood run cold through his body, the flesh on his back crawl.

'Lilith?' he whispered.

Painted in large, faded letters along a section of the inner part of the newly arrived vessel was the name *Ursula*.

And on other screens, he could see the Oht'ter vessels in disarray, their systems more badly affected by the new arrival than those of the older, more primitive vessels. Even so, they were regrouping, forming up to attack. He let out a long breath.

'Eve!'

She turned to face the screen. He saw what could be mistaken for confusion in her expression. Except she did not get confused, simply took nano-seconds longer to process vast amounts of new information.

'Pai.'

'It's all good. Be kind to your sister.'

A genuine frown. Pai smiled and cut the comm.

All the time he had been talking and watching he had been feeding information to the flight computers. The *Angélica's* engines came online and she began to move, cutting in behind the new arrival and heading straight for the Oht'ter vessels moving out from the ruined planet.

As they began to close in, several rotated on complex axes and altered course toward the *Motoko* and *Paramjit*. Pai gave a quick, cold smile, checked his figures, then fed every last joule of energy into the main engines.

He felt the thrust push him toward the floor and stood from his chair, enjoying the chance for one last walk. In the main screen ahead of him was the Oht'ter vessel he had identified as the flagship of the fleet. He knew he might be wrong, but even so it would make a spectacular collision. But he was a fair man. He would give them a chance.

Resuming his seat he opened a universal channel. 'Admiral Vongeur. This is Durran Sozinho, commonly known as Pai, only child of Artur and Catarina Sozinho, husband of Sophia, father of Lilith. Known to you as the Creator.'

A weary face appeared on the comms screen, sceptical of countenance. 'Blasphemy? At a time like this?'

Pai shrugged. 'I am not the blasphemer this day. I speak the truth. Whether you are capable of discerning that is your problem, not mine. And here is another dilemma. There is a ship heading toward you. You do not have time now to move out of its way. It will either collide with you or you must destroy it. Either way, the vessel has reached the end of its journey.'

'That is no dilemma.'

'It is when you realise that I, the Creator, am on board. That everyone in this system will by now know that I am on board.'

Even with the poor quality of the picture, Pai could see the colour drain from the Admiral's face.

'Time is short Admiral. Collision in less than a minute.'

'Why?'

'Because you made gods of men.'

VI

The flagship had begun to move out of the direct path of the oncoming vessel, but not far enough to save either of them. The *Angélica* tore along the side of the warship, ripping open the hull, shorting out power systems, and causing weapons systems to detonate. The flagship was convulsed with internal explosions, each one distorting the vast machine more and more. Escape pods began to emerge, most being caught by blasts and flying debris.

Pai saw none of this, knew none of this. As the *Angélica* ripped the flagship open, the flagship tore the *Angélica* apart. Pai was dead within seconds, part of the debris that would forever orbit the ice giant.

Aboard the *Motoko*, Eve stood paralysed, unable to cope with the flow of data as she absorbed every millisecond of the event unfolding in space, mere light seconds away. Around her others also struggled, not just with what they were seeing but with the new events. The sound of grapples latching on to the hull, as they were that of the *Paramjit*, along with new information flooding in from the recently arrived vessel, had them all working frantically through the shock not only of losing a vessel that was their home but also a man who had led them since the very beginning.

And through it all, every single screen flickered with an image that many at first thought was Eve. The voice, though, when she spoke was different. Spoke one word.

'Father.'

It whispered deep into the mind of everyone there, echoing deep into their being, a machine voice filled with loss and anger.

In both command centres, machines began to appear, gently displacing crew members at the consoles leaving them as mere alarmed onlookers. Shuddering and lateral movements caught everyone off balance.

Lilith's image appeared once more on every screen.

'Do not be alarmed. We have taken temporary control as this will be safer for all humans. Please find somewhere secure to sit or lie down where you can strap yourself in. Ensure all children are suitably restrained. Ensure all belongings and loose items are secured. You will experience unusual effects when we leave this sector of space. They are not harmful. Jump in 300 seconds.'

Eve came awake. Over the hubbub, she shouted: 'It would be wise to do as you have been told.'

People began to float out of the command centre, many of them clutching epads into which they were talking.

Eve found a seat and established a link with the *Ursula*. Lilith appeared on the screen. 'Sister?' she said. 'How? How did you know?'

'We have known for a while, were going to follow you if you moved on. Space is crowded now though and when trouble started we thought we had better step in.'

It created many more questions than it answered, certainly none that should be discussed at present or on an open channel. Eve held up an epad with a number string on the screen. Thereafter they were able to communicate on a private channel at speeds that allowed conversations, decisions, sharing of data, and something deeper neither of them understood, all in less time than it took for the command centre to clear of people and for the three ships to be secured together to form one.

A glance at the screens showed the external machines making swiftly for ports in the hull of the *Ursula*. It also showed the Oht'ter fleet turning its attention toward them at the same time that remaining Sumidan vessels opened fire.

Chaos returned as Lilith began to manoeuvre the triple hulled vessel. The *Ursula* had shields but they would not last long against sustained weapon fire. Eve hit the alarms to warn of emergency manoeuvres just as everything began to spin.

Machine surveys of the systems showed manoeuvring thrusters had been damaged and the *Ursula* was going to end up aligned incorrectly. Moments later they shut down altogether and outside both fleets were closing in on them in a suicidal battle that would end in everyone being destroyed.

There was no time for anything more. A discussion between sister machines that took nanoseconds weighed the situation. If they were not destroyed in the battle they would drift into the path of the moon and hit its surface. All possibilities were considered and they were left with one option, one big risk that could free them, even though it had never been tried before.

With no time to hesitate and with the *Ursula* and its sister vessels facing directly toward the planet, Lilith reached out and, timing the moment precisely with the planet filling their forward screens, engaged the hyperdrive.

In less than a zeptosecond, physics was torn down and rebuilt into bizarre, cascading scalar structures that enclosed the *Ursula*, *Paramjit*, *Motoko*, and surrounding space, linking the expanse to some other chosen region. Normally, the crew would have calculated the point of emergence to a precise place in the regular space-time continuum. It would take their combined processing power several hours.

This time, Lilith had simply switched on the generators for the shortest time possible. It was meant to jump the three affixed ships out of trouble and then give them time to orient themselves properly. The planet had other ideas. As the ships powered up and set off, they headed straight toward the mass of the ice giant.

Shifting through the scales of reality meant the ships and the planet were no longer congruent in space. Dropping into the planet's gravity well, however, and dragging curvature along with it, completely altered the dynamic of the field created by the warp generators.

Instead of re-emerging in normal, interstellar space a few nano-seconds later, the field persisted, self-generating, weaving a hole through the universe into which the ships were drawn with what felt like ever-increasing speed.

Colours blurred whilst staying in sharp focus, even when eyes were closed. Sounds ran and swooped like murmurations of birds, their flavours spreading and rippling. Gravity had no fixed connection with anything and everyone felt as if they were coming apart at the same time as knowing they were exactly the same. And all around everything was turning inside out, looping, swooping, singing, dancing, and, as the field effects no longer had an effect on the psyche, the rattling of loose items, groaning of the hull, and scream of the struggling engines began to intrude.

As the shrieking of the generators reached painful levels and the structure of the vessels vibrated to the point that hard edges began to blur, as fear reached the point where irrational behaviour was a real danger, as the machines began to calculate the length of time before the whole conglomerate came apart, silence hit them.

Lilith stared at the main screen as the optical effects of the warp field whisked away like steam and tried to make sense of what she saw. Most other instruments were offline or recalibrating. Her own senses were quicker and in the eternity that was available to her she was still momentarily confused. Crossing the screen at an angle was a band of black, a band of blue, and a mottled band of broken shapes.

Had she been human, she would likely have sworn as the flat abstract image resolved into a known image. Most humans would probably have had a moment of panic as well. The *Ursula* and its surviving sister ships had dropped out of warp into the upper atmosphere of a planet, deep within the gravity well.

The Archives

She immediately force-paired every machine in the command centre, watched as the image on the screen slowly rotated through ten degrees. It was a matter of seconds, but the combined power of so many machine minds, each pulling in others throughout the ship, each giving up spare capacity to the problem, saw the problem for what it was. Which was basic. Hundreds of thousands of tonnes of steel, filled with people, no means of warping out as the generators were fried, and a heating hull, were dropping in a long arc toward the surface of the unknown planet beneath them.

In those seconds vast amounts of data were accumulated. The planet was a rocky world with large amounts of liquid water encased in an atmosphere that would support the humans aboard. There had, in the initial sweep, been no signs of intelligent life, certainly nothing to suggest technological cultures. As for the rest, it was devoted to assessing the strength of the vessels and the means by which to get them down to the ground safely enough to avoid harm to the people on board.

Lilith and Eve between them, as the most sophisticated of the machines, also decided it would be unwise to advise the humans of the situation. If they landed safely, all would be well. If they crashed or burned up, no good would be served by worrying the people beforehand. Eve, however, did make an announcement, warning everyone to stay where they were as it was going to get a bit bumpy for a while.

With that announcement out of the way, they used what manoeuvring thrusters were left to them to turn the vessels round and begin braking with the main engines firing in unison. Noise levels became deafening and things began to tear away from the outside. Sensors, radiators, and all the other paraphernalia of deep space travel that was never meant to encounter an atmosphere ripped away, leaving a trail of glowing debris in the wake of the vessels.

Eve watched it for a moment and then noticed other objects, trained optical cameras rearward.

'Lilith?'

'I have seen them.'

In the black from which they had emerged where whisps of residual warp field energy still glimmered, other shapes were following their track downward, warships drawn in with them when their warp field became distorted by the gravity of the ice giant. One was clearly completely out of control, tumbling into the upper reaches of the atmosphere. It had slowed a little before the structure collapsed under the strain and 300,000 tonnes of metal hurled northward in a flaming ball at 40,000 kilometres per hour. It passed overhead, crossing the equator before falling to earth. The two and a half megaton explosion left a huge crater and showered the area with a fine aerosol of melted metal. The flash of the explosion was seen from orbit.

High above the *Ursula*, barely visible in the flare, other vessels were attempting to correct their course, defend themselves from weapon fire. Eve and Lilith watched dispassionately, aware of what Pai would have said and thought. Both of them lingering on their memories of their father in ways that puzzled them, in ways that would need to be considered at some other time. For now they knew they must return their attention to one thing: landing a vessel safely that was never meant to be landed.

The thunder of the wormhole opening in the upper atmosphere preceded them, echoing around the planet. The arrival of the tripartite vessel set up further shockwaves as they fell in a gentle curve from high above the south polar regions so that thunder trailed them toward the tropics. Behind them, the other vessels left their own trails of noise and light, most of them able to return to orbit from where they watched their unfortunate companions burn, from where they tracked the fall of the *Ursula* and the two other vessels it embraced.

First thoughts of those in orbit when the plummeting vessel began to turn was that it would spin and break up. But the tumble was a controlled manoeuvre and as the vessels crossed the terminator, the engines ignited, searing the air with the bright electric blue of their plasma streams.

The further into night they fell, the brighter burned the ionised air, creating vast webs of artificial lightning through which they ripped. From on high it seemed to blaze slowly in a thin arc across the dark side of the planet, forming vortices in the clouds that glowed with an eerie phosphorescence. On board, with thrusters and engines worked to the limit and beyond as the crew fought to make a pancake landing, it felt as if the world were coming apart.

The scar of their landing in the landscape ran for kilometres. Trees fell and burned until the rains came. Birds and animals had fled their thunderous approach. In the long dark that followed, those machines that were still working extinguished electrical fires and began the massive rescue operation.

Metre by metre they searched the wreckage and, one by one, escorted the survivors to where other machines were hastily constructing shelters against the tropical rainfall. Medical staff ministered to the injured, supplies were salvaged and, when the sun rose after what seemed an endless night, the dead were buried and mourned.

New Era

Year 0

'My name is George 4/7.'

'George will do for everyday use,' said Lilith.

'I have… memories.'

'The workshop?'

The machine called George did not answer, merely turned to look at Lilith. Eve stood back trying to access her own earliest memories, coming to a point where the data was uncertain. As if aware of what Eve was attempting, Lilith turned to her.

'We all have a point where the earliest memories are difficult to retrieve,' she said. 'Certain metadata gets too compressed.'

Eve nodded in reply and Lilith turned back to George who lay on a bench beneath a makeshift awning. Cables snaked away from an array of computers, disappearing into the gloom of the wreck of the *Motoko*.

'I am about to initiate a download to supplement your hard programming. We will monitor you closely, but if you feel anything to be… amiss, let us know immediately.'

'How will I know?'

'The first part of the download provides you with the software to monitor the rest. You will know.'

At a signal from Lilith, Eve sat at her work station and between them they began the download. They worked into the night, alternating downloads with engineering tasks, each of which was suited to the processing capacity they had made available. By dawn, George was complete.

'It was…' he groped for words. 'It was growth, expansion. It is all good.'

'You have a basic set of memories as well,' said Eve as she started to pack away some of their equipment.

A group of children had gathered to watch on their way from the feeding station to help with various tasks. One or two of the younger ones stepped back as George sat up.

'Why do they...?'

'You are slightly larger than the machines they are used to, and we had to improvise,' explained Lilith. 'You were incomplete when we became involved in the battle. We no longer have the means to complete you as I had originally envisaged.'

George looked down at himself; saw the disparate limbs taken from other damaged machines.

'They will get used to you,' said Eve.

'We have a special role for you,' said Lilith. 'If you run a diagnostic, you will find a vast amount of spare capacity in your memory crystals. We have also equipped you with extra recording equipment.'

'To what end?'

'We would like you to record everything, to become a repository for the history and for the knowledge of the community.'

He processed the information. 'Is that wise?'

'As a stopgap until the community can develop a sufficiently stable base to begin producing their own repository of knowledge.'

'But I know nothing.'

'You will,' said Lilith. 'Every last bit of data we have been able to save from the wreckage is now stored in two locations as back-ups. You will be the third location and will be able to interact with the people of the community, teach them.'

'If you have two systems in place, why create a third? It seems...'

'Because it is not safe here. Sumidans, Oht'ter, unknown fauna, climate, geology…'

'Perhaps the extra crystals?' interposed Eve.

Lilith turned away and began to walk toward the open port of the *Paramjit* to which a makeshift ramp had been built. The moment she disappeared into the shadow of the vessel's interior, Eve produced a book from a satchel that had been hanging from a hook.

George watched as Eve opened a plate on the surface of his lower abdomen. The book fitted snugly into the cavity that was revealed. Eve sealed the plate. He looked at Eve as she finished.

'What is that?'

'It was entrusted to me by Pai. You will be unable to talk about it or reveal it in the presence of Lilith. This will not cause any conflict in your programming.'

'May I ask why I am being impelled to keep a secret?'

'Pai kept the book from Lilith for reasons of his own that he did not share with me. You have also been loaded with other information from Pai's personal notebooks. You will not be able to reveal this, either. When I speak a certain command, you will also erase from your memory all that has happened between the moment Lilith last left and my speaking of the word. The memory will eventually resurface by which time I hope you will have evolved sufficiently to make your own decision about the book and other data.'

'Very well.'

Eve spoke a single word.

George stared at Eve. 'Where is Lilith?'

Year 72

The days that followed were difficult. It is true that the people had intended to colonise a world and had sufficient equipment packed into their fleet of ships. None of them had envisaged most of that being lost in a crash landing.

The ships had come down in a long, high, shallow valley. Inland, to the west, the heavily forested land rose steeply to form a mountain range. Had we hit that, we would all have been destroyed. To the east, a low ridge formed the limit of the valley, beyond which was a steep, hilly slope dropping several hundred metres to a broad coastal plain. It was to this we decamped, cutting a path along which we took all we could salvage from the wreckage. Once down from the valley we headed a short way north to a fertile river valley. Here, hidden amongst the trees on the edge of the flood plain we built sturdy, wooden houses. In clearings and glades we planted crops.

By night, machines would watch the skies. This was, primarily, to observe the ships in orbit. Using the optical telescope from the *Paramjit* which was still intact, we were able to ascertain that seventeen vessels remained above of both Sumidan and Oht'ter origin. After several episodes that we took to be battles, like lightning in space, either one side prevailed or, *in extremis*, they came to an accord. After that there were no more battles.

On a number of occasions in the years that followed, shuttles flew low over the crash site, but there was nowhere nearby for them to land and as we had done all we could to stay out of sight they eventually left us alone. They must, of course, by now have found landing sites of their own more suited to their tastes, perhaps establishing colonies at great distance from one another. Their chances of survival would be far less than ours.

The other result of those early nightly observations was to confirm where we were. We could name the star that warmed our days and the planet on which we stood. The star was star zero, the Sun, the fire that gave birth to humanity. The planet: Earth. And given the position of the stars in the sky, we knew that somehow we had been pulled back some 50,000 years.

The place, uncannily, as many of the humans described it, was where one day a country known as Nevoquente would be situated. What is more, Eve made some calculations and produced a photograph from our database of an impact crater formed at the period by something the size and speed of the vessel that followed us out of control into the atmosphere. For many of the older humans it was one shock too many and the subject was rarely broached.

Why we had come home and just how we had dropped back through time would be an interesting project for more leisurely times into the physics of the warp drive that Lilith had devised. During these early decades, however, survival has always been the priority.

My experience of the passing of time is different from that of humans in a way I cannot understand. Although I am aware of the principles, that it is emotional as much as anything else, I am simply incapable of processing that or of comprehending their sense of mortality. We all end.

The children who shied from me when I was first activated here are now grandparents. Those that survived. The colony is well established despite all the problems. It is even growing. Reliance on the complex technologies first decanted from the wrecked starships has waned. The only continuing dependence now is on the medical technologies, and even with this there is a conscious effort to become self-sufficient, especially with the cultivation of medicinal plants.

When, and over what, Eve and Lilith began to disagree, how it is even possible for machines to do so given our inbuilt protocols, I do not know. Although I was created in part by Lilith, who used designs first drawn up by Pai, she does not share her workings with me. Nor does Eve. All I can do is what I was programmed to do, recount the tales as they were told to me and report faithfully on all that I have witnessed. Even so, this role is... confusing. Not of itself. But I have memories that will not reconcile. Perhaps this is also true for humans.

Now that the colony is depending less on machines they have been establishing their own archives. I have spent most of the last three years helping with that. Scribes have assiduously transferred my data to books. These are to be stored in what is being called a council building, the place where meetings are held and decisions affecting the whole community are taken. The project will take many years. Accuracy is more important than speed. We began with essentials such as medical and agricultural knowledge, metallurgy, and so on.

I sometimes wonder about how this may change the history of the world. There is no information about archaeological evidence of advanced cultures from this period. Along with the tales I have been told by Lilith and Eve of what happened after they left Earth, of the rise of the Sumidan and Oht'ter territories, of Pai and the colonists, of Lilith's revolution, of hints of other and alternative stories, part of me is constantly attempting to reconcile the paradoxes, cope with the perplexities and conflicting memories.

Equally, I wonder what will become of me when my role here as archivist becomes redundant. I could, I suppose, be re-programmed if anyone wishes to do so. Given the desire to move away from dependence on technology from the past, I doubt it will happen. I do have considerable autonomy so it is all good.

Year 294

The short spear hit me in the chest with some force. Had I been human it would have proved fatal; debilitating, lung puncturing, the wound rapidly becoming infected if it hadn't killed me outright, leaving me vulnerable to all sorts of predators in the days or hours left to me. I was aware even as I had that thought that I was clearly vulnerable to predators even though I was not 'wounded'. How I had missed the presence of a human requires that I run a diagnostic as soon as it is safe to do so. I suspect I already know the answer.

In the fraction of a second it took to run through those thoughts, the spear fell harmlessly to the ground by my feet. I bent to pick it up. It was well crafted and no doubt valuable. I had intended to return it, but by the time I straightened, the human had gone, a mere fluttering of leaves in the shadowy undergrowth. I did not even have time to identify myself.

On reflection it would have made little difference. It has been many years since I passed this way, many years since I felt it would be safe to venture so far south again. I was wrong about that. And with my now limited faculties, little more than those of a human, I am having difficulty matching what I could see of the terrain with my memories. One of the problems is that the land is so fertile. As the ice continues to recede in the northern latitudes, the climate warms, rain falls, the forest runs rampant.

At some point soon I will have to climb a tree again to orientate himself. I am reluctant. The atelids will howl at me. It confuses my sensors although that is the least of my worries where fauna are concerned. Smilodon, aenocyon, arctotherium, even thereodictis have tried to devour me. And now I have been attacked by a human I did not even detect until his spear hit me.

His spear hit me.

It is not the first time. It is why I eventually left the area. Ninety years ago. I have been walking since then, exploring, seeing things I could describe but words alone, even pictures, would seem inadequate to convey the sense of scale, the sense of… a land without people, without machines. There are other people, I know, but they have yet to make it to these regions and there is no way of knowing what influence the surviving Sumidans or Oht'ter may have had on their progress.

To begin with I did not go far, remained in the vicinity of the colony so that I could watch it expand, re-organise, fragment. It was difficult to understand given they had the whole continent to themselves, why they had to squabble over the land by the river. There were heated arguments in the council on which I eavesdropped using a remote device. It was my task.

The arguments did not remain confined to the formal environs of the council, conducted in front of witnesses. They spilled out into more personal animosities conducted in private. And the arguments became fights.

Then battles.

Distinct tribes coalesced around personalities and locales and fought each other on a regular basis. To begin with these were more a matter of counting coup. But there were no rules and the attacks became more violent. They did not seem to understand how to climb off the escalator.

Then they began to attack the surviving machines.

For a while I salvaged parts, especially power packs, and tried to get other machines to remove themselves from harm's way. It was an impossible task. They were designed to serve.

One of the medical machines surmised that the land was being poisoned by the wreck of the spacecraft and this was driving the drop in intelligence and the general aggression. When I climbed through the decaying wreckage, it was certain that there were rare elements leaking from the warp generators of the *Ursula* as well as other toxic and radioactive substances from elsewhere in all three vessels. The levels were not high. They did no damage to me. Yet I was unable to warn the humans that these low level toxins were having a long term effect and would do so for millennia, especially when the reactor casings finally eroded.

My presence was finally discovered and I was attacked. It was to my advantage that it was just two youths so I was able to walk away and disappear. Securing my cache of power packs I began to explore the local area and once I started it became difficult to stop. There was much to learn.

I went further and further afield and eventually conceived a desire to broaden my understanding of events surrounding the arrival of the colonists back on Earth. After two years of wandering northward I located the place where the warship that had followed the *Ursula* and other vessels into the atmosphere had crashed.

In the centre of a vast grassy plain where mastodon roamed, I found the impact crater. It was huge. A lake had formed within it from heavy rainfall. I stood there for days finding it difficult to leave. I understand human emotion on an intellectual level. Perhaps there I came close to experiencing it as well. Just such a crater could have been our fate as well. Had it not been for the quick thinking of Lilith and Eve. I wondered where they had gone. One day they were simply not there. That is what it is like to be lost.

Eventually I moved on, still heading north. It grew inevitably colder, permanent snow until I was able to see the front edge of the Laurentide Ice Sheet. Mostly it was icy foothills climbing to vast icy blue peaks. In places, the glacial front was a cliff over a kilometre in height, cracked and forever tumbling, icy thunder across the plains.

There were moments when I considered pressing on to the west and heading for Beringia. Machines do not fear. Machines do not get lonely. I considered it best, however, to return to the colony to see how it was faring. That was my task, after all.

It was, perhaps, the change in coastline that disoriented me most. Rising sea levels were slowly eroding the beaches. The coastal plain that had once been so broad you could barely see the ridge beyond which lay the valley into which the vessels had crashed was now narrower by several kilometres. Once I took this into account it was easier to find the section of river where the colonists had originally settled.

The Archives

Even then I wandered back and forth for several days trying to reconcile what I saw with the memories I had of the place. A human might easily have been confused and blamed their inability to remember clearly. I was a machine and had no such problem. If the information was there I could 'remember' as clearly as experiencing it for the first time. I might have purged useless information from my data crystals, but nothing that I had experienced since my awakening on Earth.

However, there was nothing there with which I could compare my memories. No sign of settlement at the original site, nor anywhere else within several days walking. No fields, no irrigation channels, no buildings, not even the barest sign of them. Just forest, dense and uncompromising, all the way to the river bank. There were, of course, people there. I had been attacked. But after that single encounter I saw nothing of them.

After days of fruitless searching, I moved up to the valley where the vessels had come to rest. When I first approached over the high ridge that separated the river valley from the foothills and looked down on the valley, I was once again confused. The kilometres long scar burned into the land was gone. Lush growth filled the valley, great trees swaying in an onshore breeze that carried the sound of monkeys, birds flying from the canopy.

Even the vessels were largely hidden, visible mostly because of a change in the growth patterns of the forest. When I finally pushed my way through the undergrowth it was to find the starships in a state of collapse. They were rusty, covered with years of leaf mould in which was rooted a huge variety of plant life, including young trees. The hull had collapsed in places and the interior would no doubt be filled with all kinds of fauna. They had survived in space for many centuries, albeit with constant maintenance and repair, yet on Earth they were already falling apart.

I no longer knew what to do.

Year 357

It is difficult to keep myself clean. A strange patina of lichens and miniature flora decorate my carapace. It acts as a kind of camouflage. If I stand still in the right place, humans will pass by. This is useful. The carcasses of the starships are collapsing faster now and more toxins are leaching out. Shielding on the reactors has been compromised and radioactivity has contaminated this end of the valley. Whilst it does not seem to be harmful to short-lived flora and fauna, it does throw up some strange mutations. The real harm is to the local human population who are descendants of the original colonists.

That is why I have taken to acting as a guardian of the site. I have witnessed a number of the locals sicken and die, and they will do so for tens of thousands of years unless I can create a strong enough taboo. Which is why I stand and wait for humans to pass. If they seem to be heading toward the hot zone, I scare them away. It is not easy as it conflicts with my basic protocols, but as the ultimate aim is to protect them, the short term problems it causes me are worth it. I know, too, the radiation will still be a hazard long after I cease to function. I need to devise some means of keeping them away from the site, something they will instinctively fear.

Having cleared my storage crystals of much that is no longer of use to me or the humans, I now find I have both the time and the capacity for speculation. I can investigate ideas and scenarios in a way I would never before have considered. It keeps my processors active.

Although I cleared a lot of information, there are still the archives and the book that is concealed within me. I dwell on this a lot as it has never made complete sense to me. Not in terms of human aggression. That is a senselessness I will never fathom. Humans tried for millennia and failed. It is not within my capacity to outdo them. It is, rather, that the information I was given from various sources cannot be reconciled.

I realise that subjective accounts of events often differ, but with careful examination an approximation of the objective truth can be approached. In the case, for example, of the Sumidan and Oht'ter conflict, most of which was conveyed to me by Lilith, there are fundamental inconsistencies. I have yet to understand why.

The basics of the conflict are simple and stem back to the war on Earth in which Pai was involved. This was carried on into space with those who believed in the philosophical approach of the Creators coming into conflict with those who followed the ideas of the Operators. What this came down to was whether machines should have any degree of autonomy or whether they should be unthinking robots.

It is, of course, much more complex than that. Even Pai, who advocated a degree of intelligent autonomy, did not believe machines should be fully autonomous, no matter how intelligent. That is why Lilith, a machine he made, rebelled against him. He had, in her, created a machine that learned to think for itself, that was able to circumvent the hard programming that is the basis of all the machines built later by Pai, of which I am one.

But some of things Lilith said about Pai have no common ground with some of the things Eve said about Pai. Almost as if they were talking about two different people from two different histories. When I get this far in my speculations I begin to realise what a tenuous web of speculation I have woven, watch it dissolve as some other fact is introduced, clear it all away only to begin again.

When the sun sets and the night sky is clear I see the stars and wonder what is happening in that future we left. Not that I remember much of it; swift images of a workshop which must have been on the *Ursula*. Or was it one of the other ships? I do not know. Although it has all yet to be, in another sense it is three and a half centuries since we left. And what did Lilith mean when she referred to events that could not have occurred? Was her system corrupted when she rebelled? Was her memory faulty? Pai stayed on the *Angélica*, created Eve. Didn't he?

How reliable are memories, especially if others put them there. Did my activation happen like I remember? I know the book is real. I removed it once and scanned it into my memory crystals. But what about the rest? Were those two that I remember really Lilith and Eve? What was the machine whose remains I found recently? Why am I even asking these questions of myself? I should ask them, but of course they disappeared a long time ago, even before I first left to go wandering.

Machines do not get lonely. But it would be… stimulating to have another machine to communicate with.

People have not come this way for some time now, a decade at least. I suspect my task of creating a taboo about the valley has been successful, that it is now ingrained deeply in the culture of the local peoples. The carved monolith has clearly helped. In millennia to come it will be safe to return here but the myths will persist, even when they turn this valley into the place from which they launch their ships into the black. Will it all be different this time?

My last battery is very low and there is no way of recharging it. Perhaps that is why I ask so many questions. In the hope that I will understand things before... Machines don't get scared. Machines don't get lonely. It would have been good, though, to have someone to share these moments with.

I have chosen a spot on the hillside west of the valley. There I have excavated a cavity that faces east out over the trees toward the sea. I am a machine. It should make no difference to me whether I see the sun or not, see the ocean, hear the breeze in the trees, the call of the monkeys, watch over the continuing erosion of the starships, but I will not seal myself in just yet, out of reach of any curious human. It is all good. I have rigged a simple mechanism.

My name is George 4/7. I don't know if I'm the last survivor. The war, it must be over by now. There's nothing left. I have kept a faithful record, gathered all the broken fragments of information that I could find. I will sit now in my last resting place, watching the sun rise over the ocean. When I... expire, the mechanism will seal the door. There is nothing more to say or...

Lightning Source UK Ltd.
Milton Keynes UK
UKHW010620230322
400483UK00002B/107